THE BLACKFISH INHERITANCE

THE BLACKFISH INHERITANCE

THOMAS WOLFSON

Editing by Martha Gordon
Cover photo by permission of Irene Paine, www.evaandhenry.com
ISBN: 0692371974
ISBN 13: 9780692371978
Library of Congress Control Number: 2015901033
Loagy Bay Press, South Wellfleet, MA

*For My Family and Friends
With Love and Gratitude*

CONTENTS

One

RINCON AND BAYONNE

I last saw my father this past Christmas holiday. It's then and there, high up on the mountain in his shack behind his beach house, he asked me that question, that question which has caused all this grief, or a coming to terms with it anyway.

He paid our way to Puerto Rico, and naturally, we had our share to pay also. In a snowstorm on Christmas night, my wife Kate, daughter Grace, and I left New Hampshire, drove to Montreal, spent the night, and in the morning flew via San Juan to Mayaguez. From there we drove our rented car North on the western shore of the island to the small town of Rincon. It is hot.

My father's place sits right on the beach where the waters of Columbus's Mona Passage incessantly pound out their rhythm. Roosters crow next door and in the hills around the clock. Behind the house and a small coastal plain many green mountains and hills rise and fall. And in the valleys, cattle of the Brahman breed graze. Rincon is poor.

His beach house is in a neighborhood of once government subsidized cement coated cinder block structures for the poor. But the socialist experiment has failed, and slowly Americans from the States are buying up the beachfront. Houses everywhere have iron grating and gates which nightly clang shut and are padlocked with paranoid certainty. Stealing is rampant, but violence is not common.

Entering through the front door, which is rarely used, one gazes through a small living room and kitchen, each bordered on the right side by four cubicle size bedrooms, through scattered books, papers, manuscripts, liquor bottles, socks and unwashed clothes, modeling clay and plaster of Paris sculptures, out and beyond the grated veranda, through an arched twelve-foot span of half-inch P.V.C. pipe, through another twenty-foot arching span, to two magnificent drapes of Royal Palm whose trunks soar upward and whose leaves spill splendidly over yet again two more intersecting arches of P.V.C. The endpoints of these arching pipes enter into four erect columns of four-inch white pipe creating a stately pleasure-dome over the outer terrace, and upon this terrace my father, an old man, an amputee with cane, surveys the sea with its wet and wild horses foaming and fretting, and here he holds court.

"Morison is a marvelous writer. In college, maybe after, I vaguely remember reading his maritime histories, but this

Columbus book is marvelous. Thank you for bringing it to me," my father begins while nursing one of my orange and bourbon cocktail concoctions. I am warmly satisfied by his gratitude.

"And your paper on the Plymouth Colony is very good. It brings some life and scandal to that stodgy crowd, speaking of which, how's your anesthetized mother? Oh, I shouldn't say that, but God, how I struggled—for what, twenty-three years?—to create some joy, some enthusiasm for living. Imagine her hating my Jackson Pollack, weeping at the sight of it! And then to have to drag her out of that Greenwich Village apartment and that boring, boring socialist clique to move uptown to Henderson Place."

"C'mon, Pop, you can't dismiss the importance of the labor movement, or the importance of having a sense of social justice, or the fact that Mom has a lot of heart and caring."

"Soft heart, leather cunt. All that movement shit is liberation not for the oppressed masses but from her own privileged, sheltered upbringing. Did you know that she was not allowed into, never even entered, the kitchen of her own house until she was twenty-five?"

"Yes, Pop, you told me."

"God! What I had to put up with! Of course you've heard the famous wedding story, how your great Aunt Margaret came up to me not knowing I was the Jew groom and confided, 'Well, at least Abigail isn't marrying a nigger.' Imagine! The outrage!"

Two years ago I had flown down to Puerto Rico overnight to help my then seventy-seven year old father return to New York City in the spring. We had begun drinking early in the day. He had taken several codeine to ease the phantom pain in his stump. On the plane a small drunken Puerto Rican with a complexion and nose similar to Sammy Davis, Jr. stopped at our seats and pointed at me.

"You Jewish? You from Philadelphia? Hunh? You Jewish?" He laughed and walked past us to his seat. Later in the flight this same man was returning from the forward restroom as my father and I were sipping our champagne. Cordially ending our conversation, my father handed me his glass and stood up.

Pointing his cane at the man, he bellowed, "You Sammy Davis? Hunh? You Sammy Davis?" Then he lunged at the man, punched him in the jaw, and knocked him down.

Stewards and stewardesses came running toward our seats.

"He's crazy! He's crazy! The old man, he hit me!" screamed the little Puerto Rican.

Quickly surrounded, the stunned man was firmly escorted back to his seat while one of the stewardesses whispered to my father, "Thank you, sir. He's been causing a lot of trouble in the back of the plane."

With great dignity my father sat back down into his seat. "I'll have my champagne now," he said.

"You've got a lot of class, Pop," I said as we clicked our plastic glasses.

"Don't let me get off on this whole tangent. Let's talk about you. Kate and my granddaughter Grace look well. I think the little one may turn out all right," my father continues. "And yes, your paper is first-rate. How did you get it to look so good? It looks like it was done on one of those machines."

"Yes, I did it on a computer. Dartmouth undergraduates are required to buy one, so, as a liberal studies graduate student, I felt compelled to get one, too."

"Must you get everything you want? How did you pay for it?"

"I took out a loan and Mom—"

"God! You are a spoiled little rich kid."

"Well, I'm thirty-eight and it sure as hell hasn't been easy having one's way made for you in the world."

"You're lucky you haven't wound up in some gutter." We drink together. We talk. We drink some more and watch the great weight of the sun sizzle into the sea. An emerald solar flash hails the night.

Within the heavy, dark stillness the waves pound and hiss, muffled by the breathless heat. Repellant doesn't keep the tiny mosquitoes from biting. My father sleeps in the mess of his room. Little Grace sleeps after a day of playing in the sand. Kate sleeps, tired from being a mother, anxious in the house of her husband's father. A rooster crows. A lizard scurries across the floor, stops and becomes invisible through the magic of its camouflage and immobility. With a sheet drawn over my head, protection from bites, I sink at last into a dreamless sleep.

"Bincent! Bincent, where are you my baby? I got your coffee, angel."

"Here, Gloria," I hear my father answer from the back yard. Outside the metal louvered window of my bedroom an Erica palm rustles in a hot morning breeze. Water from a garden hose pit-a-pats then splashes against the dry sandy soil. Vincent's petunias are drinking. I get up, wash, and walk out back past my sleeping family, bidding good morning to a lizard here and there, and into the sunlight. A squadron of brown pelicans skims and glides over the turquoise of breaking waves in search of breakfast. I'm hungry ... for a doughnut.

"Ah, good morning, my boy. Come sit down. How'd you sleep?" my father asks. Seated in a rusty garden chair holding the hose in one hand and coffee cup in the other, he garbles his words around a large Partagas cigar. A woman is seated next to him.

"Good."

"Oh, Bincent, he's bery handsome man. How do you do? My name is Gloria."

"Hello. I'm Leon. We met once before." I hold Gloria's extended thick hand for a moment. Once a chamber maid at the Villa Cofresi Hotel down the beach where she first met my father, she now runs Gloria's Home, a rooming house for tourists next door. A Creole in her early fifties, she is heavy set, barefoot, and fond of rum. Her three or four daughters now live in Queens and Brooklyn. Every morning she brings my father a cup of coffee and in the afternoon she will often cross over from her yard to check on him and perhaps have some drink.

"So, Leon, you look nice like your brother Josh. You paint and speaka Spanish?"

"No, he teaches. He's good. They're all good," my father answers.

"Oh, that's good. So you got a brother who's a doctor—"

"Robert! The oldest! He's three doctors, now. A neurologist, an internist, and God save us, a psychiatrist!" my father interjects.

"Si, Bincent, that's the doctor with five daughters and three wives, and Leon teaches, and Josh, the middle son, he's my baby. He speakada beautiful Espanish. So, Leon, you married?"

"Yes, he's married to Kate and the girl, Grace!"

"Yes, I'm married to Kate, and Grace is my daughter. They're sleeping now. I believe you met them a few years ago when Grace was a baby."

"Oh, jes. Das right. You have a beautiful family. Josh, he's older than you?"

"Yes."

"Ah, but he has many girlfriends." Gloria laughs loudly, then stops suddenly. Looking beyond the fence of the yard down the beach, she whispers, "There she is … brujeria." An ebony-skinned woman with gray hair is walking slowly and silkily up from the sandy shore toward the public walkway which runs through the grass between my father's house and the one directly to the south. Her white muslin dress flutters in the breeze. Her face is serene and head is still as if she walks with a basket of fruit on her head. "Brujeria, Bincent," Gloria again whispers.

"Bruhairea, what!" Vincent exclaims, annoyed and not seeing.

"Voodoo, Bincent, voodoo. The police lady's coming."

"Voodoo, shmoodoo! So what! I could care less!"

When my father first bought the house, he put up a fence along the public beach access. This woman, his neighbor across the street and a local constable, disputed the boundary along which the fence ran. He obtained a court order in his favor, waved it in the woman's face, and in view of many neighbors, loudly ordered her out of his sight.

"Ay, Bincent … Leon, you know about the fence?"

I nod.

"You know about brujeria, the voodoo?" she asks.

I nod again.

"The police lady, she's got brujeria."

"I had a West Indian friend who believed in voodoo, and we hung rooster's feet over the door to protect our house. But my father doesn't need protection—"

"You're damn right!" he adds.

"Vincent's full of voodoo, Gloria. The spirits flee from him."

"Will you two stop this talk? Gloria, get out of here!"

"O.K., Bincent, I see you later." Gloria leaves, carrying her two empty coffee cups.

"Madness," my father sighs. "You'll take me swimming this morning?"

"Sure."

"Then we'll go see the new house in the mountains, my 'final folly,' the title of my latest play."

Grace emerges from the house rubbing her eyes, her blond hair sparkling in the sunlight. She wears a white T-shirt with a sailboat on it and nothing covers her little bare bug-bitten butt. Looking out at the water and up at the palms, she then notices us sitting and prances over in petite high steps. She climbs onto my father's knee.

"Pop-Pop," she says to my father, "your house is in Puerto Rico! There's sand here, and birds, and the ocean!"

"Yes, and I have many other houses."

"Cape Cod?"

"Yes."

"I was born in Cape Cod."

"Yes, and like your father, you were baptized in the same waters of Wellfleet's Loagy Bay, except your father shrouded the entire episode with some ghastly religious prayer."

"It's not gassy!" Grace defends against the sensed criticism. "Daddy, what's gassy?"

"He said 'ghastly' which means bad. Pop-Pop doesn't approve of religion."

"Pop-Pop? Why do you say that?"

"Because life is a thing of beauty and what you make of it, not a plea. It is a fight to the finish."

"Oh ... Pop-Pop?"

"Yes?"

"Pop-Pop, you have a pretend leg," Grace says with a smile.

"Yes."

"It's hard," she says, swinging her little heel against the leg from atop his knee.

"Ugh, speaking of which, you can go sit on your Daddy's leg now. How I hate that word 'Daddy.' So bourgeois. Why didn't you have her call you Pop, like me?"

"We wanted to distinguish from you. Anyway, she calls me Daddy, Dad, Leon, and Pop."

On the beach I sit, curling my toes in the sand. Once again, miserable. I wish I had religion, another God to lift me out of this despair-ridden paradise. But no, it is not possible. I've tried it before. He raised me without God, in fact trained me to disdain any of that stuff. So? Most often I am without hope. I am forever in need of this alluring, hideous father. To seek god, liberation, and love is to depart from him. That, my friends, is plain disloyalty! And thus my deepest spiritual urges seem to tear at my soul. I tell you, if life is a fight to the finish, he has me knocked out in the first round. If, as he says, man is the measure of all things, I do not measure up. I am not a man. The triumph of the will is not my victory. I have failed the standards of my class and breeding, and neither being a Harvard lawyer with Davis, Polk, like my uncle, nor a Jewish intellectual, nor an activist secure in a noble cause, nor a free spirited artist can save me. I am, simply put, a failure. A festering wound which does not heal. A wimp. I smell the sea's cyclical sweet decay and life, while Grace, enrapt in a flirtatious game of tag with the breaking surf, screams and laughs. Ah, what loveliness she is, pouring forth her soul abroad in such an ecstasy!

Isn't it funny how a distant memory will somehow vividly reappear without warning or apparent reason?

When I was ten, my friend Charlie and I had decided to do some sliding with an aluminum saucer in the snow before he went home for the night. He had come over after school to play with my H.O. trains, and even though it was now dark on this late January afternoon, we thought it would be fun to take a few runs on the steps just inside the 86th street entrance to Carl Schurz Park on the south side. The park was a familiar stomping ground in my life where often I went to walk our cocker spaniel Polly, or climb on the rocks. Since my infancy I had played in the park's playground and sand boxes, and as I grew older I liked to run up to John Finley Walk and watch the freighters ply their way up the East River, past the flashing Pearlwick Hampers sign, and through the fierce currents of Hell Gate underneath the Triboro Bridge. Sometimes the deep resonance of a freighter's fog horn would fill the silent, very early morning darkness of my bedroom, and the vision of a powerful ocean going ship bound for some distant port soothed me back to sleep. The snowy steps were in eyesight of the front door of my house.

"Neato!" Charlie exclaimed seeing the saucer run. "I can't stay long cause I'm supposed to be home. But let's go!"

"All right!" I yelled as I ran to the top of the stairs tugging the silver dish. "Watch this, Charlie!" Seating myself firmly in the aluminum saucer and holding both straps tightly, I rocked over the top step with just enough momentum and careened down the three flights of steps, halloing all the way.

"My turn!" Charlie shouted excitedly, grabbing the saucer and running up the stairs. I followed him up into the darkness at the top.

Just as Charlie was seating himself in the saucer, a dark figure emerged from out of a shadow, walked slowly toward us, his steps crunching in the crusty snow, and spoke.

"You shouldn't be hangin' around here," he said with agitation, his pimpled face coming into view. His hands were thrust into the pockets of a black leather jacket with a turned up collar.

"How come?" Charlie said, looking up from his cross-legged position in the saucer.

"There's going to be a rumble. There's a gang fight goin' to happen, and you could get hurt," the young man said menacingly.

"Well, we just live across the street, so we'll get out of here. Let's go, Charlie," I said.

"No. You stay with me. It's not safe. I'll protect you. Come with me."

Scared, Charlie and I reluctantly went along, our sparkless eyes meeting, resigned to our inability to make a run for it. Up the walkway away from the steps and further into the park, turning left and up into the elevated, dark promenade and sitting area adjoining the playground where my mother had swung me and watched me at play in the sandbox and where a snot-nosed bullying toddler had once frightened me terribly, across the crunching snow, to the flagpole, to a bench, we walked. Only the lights of the apartment buildings on East End Avenue and the occasional flicker from Gracie Mansion across the way sparkled through the bare winter branches. All the rest was darkness and there was no gang.

He sat between us. He took out a knife. He said, "You'll do what I say."

First he made Charlie, then me, then Charlie suck on his pecker. Then he made each of us masturbate him.

When it was over, and he had wiped himself off on Charlie's new sweater, he said first to me, then to Charlie, "You got any money?"

I gave him a quarter.

Then he said first to me, then to Charlie, "You got a watch?"

Charlie gave him his watch.

"You stay here for ten minutes. If you move, I'll kill you," he said pulling up his collar against the cold. "Ten minutes," he said again and left. We sat silently and in a minute or two we saw the distant silhouette of his figure sprinting silently toward and disappearing onto John Finley Walk. Charlie and I walked quickly out of the park, carrying the saucer.

"I'll see ya later, Charlie."

"Yeah, see ya," he said, walking to the bus stop.

"Their stories don't match, sir. He's sayin' he was on his way to the bus stop, and your boy's sayin' they was playin' with the saucer. No match, and unfortunately, these kind of things happen all the time. But we'll do what we can," the detective said to my father.

My father, not without caring, made light of the episode to de-emphasize its emotional impact. "It's happened. What can you do?" he said.

I didn't feel particularly traumatized by it. It was an out-of-the-ordinary, intense event, I thought, one in which someone had taken an unusual interest in me. I knew I wouldn't forget what had happened, and I thought maybe I could write about it someday. And revealing the episode had created a moment of intimacy between me and my father; I felt important. I don't know what else.

Kate gets up and joins us on the beach. We eat banana cake and a stale doughnut. Grace plays. We watch.

"So far, no frontal assaults, Kate. Just a few lateral attacks and covert disruptions. Last night he said he was looking for signs of genetically inferior qualities in Grace passed on from your family. You know, the same Bayonne bullshit."

"That bastard. What great stock does he think he comes from? Bayonne! I've never set foot in Bayonne!"

I must explain the Bayonne epithet. Six years ago in January it was born. Sitting around a large round table in a chandeliered dining room of New York's Cosmopolitan Club, my brothers Josh and Robert, Kate, my mother, her fiancé, and her sisters Mimi Chandler and Eleanor Farnsworth were celebrating my mother's pending wedding to Jack Weldon, a labor reporter and Movement friend of more than forty years. Regressing to familiar sibling responses to a formal family occasion, my early middle-aged brothers and I secretively began making faces at one another to ease our boredom. Then Josh casually lit up a joint as if it were just another cigarette and nonchalantly passed it to me. I took a hit and nonchalantly passed it to Robert. Robert smoked and passed it back to Josh. Of course, this was all very rude. But the ritual went entirely unnoticed, making it all the more invigorating.

"You know something," my doctor brother Robert quietly said to me, "that wife of yours is nothing but a manipulative

Bayonne street hustler. You guys could have come to Mom's for Christmas dinner at one o'clock instead of four. But no, she had to be with her family in Jersey, which ruined Christmas for my kids. Christmas is supposed to be for the fucking kids," he whispered.

"I don't know what you're talking about. We made every effort to fly back here from California and please her family and mine. We had two Christmas dinners in one afternoon, for Christ's sake," I whispered back.

No more was said at this time. An appropriate response would surely have disrupted my mother's joyousness after her long period of unhappiness and loneliness. But the insult to my wife registered. Bayonne, in my imagination the oil-slicked, methane-infused essence of the worst of New Jersey, a toxic industrial waterfront with divisions of aligned cargo containers and heaps of garbage, more low than Hoboken, Elizabeth, and Jersey City, and less renowned than the stink of Jersey Flats, where lonely, horny merchant sailors far from home seek a corner bar and a girl in empty, broken-down neighborhoods, is by any standard an insult.

Now Kate, having cultivated out her Jersey accent, gone to college and graduate school, become an English teacher, and then a marriage, family, and child therapist, is certainly the star of her family. Yes, she has elevated herself out of the peculiarities of her Irish Catholic immigrant heritage—her grandmother's domestic service to the Park Avenue wealthy, her cousin's twenty-three years of

Schaeffer Brewery truck driving, the lone picture of Christ exposing his beating heart on a bare living room wall. But this process of nourishing an evolving identity did, in fact, begin with her father William O'Hara, not of Bayonne, but of Brooklyn.

William married one Helen O'Hara (same surname, but unrelated) and went off to war. A tail-gunner on a B-17, William was ordered to bail out over Germany after the plane got hit and caught fire on its last mission. The plane, however, limped back over the Channel to England, and William parachuted into the arms of his Nazi captors. Without a plane, the Nazis were convinced he was a spy. In his eighteen months as a prisoner of war, William was lined up three times in front of a firing squad and shot with blanks. This psychological torture was designed to extract a confession. With nothing to confess he was finally freed by the Russians. He returned to the States and began living his life, as he said, "on borrowed time."

On the G.I. Bill this same Bayonne-slandered William took his wife Helen up to Burlington and attended the University of Vermont, majoring in music. They produced their first child Kate in Rouces Point a year after the war's end. After he graduated, they moved back to New York City. William attended Columbia Teacher's College, received a master's degree in music, and then moved out of the city where he raised a family not in Bayonne but first in Ridgefield Park and then Bogota.

William worked for the next twenty-two years as a music teacher at East New York Elementary School. To support his two sons and two daughters, he supplemented his income by working as a janitor, milk truck driver, and private music teacher. Every year at Christmas he took his fifth grade students to New York's Port Authority Bus Terminal to give a free choral concert to the commuters rich and poor, vagrants, hookers, and runaways. In 1977 at the age of fifty-five, William had a massive heart attack and died. A Bayonne slur this honorable life need not endure.

Now if the Bayonne aspersion (and my apologies to Bayonne for the elitist sullying of your good name) were born at the Cos Club, it was conceived a year and two months earlier. My family had had the opportunity of meeting the O'Hara family less William in late 1980. Kate and I had flown back from California to attend a party given by my mother in honor of our marriage, and all those previously seated at my mother's Cosmopolitan Club engagement party were present. Even my father put in a flamboyant, whirlwind appearance in the apartment of his ex-wife to honor his son and new bride. In walked the O'Hara brothers, Brian and Sean, sporting not velvet-collared fine wool overcoats but bulky Robert Hall polyester jackets. With awkward smiles and withheld Jersey accented voices they congregated along with their overweight sister Maura and her stocky Italian husband Anthony Gridone underneath the Adelaide Chase oil portrait of my mother and grandmother.

"Aren't they cute!" declared Aunt Mimi. "How Irish they look! How grand! Why your grandfather would be tickled pink!" My grandfather for many years had employed Irish maids, and late in his life he had grown quite fond of Ireland and the Irish. At least, I suppose, I hadn't married a nigger.

Well, if this Bayonne matter was conceived and born in a milieu of matrimony and holiday cheer, the intended slur was soon challenged in that somber moment when a loved one approaches life's final curtain. Two months after my mother's wedding, my father was walking home down 86th Street toward East End Avenue when pain in his right calf forced him to rest atop a garbage can. Unable to continue walking, he hailed a cab. The driver helped him into his house. He called his friend, Dr. Begner, who came right over, examined him, and then ordered him to New York Hospital by ambulance. I received a call in Ventura, California from my brother Josh.

"The old man's in real bad shape. He's in the hospital. You'd better come back here."

Not since my mother moved out of our house ending our family seventeen years ago had I felt that familiar grave stillness of an inevitable, dreaded event. I took a taxi directly from Kennedy to the hospital. My brothers met me in the corridor outside of intensive care.

"How's he doin'?" I asked Robert, the doctor.

Through exceedingly rare teary eyes, he shook his head and answered, "Not good. Two aortic aneurysms, one in the arch, one in the diaphragm. They're a ballooning of a weakened main artery wall. The arch carries all the blood to the brain. If the one there goes, he's finished."

"What about the other?"

"He's just out of surgery. They clamped it to keep it from blowin'. It was throwing out sclerotic material, paste like stuff, which was clogging up his right leg."

"Can I see him?"

Robert shrugged and said, "He looks awful. He's in there. Go ahead."

I found him through a web of tubes, barricaded by humming, clicking equipment which glowed green in the dimly lit room, lying there, face up, eyes closed, mouth open, tubes in nose and arm, inflated—inflated like the block-long Macy's Day Parade Bullwinkle I had come across on acid when returning home one Thanksgiving pre-dawn morn in 1968, tied down and resting between Central Park West and Columbus on 77th Street. Cut the lines and he would have floated up and away over the city lights. I held his hand for a moment and left.

My brothers and I had pizza across the street. I had a couple of bourbons with ice, a dash of bitters and a twist. We then went to Robert's hospital-subsidized apartment on Fifth Avenue down the block from Mount Sinai. He lived there with his second wife (a Jewish nurse from the Bronx distinguished, my father would say, by an accent lacking cultivation) and the second and third of his now three daughters. The wife and daughters were asleep.

"Oh, wow, Slade! You've got a computer!" Josh said with delight. Slade, a gun slinging hero of a fifties grade B movie, was a nickname given by Josh denoting Robert's more sinister, James Dean qualities. "Let's play!"

"Let's smoke," Robert said.

"All right!" Josh rejoined with enthusiasm.

With some background rhythm-and-blues rumbling in hypnotic cadence, we passed a joint. They huddled over the monitor, their heads bopping in time to the music, laughing. I drifted off to the other side of the living room and stood looking out the window.

"Oh, Papa," I thought, "has your time come?" Outside the lights in the Central Park blurred, then swam in abstraction.

I turned and faced my brothers. "These idiots," I said to myself, "have they no feeling? Our father is dying, and is there no communion? Just computer goonery?" Surely I had had an eleven year reprieve in Los Angeles from my father's meddling, from the teeth of his psychoanalytical buzz saw, but had their suffering or discomfort been so intense as to produce glee at the moment of his departure?

Robert spun up out of his seat and around in a circle, twirling his forearms around one another and rocking up and down in time to the music.

"We are all atoms, yes atoms," he chanted, "swirling in the universe. Atoms meet and atoms are repelled. Atoms, yes atoms. We are all atoms."

I stepped toward him, suddenly determined to confront what I considered to be his sociopathic disconnect from reality, his lifelong hostile, at times violent interactions with me and other family members, and the resultant lifelong fear I had of his bullying. And, most importantly, I was determined to confront his recent disrespectful characterization of my wife.

"I don't understand why you called Kate a Bayonne street hustler."

He stopped dancing. "Because that's what she is. She manipulated the whole fucking Christmas Day schedule—"

Immediately I knew he was about to reiterate his ridiculous, contemptuous accusation made at the Cosmopolitan Club that Kate had ruined Christmas for his daughters by first visiting her family in New Jersey and only later in the day celebrating the holiday with his girls at my mother's apartment.

"I don't know what you're talking about."

"I'm tellin' ya, she's a fuckin'—"

"You're full of shit!" I erupted in a rage while grabbing his shirt.

He shoved me in the chest with both of his arms. "Keep your fucking hands off me!"

"Insult my wife, asshole, I'll kill you!" I roared, lunging at him. With one arm and fist wrapped around his back, I pulled the hair on the back of his head with my other hand while he pummeled at my ribs.

Josh jumped out of his seat, shouting, "Cut it out, you guys!" trying unsuccessfully to break up our furious, inseparable embrace.

"I'm strong now, you shit!" I screamed, as our violent waltz whirled us out of balance, and we crashed onto the mahogany coffee table, collapsing it.

For a moment we lay there, stalemated with his finger between my teeth ready to be bitten off and his thumb dug into a socket ready to gouge out my eye. We released our holds and stood.

Sylvia, Robert's wife, entered the room, shouting, "What are you guys doing, for God's sake, still fighting twenty-five years later?"

"I'm through with you!" I bellowed at Robert. "You've brought nothing but pain to my life! You make me sick!"

I picked up my coat, went to the front door, and turned, adding one concluding malediction. "It's over!" I said, as the door slammed behind me.

I spent the night in Josh's apartment. In the morning I called Robert. Of course it wasn't 'over' last night. I had scarcely seen him for two decades. I apologized for breaking the coffee table. We agreed to split the cost of repair.

The morning sun was white, clean, and without heat. I walked up 79th street, around the Museum of Natural History, and into Central Park at 77th Street. After the weighty events of the previous evening the bitter cold was bracing, not uncomfortable, and the familiar lake and Delacorte fountain and music shell seemed new after my long California absence. Exiting at 72nd Street, I side-stepped a cushy, navy blue canvassed perambulator with spoked off-white wheels briskly pushed by a red-faced governess and continued walking south on Fifth Avenue. A sable-chapeaued gentleman in camelhair greatcoat hailed a taxi while holding the adoring hand of his daughter. Perhaps they were going to the zoo or Rockefeller Center. At 70th Street an old man stooped over his smoky, sweet-smelling cart, tending coals and vigorously arranging chestnuts with tong-like fingers. I crossed the street toward Madison and entered the warmth and silence of the Frick Collection.

My heels clicked against marble floors as I entered the inner sanctum of the steel baron's mansion, where the softly reverberating souls of Bellini, Rembrandt, and Ingres mingled with the gentle splash of a fountain in an enclosed verdant courtyard. I sat on a bench against one wall and listened.

Bayonne receded. I had at last defended my honor and the honor of my wife and her family. No invasive scum from the past could again threaten to pollute my present. Yet, I am sure, my antisocial personality-disordered brother had not really known or was unable to control what he was saying. I sighed and thought of my father. Like a mist, sorrow returned, adding itself to the ethereal mélange of the room.

My father did not die this time. His condition stabilized, but the circulation in his right leg deteriorated. We talked almost daily on the phone. The doctors had advised against operating on the aortic arch because of the high risk of stroke or cardiac arrest while on the heart-lung machine. To leave it untreated meant instantaneous death should it burst. My father simply said, "Fuck it! What better way is there to go?" and hoped that the aneurysm was strong, perhaps even calcified. Within a month, however, his leg became gangrenous and it was amputated below the knee. Immediately prior to the leg operation when there was continuing doubt about his ability to survive another trauma, I spoke again with him from my office in California.

"Well, Pop, if you get there before I do … "

"I'll be waiting for you," he answered weakly.

"I love you, Pop," I said.

"I love you, too."

He pulled through and we continued our conversations while he recuperated and learned to use and adjust to a prosthesis at Burke Rehabilitation Center in White Plains. After purchasing a lower right leg from a run down mannequin factory in downtown Los Angeles, I planned on creating a ruby and emerald-sequined object d'art for Long John Silver in anticipation of a summer visit. Although the effort helped me adjust to the idea of a legless father, I decided against giving him the thing. He seemed so very vulnerable. In the course of our talks, I filled my father in on some of the details he missed in his five-month ordeal. The Bayonne episode was one such detail.

"Isn't that great?" he said in reference to Robert's remark. "What an astute, distilled observation! What chutzpah!" he chortled.

"I found it insulting and I kicked his fucking ass!" I retorted disbelievingly, exaggerating my part in the fight for emphasis.

"You and Kate both take him too seriously. What he said was correct. Kate is an essentially low person."

"Aw, shit!" I said, dropping the conversation for fear of exploding his aneurysm.

So much for Bayonne. I wash down the last of the banana cake with coffee. I say to Kate, "It's just part of the price you pay for a tropical paradise respite from the northern deep freeze. You can't take him too seriously. Let the winds of heaven blow between you, as the Viking Runes say. You know, you do your thing, I'll do mine, and if we meet, how beautiful or some such Fritz Perls horseshit."

We laugh. Looking up from her cakes and sand castles, Grace laughs, too. A wave rolls over, breaks, and races up over her back toward her creations, flattening them at the apex of its advance, then retreats. Stunned by the assault, she drops her jaw. Our jaws drop, too. She looks up at us asking with her eyes 'Should I cry?" then shrieks with delight. We all laugh.

"Robert! Josh! Leon, my boy!" The sound of my father's voice, habitually naming each son in order to discern by elimination just which son is now present with him, carries over the fence down to where we are sitting. "My swim!"

"O.K.! I'm ready!" I call back. Taking Kate's empty cup, I stand and head up to the house. "I'll see you in a few minutes, honey."

On the veranda seated on the end of an improvised daybed made of plywood and four-inch foam, my father unstraps the rubber socket of his artificial limb into which fits his stump. He removes two white wool socks and sighs with relief.

"God, you'd think in this age of flaunted technological advancement some idiot could invent a comfortable leg. In my bedroom, dear, on the floor," he points in the general direction of his room, "my swim leg."

I enter his room which is in incredible disarray. Unmatched socks, orange plaid pants and a green seersucker sports jacket bought in some thrift shop, several handkerchiefs, gaily colored, torn undershirts, a bathrobe, more pants, a purple shirt cascading off a table, all meander through mountains of greasy bed sheets, past opened books, a plastic urinal, scribbled pieces of paper, a phone off the hook, a bag of pills, an unfinished scotch and water in a plastic glass, around, across, and underneath the bed, through an unused walker, by old shoes and sneakers everywhere like river bottom boulders and stones ready to trip your feet, and from it all, remarkably, emanates that never-thought-it-would-arrive musty smell of old man-ness. There, buried beneath this everyday debris in a corner, barely distinguishable from the other shoes, a worn, black sneaker stiffly protrudes upward, and in it is snugly planted the made-to-look-lifelike plastic swim leg.

"And bring me a number three and a number five sock in the bag hanging on the doorknob."

"Right." I return with the socks, numbered to indicate thickness, and the leg.

"Number two, three, five, ten, they make no difference. Always the pain, the phantom pain." He grimaces as he pulls on the socks and the leg.

"You mean after all this time your foot still hurts?"

"Yes! My foot, my toes! And they no longer even exist! Fascinating! Come, my boy, to the beach!" Wrapping a self-designed, ankle-length piece of purple curtain fabric around his waist, held together by Velcro, and draping a large yellow beach towel over his red undershirt, he now slowly walks with a wooden cane in each hand off the veranda toward the water. I follow as if in a ceremonial procession.

A moment later we stand at the crest of the beach. A breeze blows through his white hair and flutters his garments. A tight smile of pleasure appears in his eyes. He inhales the salt air. He gazes at the sea with unmistakable determination. He is Rodin's Balzac.

I hold his arm and he uses his canes for balance against the surf. A wave breaks. Then proceeding forward, casting aside the canes and diving into the next wave, he swims.

I stand. Holding the canes like a baby, I watch. The water swirls about him and pulls at my feet and legs.

Twenty years ago winter is bleak in Madison, Wisconsin. When you get off the Northwest Orient plane leaving behind New York City which you thought was cold, the instantaneous crystallization into ice of the natural moistness within your nose lets you know right away this is some ungodly, arctic environment. Lake Mendota freezes over four feet thick and everywhere the ground is bone and head-cracking hard. Now, instead of walking around the lake to visit Picnic Point and its tranquility, I take direct walks out across the ice. Except for three or four ice boats and a few solitary walkers, the lake is barren. A mile away in front of the student union sails flutter. Winter is a bitter time here and for the most part students keep bundled up within themselves.

However, as the days warm and songbirds and the buds on trees and bushes re-appear, spring brings student unrest. For a while I have been having weekly therapy sessions with Dr. Kepecs. One day after talking with him about my lack of direction, alienation, and anxiety, I leave his office and walk around the corner into a river of protesters flowing toward University Avenue. This is not terribly surprising since riots have already gone on for three days and now National Guard troops have occupied the campus to restore order and break the student strike. Opposition to the war and the international corporate conspiracy to oppress the Third World and the American working class permeates the air like the smell and feeling of the new season.

There at the head of the parade is my friend Neil Koestler, gleefully and self-deceivingly claiming responsibility for this particular action, but really he is a lanky, ineffectual buffoon and public nose picker who comes from a painfully dull, lower middle class upbringing in suburban Philadelphia. He couldn't possibly have brought together the thousands of students participating in this march. Neil has immersed himself in Communist rhetoric as if lost in some cult, supported by a workable language and a "concrete" interpretation of the world and his place in it, the Marxist-Leninist-Maoist ideology supplanting his tortured individuality and inviting him to conform with a new rejuvenated purpose. Just look at him up there walking like a jerk, a fool, but I like him.

I join in next to my friend, and as we walk toward confrontation with the tear-gas-armed troops at the bottom of the hill, Neil greets me.

"All right! All right! Power to the people!" he exclaims. God, what a jerk!

"On strike, shut it down! Hell no, we won't go!" I offer up, and together we laugh like two jerks in the excitement and disruptiveness of the moment. Someone points to some dumpster garbage bins next to the Engineering building, and a few reckless hooligans, heightening the growing tension, dart over to them and rumble them back to the head of the parade. They will be our protection and our battering rams.

Behind us nearly five thousand students march twelve abreast. There is still killing going on everyday, every moment. Human beings are senselessly dying, and we're next. My hands join the others gripping the edge of the dumpster, and the chant "Hell no! We won't go! Hell no! We won't go!" urgently resounds for blocks around, and our hearts beat faster. We break into a trot, increasing the tempo and volume of our chant, our dumpster spearheading the assault. My mind screams with the words "No more fucking war, assholes! Fuck your stupid game! Fuck all the shit of our lives! Fuck all the shit of my life! You fucking creeps, go ahead! Shoot your guns! I don't care! Charge!"

Then, "Thud! Thud! Thud! Thud!" in rapid succession the soldiers fire and "Clang-poof! Clang-poof! Clang-poof!" canister grenades of pepper gas metallically crash on the pavement and explode all around us, instantaneously smashing the assault. Our exhilaration and heroic stupidity, the fire of our fight, are suffocated and extinguished, sending each of us scurrying and gasping for our lives. Some of us rush into an adjacent building.

Running through hallways, I find hidden refuge on a cool, dark, classroom floor. Afraid and alone, resting for an hour as my heart subsides, I walk home in the early evening darkness. I am invisible to those around me.

I think of myself as a child. Every Sunday, sometimes sooner, asthma shrinks my lungs and my hold on life. Every Monday in the fourth grade I am absent from school. In the very early hours of the morning I climb into bed with my mother. This comforts me. I think my father, who is in the other bed, is disgusted by me because he does not want a sick, mama's boy. Pop gets up very early and works in the garden. I would really like to help him. Sometimes he lets me weed.

Beginning in the summer, I get an apartment on West Washington and Mifflin. Willie Davis, the black student leader who led the spring strike, lives upstairs with his white wife. Sometimes she comes downstairs to borrow a food strainer to sift their grass. Feeling flattered and somehow more connected to the Black Movement, I gladly donate the utensil.

There was a time when the color disconnect was nonexistent, when Ernie Warner and I were kids and good friends in Warwick where we had a weekend house outside the city. He lived down the road with his mother Mona, father Big Ernie, Uncle Jim, Little Jim, Little Walt, Aunt Sylvia, Little Abe, Uncle Abe who used to sit in the outhouse for hours on end sipping his pint of whiskey, Haddie, Hodgie Baba. We rode bikes, went to the drive-in movie theater, played at the dump, crashed old baby carriages into the chicken coop, caught frogs and turtles, all went fishing together in his family's '51 black Buick, picked mushrooms, wore Hop-a-Long Cassidy chaps and cowboy hats together. Sometimes Mona would yell at all the kids, make them go into the field to get switches, and line them up for a licking, at which time I'd make haste for home as the small parade of children broke into a chorus of tears, even before their legs were stung. Then later I'd always visit Ernie over quiet pebbled circles in the creek beneath the bridge, and we were friends forever.

How is it that one comes to think of himself as a shit?

Following my father's morning triumph over impending atrophy and rigor mortis, we sit on the outer terrace beneath the arching PVC dome. Kate is making sandwiches with Grace. Gloria crosses over from her yard, her heavy feet patting on the walkway.

"Is it too early for drinks?" my father asks, his eyebrows playfully bobbing up and down as he dabs dry the last few drops of water from his swim.

"Hell, no. Hi, Gloria," I say on my way inside.

"Hello, Leon. Hello, my baby," she says to my father. "You takeda nice swim, yes?"

"I swim ... Nice? No. Necessary? Yes. This heat is unbearable! The view is the same. The waves won't stop pounding. I'm trapped in paradise! A prisoner of my condition! Thank God, my son is taking me out of here!"

"Oh, Bincent, you leabing me?"

"No!" he shouts, irritated by Gloria's clingy misinterpretation. "Not you! He's taking me for a drive up the mountain to my new house!"

Kate and Grace bring out the sandwiches along with a glass of milk and a ginger ale. A few minutes later I follow with three drinks of Jim Beam whiskey, orange juice, bitters and crushed ice. I hand a drink to my father, and as I give one to Gloria, he exclaims, "Not my Jim Beam! This Puerto Rican bitch can't tell the difference! Give her rum, that's what she likes, it's cheaper!"

"Oh, thank you, Leon. It's O.K., Bincent, this is nice," Gloria says, eagerly sipping the drink, feeling coddled by Vincent's roughness.

I shrug, offer a "Cheers," and drink. We eat our lunch.

Gloria returns to her house. In this hottest time of day we all nap. My father snores in the darkness of his room. Grace, her cheeks flushed, sleeps soundly in her tee shirt on top of the sheets. In my room on the bed where an ever so slight breeze slips through the louvers cooling her sticky, salted white body, Kate waits. Quiet early afternoon sounds—voices, a crowing rooster, the sea—murmur off the street through the heat and into the room. We make love silently, the intensity of our thrusts heightened by the hush, which would amplify, like sound through water, our pleasure-filled sighs. Looking into each other's eyes until overwhelmed by feeling, we, too, then sleep.

After splashing water on my face and taking a handful of stubby rough cigars (made in Rincon by an old man) from a package in the refrigerator, I join my father on the veranda. He is splashing on some Russian Leather cologne, used not as an allure but as a smelling salts on his beard and moustache. He ties a red bandana around his neck, puts on the dark glasses which hang on a string around his neck, adjusts his straw hat, and through his teeth which bite on a cigar, he says, "Ready? To my Final Folly!" With difficulty he walks with his cane to the rented car and seats himself.

We drive three blocks away from the beach and out of Parc Estrella, the formerly government-subsidized neighborhood, to Highway 15.

"Turn left here. I want you to stop for a minute and meet my man, Pedro Romero, before the whole fucking island becomes a mall. He's Rincon's last authentic artisan."

We drive a few hundred feet and turn into Mr. Romero's place of business where new cement castings of columns, fountains, Virgin Marys, and other yard adornments are neatly lined up.

"Hey, Pedro, my boy!" my father calls to a thin old man in a white tee shirt wearing a very large straw hat. The dark skinned man saunters up to our car, stares without expression at us, and sucks on a Marlboro.

"Pedro, this is my son, Leon." The man nods and limply shakes my extended hand which I reach out through the window.

"I told him you do good work, that you're a good artist, a bueno artiste," my father adds with an encouraging smile.

Again the man nods, still without expression.

"Have you got any broken old pieces to add to my ruins? Something with a patina, my boy?"

The man slowly points at the neatly lined up items and says dryly, "All neuvo."

"Where did you get your molds? Did you make them?" my father asks, increasing his volume and enunciation.

The man sucks again on his cigarette and answers, "Connecticut." He flashes a toothless, white-stubbled smile.

"Let's get out of here," my father says to me with exasperation. He compliments the man, "Bueno artist! (Drive!) Bueno travallo!" He forces a smile, drawing his fingers together and rocking his hand at the wrist in a gesture of feigned appreciation.

"God!" he adds, as we drive down the road in the direction from which we just came.

We pass Roho Lumber and Building Supply.

"Turn left, here!" my father cries, and we enter a very narrow paved road cut like a trench through ten-foot high rows of sugar cane. Planted across the narrow coastal plain, the cane obscures our vision for half a mile, until abruptly we climb upward, our transmission knocking and clinking like chain on a cogwheel, the cane falling beneath us as the road ascends the winding crest of a mountain ridge and plunging escarped valleys slice at the wheels on both sides of our vehicle. Below on valley floors dots of cattle vie for the shade of palm trees. We climb and dip upwards for several miles, passing houses on stilts. We enter a small hamlet perched on one of many mountaintops. On the right is a small market. On a rise a few hundred feet beyond is an empty bar and dance hall supported by six square, poured concrete pillars, some as tall as twenty-five feet, planted in the side of the mountain. It is called El Danube.

We pass the bar, following the road sharply to the right for another hundred feet to where it makes a steep descent on the edge of a valley. Here there is a small faded green adobe house, quite dirty, owned by a very old lady, and next to this house, squeezed between the narrow road and the precipitous slope, a wooden house with faded, chipped and peeling yellow paint and a rusted tin roof, a shack really, sits with its valley side also on square concrete stilts. This house is my father's Final Folly.

We park in a half space on the downhill side of the house just big enough to let another vehicle pass, where a brake failure would most definitely mean the end of your car, if not your life. We get out and breathe deeply, relieved at our safe arrival. Quite different from Parc Estrella's seascape and pounding surf, the heavy presence of quiet is startling, and when you now look out, the sky silently enters through your feet, lifting you up to the edges of the blue sky dome which drops beyond the falling hills and mountaintops to the distant horizon of the sea.

"What a view, Pop! Are you sure this Final Folly isn't the home of Apollo of Mount Parnassus?"

"Ahh, I'm glad you know something, my boy. Come in. Do come in," he says, opening the door.

We enter a twenty by twenty-four-foot room, recently opened up from two or three smaller rooms with three dark, exposed wooden walls and a weathered delaminating plywood floor littered with mouse droppings, dust, and rubble. The fourth wall on the right is made of corrugated metal roofing painted with purple enamel. Incongruously sitting within this wretched space along the right-hand wall is a five-foot-wide, four-foot-deep, twenty-foot-long aquamarine, empty concrete swimming pool in which scurries a trapped mouse.

"God! Pop, what's to keep this pool from tumbling down the mountain?"

"My man poured four concrete columns underneath it. Then he jumped up and down in it to convince me of its strength. At least I'll be able to swim alone, and if it collapses, so I'll wash down the mountain!"

A door in the left-hand wall leads into a dark kitchen area with some rotting cupboards. Through another door in the same wall sits a filthy, lidless toilet bowl and a shower base without a stall or curtain. A twelve-foot-wide, floor-to-ceiling opening sawed into the back wall allows light to pour in, and outside this future doorway a covered plywood deck rests atop twenty-five-foot-tall concrete columns sunk into the sixty degree grade. Two chairs and a wobbly table sit on the deck. Far below a lone Brahma cow stands in the shade of a cluster of palm trees. And looking out is the view.

"Ah, good! They didn't steal them," my father says tearing open a package of lavender bed sheets. "We'll hang these, my boy, on the roadside wall. It's cheaper and easier than paint or windows, and they'll ripple along with the metal wall and the water. Rippling light, rippling air, rippling water. Alive, as they say!" He hands me a package of tacks and in a few minutes the sheets are hung.

"Perfect madness!" my father declares. "And now, shall we sit on the deck and have a ... Ach! We brought nothing to drink! What shall we do?"

"I'll walk up to the market and buy some rum and ice."

"Ah, good thinking. Here, take some money. Buy a dustpan and some club soda, too. I'll sit here and smoke my cigar."

Outside I breathe deeply again and walk up the hill. I feel like I'm in another time, and most definitely this is a different place. There are no gringos here. I pass El Danube where through the white metal grating I see many picnic tables around the empty dance floor, and behind the bar a man swabs a glass and holds it up to the light. I walk down the road and into the mercado.

I find the rum, ice, soda, and dustpan, and the woman responds favorably to my request for two cups.

"Do-you-have-any-peanuts?" I carefully enunciate to the woman.

"Pea?" She smiles hesitantly and shakes her head.

"Peanuts," I say again.

"Penis?" she asks with widening eyes and a broad grin.

"Pea-nuts. Nuts. Nuts to eat," I mime a picking of nuts from my hand and munching action.

"Ah, si," she laughs and points to peanuts on a shelf.

"Gracias," I say, receiving my change.

"Gracias, senor."

I walk back to the house, pulling a stubby cigar from my shirt pocket and lighting it. I could live here, I think to myself.

"So, my boy," my father begins as we sit side by side admiring the view and sipping our stiffly poured drinks, "how do you intend to recoup your life?"

Aha. There it was. The question. Loaded with the assumption of a lost life. A failed life. Is not a dig leveled at a son a dig at one's self? This question was more than a dig. Was it love or murder?

"Well, I'm going to write," I said awkwardly, as the silence filled with his unspoken criticism.

And this, my friends, is my beginning.

Two

THE FINER LIFE

Standing on a chair atop the brownstone stoop, I admired the glistening brass knocker against the dark green door. I carefully poured more Noxon polish on the blackened rag and dabbed it on the numbers 5, 4, and 9. The warm spring sun made this first outdoor chore since snow shoveling all the more enjoyable. Tiny leaves transforming the sycamore buds filled the air with expectation, and chirping sparrows flitting in and out of the bushes in front of the four story brick house were joyous. Mothers and governesses with carriages and strollers, nuns from the Misericordia Hospital, gentlemen with dachshunds or cockers and newspapers tucked under their arms, laughing tots on tricycles and nine year olds, like myself, haloing and roaring by on two wheelers, all streamed steadily by, stopping at the corner of 86th Street and East End Avenue, then crossing into Carl Schurz Park.

I buffed up the numbers to a gleaming shine, jumped off the chair and bounded down the stairs and into the middle of the street for a better view of my completed work. What a miracle was worked by the spots of golden luster, like deep red lipstick on an aging mother! Although its bricks were fading and in need of some paint, the narrow, seventeen-foot wide Queen Anne house, destined to be an historic landmark, held its own among the other three houses to its right and the one to its left on Henderson Place.

To make up for its less than pristine condition, my father had added a few cosmetic flourishes to the facade which set the house apart—a fine English knocker; nine panes over nine double windows on all of the upper three floors, including the third floor dormer set against the mansard slate roof shared by my brothers' bedrooms; purely ornamental metal shutters on the first two floors; white window frames rather than the typical black or dark green frames of the neighbors. The house, irrespective of the internal chaos both natural and unnatural to a family of five, was one of my father's pinnacle life achievements.

Of course, any steps along the road from poverty are an achievement, but for a son whose Russian Jewish socialist father had eked out a living by selling newspapers on street corners in Far Rockaway and whose mother worked as a seamstress and scavenged dead fish off the beach for dinners, my father's 1943, $7,000 purchase of this house, located just two blocks from Gracie Mansion, was a proud moment. Had his parents been alive, they would have yet again marveled at his success. Nonetheless they had lived long enough to see him well on his way to prosperity, even if he was a little wild, graduating on scholarship from the Ethical Culture School (where, he said, so many of the children had been intimidatingly rich) and Alexander Meiklejohn's Experimental College in Madison, Wisconsin, and authoring at the age of twenty-seven a Broadway play with his name on the marquee in lights during the 1937 season. For paternal advice on the house purchase my father had thus consulted his wealthy and distinguished father-in-law Robert Ward Chandler in Boston. And much to the chagrin of my mother who had wanted to stay downtown in their Greenwich Village apartment surrounded by artists and Norman Thomas political idealists, my grandfather had advised that making the move was sound and the only proper thing to do. So, five years before my birth and in the year of my brother Josh's birth, my father, my mother and my three month old brother Robert moved uptown.

I walked back onto the sidewalk and up the first step of the stoop, when suddenly I was stunned and drenched to the bone by a bombardment of several gallons of icy water, a wastepaper basketful at least, followed by peels of my brother Josh's hilarious laughter cascading down from his third floor window.

"Oh, Josh! You, bum! I'll get you for this!" I screamed, racing into the house and up the stairs. "Here I come, you cocksucker!" I hurled myself around a fat baluster on the second floor and continued up to the third.

"Leon, now you watch your mouth, or I'll be washin' it out with soap," Virginia, our black housekeeper and cook warned from my parent's second floor bedroom where she was gathering up laundry.

"Quiet down out there!" my father shouted from behind the drawn curtains at the doorway to the living room (also on the second floor) behind which he clacked away in seclusion on his typewriter.

In a last burst of energy and out of breath, my feet and hands alternately slapping the steep steps, I reached the top floor and charged toward the bathroom.

"Shut the fuck up!" Robert yelled from his bedroom as I passed. In the bathroom I saw Josh's feet go up the ladder and into the skylight well where he was frantically trying to unlock the cover and escape to the safety of the roof.

"I've got you now!" I laughed hysterically as I filled a glass with water blasted from the faucet, doused my brother's legs and butt, and filled the glass again, splattering water all over the room.

"No, no, no! I give up! Uncle! Uncle!" Josh cried.

Robert came into the bathroom, slugged me in the arm, and said again, "Now I said shut the fuck up, fathead! I'm trying to read!"

"Don't fuckin' hit me," I screamed, lunging at my oldest brother, my arms flailing. He laughingly quashed my assault by holding me at bay with a straight-arm and hand clasped over my head until my unconnected jabs and hooks subsided, and I, too, could only laugh at my helplessness.

"All of you, outside!" my father commanded from downstairs.

"Yeah, Leon, get the crutches and a cup," Josh said excitedly. "I've got to see you at work at least once before going back to school." Josh had just returned home yesterday, a Friday, for Easter vacation from his Putney, Vermont boarding school where he was in his freshman year.

"Oh, no. Not that again. Go get a football in the cellar, Leon!" Robert ordered. As the oldest sibling, sixteen and a sophomore at the Van Janssen School for Boys, Robert was not as interested in the shenanigans of his younger brothers as he was in cars, sports, and girls.

I changed my shirt. Then the three of us barreled downstairs. Josh and Robert went out the front door, and I went down into the basement where my mother was at work in the kitchen, doing dishes in slow motion, oblivious to the recent commotion upstairs, chewing on her tongue and singing "Danny Boy."

The bottom floor or basement was located beneath street level. In back of the house, just outside our kitchen, was a claustrophobic backyard, filled with soot and dog and cat shit from our cream-colored cocker spaniel Polly and cat Cosmo. Access to it was shared by two adjacent houses. In the middle of the yard sat a bronze female nude, shat upon by the pigeons and sculpted, my father proudly informed us all, by his former lover Sonya Little, an older artist of some repute who had lent to my young father some of her passionate distinction before being debilitated by a stroke. Thence abandoning that relationship, my father was saddled, so we were taught, with my more boringly conventional yet distinctively upper crust mother. But, he told us, she had been good in bed, and only recently had references to her and her sisters' juiceless lack of passion—a family of "leather cunts"—become commonplace.

A rarely used door into a dark cellar on the left belonged to our neighbors the Polks. Sammy Polk, a Madras bow-tied Wall Street lawyer with straw hat, was the father of Josh's friend Johnny, a former classmate at Van Janssen (now at Milton Academy). Leaning our backs against the mansard roof, we used to edge along the eight-inch wide ledge from Robert's third floor bedroom to Johnny's. What was most unusual about Sammy was that he had sailed the family yacht from Pocasset to Bermuda one January and had never been heard from again.

Another door cut into a tall fence opened into the Bramante's backyard across from our kitchen. The Bramantes, art collectors and musicians, were exotic people but not really friends of our family. He was handsome like Errol Flynn, and she had a high forehead and lots of long black hair wrapped round and around in a bun off her left ear. Once their backyard door opened and Segovia and Carl Sandburg both peeked into our yard.

Running the fifteen feet from the Bramantes to our kitchen door was another six-foot high fence separating us from the Byrd and Cox's backyard. Robert and Betty Byrd were old and proper people who were driven by chauffeur to their weekend residence on Long Island. They had a somewhat moronic and dependent son Dannet in his late twenties who had a long, unfortunate history of seizures. Sometimes Dannet would appear at our adjoining basement doors underneath the stoop, often with an abrasion on his forehead from a recent fall. Grabbing me in a headlock or pulling my hair, he would slowly say, "All right, kid, now I've got ya." Then he'd rap me over the head with his knuckles or push snow into my face. He wanted to be friendly, I think, but he didn't know how. One day Dannet jumped or fell off the roof and simply ended it all.

Next door to the Byrds and sharing the same yard, the Coxes lived. Dean Cox was in advertising and had created a well-known campaign for a major brokerage house using a "nest egg" motif. His wife's name Priscilla I always associated with White Rock sarsaparilla, the soda I shared with their daughter Bee Zee while eating peanut butter-on-spoon snacks. After climbing the fence, my brothers and I would play "flies up" with Bee Zee and her older brother Schuyler, using a pink Spaulding rubber ball bounced off a brick edge in the narrow yard. After school, especially in our 7th and 8th years, Bee Zee and I would engage in exploratory sexual activity, playing doctor and placing "medicinal" beads in every orifice, lying naked in bed pretending to be infant twins, or lying on top of one another as husband and wife. When I told my father about our games one evening at a family dinner, he had said to my embarrassment or pride, "Imagine, my youngest son fucking at his age!"

After rummaging through the cellar—a small room off the basement hallway filled with junk, boxes of my father's old manuscripts, the furnace and hot water heater—and finding the football and the crutches, I went back into the kitchen to check on my mother.

"Hi, Mom. Josh drenched me again with a wastebasket of water."

"Oh, that naughty boy. He's so childish! Really!"

"It's O.K., Mom. I got him back with a few glasses of water. But Robert punched me."

"I don't know what I'm going to do with you boys!"

"Don't worry, Mom. We'll be O.K.. We're going outside to play football and do a little begging and falling."

"Oh, dear. You're all so odd!"

I grabbed a metal cup from the sink, stood on my toes, kissed my mother on the cheek, and went out of the kitchen into the fifteen-foot-long, four-foot-wide hallway leading to the door underneath the stoop. Robert and I often played some furious games of soccer in this hallway. On my right was the narrow, winding stairwell. Next to the stairs was a closet filled with hundreds of files and papers—income tax returns, old newspapers with pictures of F.D.R. and Truman, letters and stacks of back issues of *The Progressive* magazine. My mother spent hours in this closet, almost daily, organizing, filing, reshuffling, sorting, boxing, talking to herself, reorganizing, muttering, and weeping. It was a place she entered, along with the bathroom, to collect herself and have some privacy.

I took one of my father's old, moth-eaten overcoats from its hook and put it on. The hem came within half an inch of the floor. Tucking the football under one arm, with index finger stuck through the cup handle, and carrying the crutches in the other, I walked past the closet and the cellar room on the right, out the front door and up onto the sidewalk.

"Bout time, fathead. Look at that coat! Oh, no!" Robert laughed. "C'mon, let's play football."

"No, no, Robert, wait awhile!" Josh coaxed. "Let him do his work. C'mon! Watch this."

I tossed the ball over to Robert, pulled the coat collar up high around my neck, and laboriously made my way on crutches down to the corner on East End Avenue, while my brothers looked on from a distance. Leaning against a lamppost, I pulled my left leg up and tucked it behind me against the post. I hung my chin down to my chest and began extending the cup to curious, if not alarmed, passers-by. Some people chuckled, believing the activity to be a joke. Others approached cautiously and dropped a nickel or dime into the cup. Every so often someone stopped and asked if I was all right. Always I kept my head down and only grunted in response. After fifteen minutes, feeling my interactions were too few and lacking intensity, I made my way with cup in pocket up the block. I eyed a middle-aged, well-dressed man spryly walking in my direction, and just as we were about to pass one another, I collapsed in a heap at his feet.

"Hey! Are you all right, fella?" the man asked, leaning over me. "Let me give you a hand."

"Gee, I guess I tripped," I said, relishing his kind attention and the firmness of his grip in my hand.

Pulling me effortlessly to my feet and steadying me back onto the crutches, he said with a smile, "Now there you go. You watch yourself."

"Thanks, mister," I said. Although in the distance I could see my brothers doubled over with laughter and stomping around in a circle, I was well satisfied with the exchange and didn't think it funny.

For the rest of the morning, after tossing my overcoat, crutches and cup down into the basement entrance beneath the stoop, I played football with my brothers, mostly monkey-in-the-middle, and, of course, I was the monkey.

After a lunch of burned toasted Velveeta cheese sandwiches and Hershey's chocolate milk prepared by my mother, Josh went over to Johnny Polk's, and Robert and I went over to the park. For more than an hour, we walked, like tightrope artists, atop a four-foot high, inch and a half wide iron fence surrounding the rectangular green between the 86th Street entrance and the circular steps leading up to John Finley Walk and the East River. For my brother and me, it was a moment of concentrated, silent communion, and an opportunity to perform for mothers and their babies, old men, nuns, and the German, Irish, and Slavic old women from the neighborhood railroad walk-ups sitting on the benches, resting swollen ankles with rolled down Supp-Hose stockings in heavy, black, open-toed or Dr. Posner's Flex Arch shoes, quietly talking in broken English and enjoying the sun.

Robert went home to read, and I spent the rest of the afternoon climbing rocks, outcrops of Manhattan schist behind the benches and walking along John Finley Walk from where one could see the swift East River tidal currents, funneled from Long Island Sound, swirling underneath the Triboro Bridge. Great freighters, when plying through Hell Gate underneath the bridge where the Harlem and East Rivers meet, were often carried sideways by the treacherous waters. And just at the moment I thought they might run aground on the rocky banks along the F.D.R. Drive, their powerful, steady engines would head them south between Carl Schurz Park and the flashing Pearlwick Hampers sign in Queens—sometimes with their deep foghorns intermittently blasting—down past the Con Edison stacks, underneath the Queensboro, Williamsburg, Manhattan, and Brooklyn Bridges, and through the Narrows to the Jersey Shore and beyond.

I walked down the walk toward the fireboat, docked at 90th street beneath the back lawn of Gracie Mansion where the mayor lived, circled around the park to 88th Street, and exited onto East End Avenue. Before returning home, I snapped off one more Buick emblem from the trunk lock of a parked car, and put it in my pocket. Of late I had taken to collecting these lock covers and Mercedes hood ornaments, feeling adventuresome, naughty, and successful, like a pirate acquiring booty.

"Boys!" my father commanded, "I want you all wearing sports jackets and ties; we're eating in the dining room. You may all join me for a cocktail in the living room. Leon, first wash your hands," my father said to me directly as I ran past the living room on my way upstairs.

"Right, Pop. Pop? Make me a cocktail, too! You know, one of those special ones!" I said, referring to a bitters, club soda, and sugar drink he had made for me on other occasions. At least it tasted sufficiently awful and had a pretty enough color to pass as a cocktail.

In a few minutes my brother Josh and I stampeded down the stairs and into the living room. My father sat on one end of the skirted Chippendale sofa, looking very dapper with his neatly trimmed black moustache and Havana cigar in one hand. The dog Polly slept at his feet. He acknowledged our presence with a quick raising and lowering of his eyebrows while puffing on his cigar and gazing contemplatively across the small but charming room into the crackling coal fire.

A Louis XVI white marble and ormolu clock ticked atop the black and white Venetian marble mantelpiece. Set back from the mantle on each side of it stood two satinwood and marquetry side tables, Chinese famille rose oviform lamps on both, and on one two small busts, Voltaire and Rousseau.

In front of the fireplace Josh sat in one Louis XV carved and gilded wood fauteuil and I sat in the other. Behind me on a corner pedestal a Lehmbruck cast stone male bust with fist pulled to its chest looked out over the room. Behind my brother a small window seat in front of gold drapes was flanked by narrow bookcases containing volumes by Freud, Plato, Balzac, Dostoevsky, Tolstoy, and several of my father's own novels.

Two small early Empire armchairs faced one another on each end of the couch. Between the chairs on the coffee table an eighteen-inch high David Smith metal sculpture stood. Hanging behind one of the chairs was a small Dubuffet painting of three men in the desert. Next to the painting was the liquor closet and bar. There hung photographs of my father with famous people along with framed letters of thanks and praise from them, a brown and white picture of his white-haired father with a grand moustache, looking like Mark Twain, sitting in a rocker and cupping his ear to hear, and a picture of his little mother less than five feet tall.

Behind the other Empire chair next to my father, another closet with firmly shut door was stuffed, because of lack of space in his bedroom, with my father's eclectic wardrobe and an enormous pile of matched and unmatched shoes, including patent leather opera slippers. Occasionally the closet also contained an unopened bottle of cheap Bellows scotch or Ten High bourbon to replenish an almost empty Chivas or Bonded Old Grand Dad 114 bottle in the liquor closet.

"Your drink is ready in the closet, Leon. Where's my other son?"

"He's reading. He doesn't want to wear a jacket to dinner, either," Josh said.

"Trou-ble," my father said melodically, the pitch of the second syllable dropping down from the first. "I've got a low thug in the making, children. If he were reading something substantial, I might be able to excuse him. But *Hot Rod*? And you, Joshua. your school sent me their—shall we say—rather disappointing report. One of the advantages of going to this progressive school is they communicate about you rather than simply allotting you a grade. Fighting with water-inflated bicycle tubes is not my notion of elevated, progressive, and expensive education, yes? I was pleased that you do well in farm chores and skiing. With such an education you'll go far in life. Clowning around, my boys—and this goes for you, too, Leon; I also got your disastrous report—will land you in the gutter. I expect a more serious performance from both of you. Achievement is the measure of man. Now, enough said."

"Sorry, Pop," I said.

"Don't apologize to me! You haven't done anything to me! I could care less! It's your life! You change it! Do it!"

"Sure, Pop. Okay. I'll try harder."

"Oh, man, I should have skied the head wall at Tuckerman's Ravine this vacation," Josh said.

"Hey, Pop," I asked, moving the subject to safer ground, "are we going to listen to DaKoven tonight?"

"Of course."

"Who's he, Leon? Sounds like a real dink," Josh said.

"Every Sunday Pop and I listen to *The Dakoven Concert* on the radio at nine o'clock. He plays Vivaldi," I said smugly, hoarding what I felt was a privileged father-son moment of intimacy. "See what you've missed going away to boarding school?"

"Oh, wow. I really see."

"You'd do well to listen to Vivaldi, Joshua. Where's your mother?"

"I don't know. I guess she's downstairs helping V.A.," Josh answered, using the abbreviated form of Virginia. Just then the sound of soft, slow-moving footsteps and quiet humming, mingled with heavy breathing, drifted into the living room, and in a moment V.A. appeared, filling the doorway. She wore a white work dress with a plain gray cardigan sweater. While cracking her Chiclets, she caught her breath.

"Whew! Snapper, babies. We got red snapper. Fresh from 9th Avenue and 39th Street. Mr. Perlman? Your dinner is served!"

In the four years V.A. had been with our family on a mostly full-time basis (occasionally she "moonlighted" a couple of times of week for the Diamonds on Park Avenue), she had become an intimate family member. One Sunday she had taken our entire family to hear "her Adam," and all of us took a taxi up to the Abyssinia Baptist Church in Harlem and listened to Adam Clayton Powell preach. She was adept on the Ouija Board, startling us with summoned up names of ancestors, birthdays, and forgotten places. She spent hours alone in her top-floor room, filling page upon page with "spirit" writing, mysterious communications from another world received through her hand which moved across the paper on its own without her looking. This writing she never shared.

"How nice, Virginia!" my father exclaimed. "You went all the way down to 39th Street for the fish?"

"Yes, sir. The best market, the only market for good snapper, u-hunh!"

"I don't believe it. You break my heart!"

"You better believe it, and don't be havin' no heart attack and waste my fish. I'm bringin' it up now," she said and went back down to the kitchen.

"Robert!" my father bellowed.

"All right, all right, I'm comin'," he answered. We could hear his reluctant steps clumping out of his bedroom and down the stairs. In a few seconds he stood in the doorway, jacketless. With his head hung low from slouched shoulders, he peered up suspiciously through a precisely coifed spill of black Brylcreamed curls and into the room. The rest of his hair swept up and back, shining like chrome on the fins of a late model car. Small for sixteen years, he weighed only a hundred and twenty-five pounds, but he was extremely quick, had worked out with barbells, and had made the varsity football team as a starting halfback.

"Your jacket?" my father said.

"I don't need no fuckin' jacket," he answered.

"Whoa! James Dean!" Josh declared gleefully.

"You're not to use that language in this house! And if you care to eat, you'll wear a jacket in the dining room."

"I don't care. I'd rather have a hamburger at the Camel coffee shop instead of some phony bullshit."

"What is your problem?" my father asked with feigned exasperation.

"What's yours?" he quickly retorted.

My father turned to me and asked, "Could it be his size?" which I answered with a quick shrug while he continued, "My brother Sidney was small and always had to act the tough guy ... Quite sick." He puffed on his cigar.

"Eat it raw, man," Robert said under his breath.

"Oh, wow! What a rock!" Josh blurted out, slapping his knee.

"Hey, shut the fuck up, Josh!" Robert warned.

"Eat it raw?" my father asked Robert. "Is this some sexual perversion? Are we talking about some sense of inadequacy, some deep seated inferiority complex, resulting, perhaps, from the smallness of an increasingly significant part of your anatomy?"

"Stick it!" Robert answered.

"Ah, 'stick it,' he says. I see."

Robert angrily thrust his middle finger up at my father and went back upstairs.

"Charming. Shall we go to dinner, children?"

Down the winding, red-carpeted stairway, past our reflected selves in the landing mirror panels, we proceeded. On the first floor I paused at the Orozco painting of a woman who, having discovered a crouching male intruder inside an open bedroom window, is fleeing. How curious that this familiar scene, observed almost daily throughout my life, was growing increasingly more meaningful!

Josh and my father went to the right at the bottom of the stairs. They passed the wooden Noguchi sculpture and the marble Jacopo Sansovino of the Virgin Mother and Child, went into the front sitting room where the mirror around the mantle piece reflected a tunnel of crystal chandeliers in the opposite mirror behind the George III window seat, and then they walked back around and past the *White Angel* Pollack (How my mother hated that painting for its apparent lack of sense!) and into the dining room.

I, on the other hand, turned left. Pushing open the swinging door, I entered the enclosed first floor landing. To my left the stairs continued to wind down to the basement and kitchen. Straight ahead a servant's door opened into the dining room. And to the right of this door another small door was cut into the wall several feet above the floor. This door I opened. Climbing into the dark dumbwaiter shaft, and grabbing hold of the old hemp ropes, I lowered myself down into the basement.

"Hi, Mom, need any help?" I asked, bursting open the door into the kitchen from atop the dumbwaiter.

"Heavens!" My mother cried.

"Leon, you get out of my dumbwaiter!" V.A. ordered. "You be upsettin' my snapper, I'll tan your hide!"

"Leon, really! Here. Carry this bottle of wine up to your father and sit down. We'll be right up."

Though approaching a theatrical gaudiness which minimized its shortcomings of dust, darkness, and worn carpeting and seat covers, the dining room really was quite splendid. Waves of red satin drapes plunged from ceiling to floor on the far wall. A mahogany dining table with eight chairs and a sideboard—all Regency—were the principal furnishings. They had been a wedding gift from my mother's parents. On the sideboard a pair of George III cluster-column candlestick lamps cast a soft, dim light. The flickering glow from the pair of six-light bronze candelabra on the table, reflected in the convex gilt mirror hanging on the wall behind the foot of the table.

Also reflected like a kaleidoscopic spray of colorful jewels was light from the room's most spectacular display of artistic expression, a Fifteenth Century Belgian, nonreligious stained glass window of two maidens dancing around a fountain. Bordered by drawn and raised curtains, as if on a stage, and lit from behind, the window filled the space above the fireplace mantle and had the ability, I thought, of thoroughly transporting dinner guests to another place and time. For as long as I could remember, my father had promised the window to me. "It's in my will," so he had said. It was known as my window. Robert had been promised the Lehmbruck, and Josh the David Smith.

Finally, a small wooden statue with a patina hundreds of years old—the figure of a woman (probably the Virgin Mary) with extended arms—stood on a pedestal near the head of the table by the satin drapes. She seemed either to be blessing or pleading with those seated at the table.

"Ah, the vino, my boy. Sit, Leon," my father said from his seat at the head of the table beneath the wooden statue. He examined the bottle. "A '55 Lascombes. A little soon for this, but no matter."

"I thought you're supposed to have white wine with fish, Pop," I said, pulling in my chair underneath the stained glass window. Josh sat opposite me, shaking out his napkin. Next to him Robert's chair remained empty.

"Ach, that's all shit. You have what you like. I like red. And should the sensibilities of the anal retentives be aquiver, let them be assuaged by the fact that Virginia has made her snapper with a red sauce."

Although the meaning of such sweeping Freudian condemnations escaped me, I was impressed by and understood their authoritative tone. I was learning that somewhere beneath rejected propriety lay some mysterious and awesome code, all the more superior because it emanated from my father.

"Bravo, Virginia!" my father exclaimed as V.A. carried in the parsley-adorned rice and fish platter. My mother followed with a tureen of buttered baby peas, seating herself at the foot of the table underneath the convex mirror. Passing the fish before my father for his approval, V.A. then served my mother, my father, Josh, and then me.

"Well done, Abigail," my father addressed my mother, "for a girl who never set eyes on a kitchen until she was twenty-five."

"Is that true, Mom?" Josh asked.

"No. Your father exaggerates everything," she answered, slightly perturbed. The youngest of four sisters, my mother had grown up in a well-to-do but not stuffy family. Her father, Robert Ward Chandler, now eighty-six, was the son of the Newburyport shoe manufacturer Elisha Dunster Chandler and grandson of the hardworking Ipswich farmer Nathan Dane Chandler who, according to the presiding minister at his funeral, "was a God fearing man and had no patience with them that weren't." Upon graduation from Harvard and Harvard Law, he built one of Boston's most prestigious law firms, Chandler and Wade.

"Of course I saw the kitchen," she continued, "but we had servants, and Mother didn't want her children in the way. She wanted us engaged in more productive activity." She leaned forward and spooned out some peas onto my plate and then Josh's. She began biting on her tongue which protruded a bit out of the corner of her mouth, a nervous habit indicating preoccupation with something other than the task at hand.

Her mother, also named Abigail and now deceased, had been a cultivated woman and had seen to it that all her daughters learn stringed instruments for quartet playing, attend the finest girls' academy in Boston, The Winsor School, and complete their educations at Vassar. But lovely as she was, my mother had been a sad little girl, dominated and bullied by her rather masculine sister Mimi, three years her elder and a severe violinist, ignored by Agnes, six years her elder and Warden-to-be at Vassar, and overshadowed by Eleanor, nine years her elder and one of the first female pediatric medical students at Johns Hopkins. Often left alone to play with her dolls, my mother had told me that at times she felt like an addendum to her family and oppressed by the trappings of her social class.

"Hey, Mom, this fish is pretty good," I said with a full mouth. "I'll tell V.A, too."

"Awful fish," my father countered. "An utterly bland, flavorless fish. All I taste is the red sauce, which isn't bad. I don't understand what people see in snapper. I like a real fish, like a mackerel!"

"Yeah, I like them, too!" I exclaimed. "Like we had on Cape Cod for breakfast!"

"That's disgusting, Leon. You would like something like that!" Josh teased.

"Hey, eat it raw, Josh!"

"Boys? Enough!" my father ordered. "Leon, go tell your oldest brother I'd enjoy his company at dinner."

I got up from the table, went through the front sitting room and around to the stairwell. I yelled up my father's message and returned to my seat.

"Hey, Mom, you look pretty good. Wha'd'ya, go to James's Beauty Salon today?" I asked, remembering that one of my favorite activities when a younger boy was going to the York Avenue beauty parlor with my mother. James had always been real nice to me, and the other ladies had thought I was cute and charming.

"Why aren't you sweet for noticing? What a good little boy!"

"Enough of the emasculating praise, Abigail. A mere 'thank you' will do. You can't continue to cling to the past and keep him there as well. He is irrevocably growing up,

I hope. And you, my wife, are also gaining in years, as, no doubt, your bimonthly 'touch up' at the parlor attests. He doesn't need any more of that 'goodbye, goodnight, yes' crap," my father said, referring to a bedtime ritual still performed from time to time between me and my mother. Following the reading of a story or two by my mother, an extended back rubbing "wub," tickling "tickoosh," and scratching "skish," a regular feature of my earlier childhood had been the sharing of the words "goodbye, good night, yes" spoken in unison with my mother. They brought an intimate conclusion to the day and were my final preparation for slumber.

"Oh, wow! Things haven't changed much around here," Josh said.

"Precisely," my father said. "But we're trying, are we not, Abby?"

My mother, without acknowledging my father's question, began to push all of her peas into a neat pile with her fork. More quickly she picked them up and chewed without looking up. "Thank you, Leon," she said.

Robert sauntered into the room. He was wearing a sports jacket. He sat next to Josh.

"Ah, just in time, my boy. A little wine for my boys. Pass me your glass, Robert," my father said, pouring some of the Bordeaux first in Josh's glass on his right, then in mine on his left. He then filled Robert's glass, handed me the bottle, and told me to pass it to my mother.

"A toast!" he continued, raising his glass. A high-pitched resonant ringing filled the room as Josh swirled his wine-dunked index finger around the lip of the thin crystal glass. "Come off it, Josh," my father said with exaggerated exasperation, annoyed with the interruption. "Didn't I teach you any manners? Haven't you learned anything at that school?"

"Hey, that's wild!" Robert said, following Josh's example. I, too, dunked my finger and tried to make the pure sound. Soon a lovely harmonic chorus sang out in the room. My brothers and I swirled and smiled at one another for the momentary joy of it.

"Enough!" my father cried.

"But I learned it in school! In science glass! C'mon, Pop, put more wine in my glass and it will change pitch!" Josh implored. My mother smiled broadly.

"Yes, yes, I know. Mozart wrote an adagio for an instrument called the glass harmonica based upon this very same demonstration. Quite lovely. You'd all do well to listen to it sometime. But this is neither science nor music class, is it children?" He gave a mock chuckle. "No, in case you'd forgotten, this is the dining room, and I wish to propose a toast. Now, stop it!" We stopped. "To my middle son upon his return from school! To Josh! Welcome!"

"Welcome, Josh! Let's clink!" I exclaimed.

"C'mon, Abigail, glass up! Show a little enthusiasm! A little adult passion for your middle son," my father chided mellifluously.

"Hey, hey! Wha'd ya say! My kid brother's returned to the den of iniquity! Not too swift, right, Josh? Yeah, to Josh! And to Mozart!" Robert toasted.

"Hey, gee, thanks, brother, oh, Wild One."

"Robert, clink!" I said, leaning over the table and thrusting my glass between the candelabra at Robert. Instead of that wonderful bell-like ringing, my overly forceful, excited motion brought the awful sound of shattering glass, and the small explosion left Robert's extended, glassless fist bathed in red wine which now dripped and pooled on the white linen table cloth.

"Oh, Leon, really!" my mother shouted.

"You dumb fuckin' fathead, Leon!" Robert yelled, jumping up from his chair, reaching across the table, and striking me with his knuckles on the side of the head with lightning-fast, Floyd Patterson agility.

"ENOUGH!" my father bellowed. "Robert, you're not to hit! Get down in your chair. It was an accident." His words would have soothed my wounded, tearful feelings, even lessened the pain of the rising bump, had he not sarcastically added, "Twenty-dollar Steuben crystal is not irreplaceable; we're made of money."

With her foot my mother found and pressed down on the buzzer hidden underneath the carpeting, and soon V.A. appeared. Interspersing an occasional "uhunh" and an "oh, my, mm-mm" within her quiet, gum-clicking hum, V.A. picked up the broken bits of glass, dabbed and then salted the spotted linen. After placing the wooden salad bowl filled with greens next to my mother, she then began clearing our dinner plates and replacing them with blue glass salad plates. My mother tossed the salad.

"Oh, man, more of the old lady's pukey sour dressing," bemoaned Robert. "C'mon, Mom, how 'bout some blue cheese?"

"'The old lady, the old man,'" my father mimicked with a screwed up face. "You feel so young, so little that we should be so old? Always hostile, always disrespectful. For what? Your mother's French mustard dressing happens to be one of the few things she does well."

"Yeah? Well I don't like it."

"Then don't eat it!"

"How come we always eat salad after the main course?" Josh asked. "At school we always have it before the main meal."

"We eat it," my father answered, "after the main course in order to cleanse our palates—the European way. Before the main course is the California way which is quite senseless and gauche."

"How come we need to cleanse our palates, Pop?" I asked.

"In order to fully taste and appreciate the subtleties in flavor of the next dish, we need to remove the lingering flavors from the preceding dish. Eating and cooking are an art, my boy."

"Well," Robert interjected, "I'll be sure to keep my palate dirty to cover up the taste of the shit we get around here!"

"Enough!"

"Yes, Robert, really!" my mother said. "That's so unnecessary. I try. I really try … on top of my job," she added meekly, referring to her work as a secretary for the National Sharecroppers Fund, one of many jobs she had held on behalf of the downtrodden. "And I don't get one iota of appreciation from any of you."

"I appreciate you, Mom," I said.

"Oh, yes, I know. You're such a good boy—an angel."

"Ach, here we go again!" my father shouted.

"Him? An angel? He's a litttle thief and con artist!" Josh added laughingly.

"You're going to kill him, Abigail, with that baby, shmaby stuff," my father said with disgust. "And you'll do it with that deadening, guilt-ridden, fatal innocence."

"I'm not killing him … Why don't you all leave me alone?"

"Is that a reverse way of saying you want to leave? Well, then, leave why don't you? I know that's what you're going to do, Abigail."

"I'm not leaving."

"Hah! How many millions will your father leave you? Just wait. When that money finally comes to you, you'll flee!"

"What money? I don't know what you're talking about," she said sheepishly.

"I don't believe it! There it is again! Innocence! Boys," my father continued, pausing briefly to sip on his wine as V.A. came back into the room, cleared the table, placed a stack of five Limoges desert plates in front of my mother, and exited. "Did I ever tell you how I found your mother wandering in tears around the grocery store after Robert was born? She did not know how to shop! She was at a loss because no one had ever taken her shopping! Tell them it's true, Abigail!"

"It's not true."

"I don't see why you put up with this shit, Mom," Robert said. "You ought to leave."

"Yeah, Mom," Josh added, "How come you don't get pissed?"

"She can't get pissed!" My father cried. "She's still an innocent little girl playing alone with her dolls in Jones' Mansion!" Jones' Mansion had been her five-foot-high colonial style doll house set off in the woods on her family's weekend estate in Ipswich on the North Shore. There she had spent hours playing with the fanciful Jones doll family. Only last summer my mother and I had rediscovered the little weed and brush-hidden dwelling. Pushing open the door, we had found the Jones family—their mouse nest innards spilling into the droppings all about—still sitting amongst their furnishings and molded, flaking books, as they had been left forty-three years before.

"She's buried in the past, boys!" he continued as she scratched at the eczematous inside of her right elbow. Tears began to well up in her eyes. "Passionless, save for a miniscule touch of idealistic socialism. But even that is an ineffectual, fanciful yearning for her own control, not her father's and his class trappings, over her own means of production, creativity and aliveness! Yes, Abby? But the truth is, we're drying up, aren't we? It's what we call the L.C. syndrome ... Leather, boys, leather," he said melodiously.

"Leave Mom alone, Pop," I said, "or I'll leave the table."

"But children, it's true! I tell you, it's all true. Don't be charmed by that little girl innocence! It will kill what is dearest to you, as it killed my third son, your brother John Ward!" he shouted, referring to a brother who had died on his first birthday a year before my birth. "And believe me, it was no crib death! He'd been running a fever all week while I'd been in Hollywood, but did she do anything about it? No! A hundred and three and a half temperature and no doctor! And in the morning he was cold, blue, and gone! Tell me it's not true, Abigail! It's your goddamn fatal innocence that killed my son!"

"GODDAMN YOU!" my mother screamed, standing and lifting the desert plates over her head with both arms and hurling them down to the floor where they smashed to pieces. "Goddamn you, Vincent! You were there, too! You had come home!"

"Ahh, a little passion, a little life at the expense of fine china may be worth it, don't you think, children?"

Just then the dining room door opened and V.A. walked in carrying a shining silver tureen. "Mousse au chocolat, babies! We got—" She stopped short at the sight of the broken dishes. "Shew! We had—"

"Don't bother, Virginia, just don't bother," my mother said, leaving the room with tears flowing down her cheeks. She went down the stairs.

"Incredible bullshit," Robert said, standing and tossing his napkin on the table. "Welcome home, Josh." He laughed and went back upstairs to his room.

"Yeah, right. This is great. I'm going over to Johnny Polk's. See ya later," Josh said on his way out.

"You can bring me some of your coffee, Leon, in the living room," my father said. Lately, I had concocted a special brew for my father's demitasse which included a little Bosco and a pinch of salt. He liked it.

My father retired upstairs. Leaving V.A. in the dining room, I went down into the kitchen to make the coffee in the aluminum drip pot. As I boiled the water and measured out the coffee and Bosco, my mother sat with her head buried in her folded arms on the table. She said nothing while I worked.

"Don't worry, Mom. It'll be all right," I said. After pouring the boiling water into the pot, I touched her shoulder. "I love you, Mom."

She looked up and said through reddened eyes, "You are a good boy, a very good boy."

I kissed her on the cheek and carried the coffee up to my father.

"Excellent coffee, my son," my father said, sipping from the tiny cup and admiring the fire. The dog Polly lay sleeping at his feet.

"Can I snip and warm up your cigar, Pop?"

"You certainly may."

In the liquor closet I took a metal-encased Don Diego Las Palmas out of its box and sat with it in one of the small Empire chairs. "Are you going to get a divorce, Pop?" I asked, unscrewing the small cylindrical humidor, then taking the cigar clipper from my father's outstretched hand.

"I think not," he answered while I snipped out a wedge of tobacco from the cigar's end, put it in my pocket, then slid off the paper ring and put it on my finger.

"Good ... Pop, can I have the tube for my collection?"

"Of course," he said, handing me a book of matches.

"It's not crunchy, Pop," I said, rolling the cigar next to my ear. I put the cigar down in my lap and lit a match. Then picking it up again, I rolled it back and forth through the warming flame. I handed my father the cigar and was about to light its end when he gently waved the flame away.

"A gentleman lights his own cigar."

"Oops. I forgot."

"I think before our radio show begins you had better walk this poor dog. She hasn't been out in hours."

"Oh, yikes! What time is it, Pop? I've got to meet Ajeet!" I said, charging out of the room and up the stairs to my room.

"Who's he?" my father called after me.

"He's the Indian ambassador's servant," I yelled down to my father. "He lives across the street in the apartment house. His master works at the U.N. and he doesn't speak any English. He's my friend. We walk the dogs together," I shouted, rummaging through my drawers. I found my recently acquired corncob pipe which I got in trade for four Buick emblems. I reached into my pocket, pulled out the cigar wedge and added it to a one-inch-high glass tempera paint jar. The jar was almost filled with the tobacco wedges. I bound down the stairs past the living room, called for Polly, and flew down the next flight of steps to the vestibule with the dog in pursuit. I threw on a jacket, leashed the dog, and went out into the cool night air.

I could see Ajeet waiting with his little dog across the street. He stood under a lamppost a few yards from the apartment house awning. His white, toothy smile almost glowed in contrast to his dark brown skin and jet-black hair. He was very, very small.

Two weeks ago my mother and I were returning home from grocery shopping when, instead of going into our house, she had taken me over to the apartment building. It was dark in the late afternoon and a small crowd of ten or twelve people had gathered underneath the awning. A shiny black limousine was parked at the entrance, and a chauffeur stood nearby. In a moment a little dark-skinned man wearing a brimless white hat, a long white shirt, and stocking-like white pants appeared in the doorway. The small crowd burst into applause, and the man clasped his hands together as in prayer and bowed to each of us, including me, while smiling broadly. He then entered the limousine and drove off. My mother told me that the man's name was Jawaharlal Nehru, Prime Minister of India. And she also told me that he had been a close friend of a very great man named Gandhi who had some very interesting ideas about getting along with one another.

Ajeet and I smiled at one another and walked our dogs together across East End Avenue and into the park. In a moment I said to Ajeet, "I have something for you." I then presented him with the corncob pipe and the jar of tobacco wedges. He smiled at me, took the gift and bowed, smiled and bowed again, and I smiled back at him. For the next quarter of an hour we walked, enjoying the spring evening as we had over the past few weeks and would continue to do until summer arrived and our ways would part.

At John Finley Walk, where other walkers and their dogs strolled in the darkness from lamplight to lamplight, we stood silently with our sitting dogs, looking out at the black, swiftly flowing river and the lights of the Triboro Bridge, Queens, and the flashing Pearlwick Hampers sign. Momentarily, a deep and great blast from a freighter's foghorn resounded from the river, echoing through the building canyons of Yorkville, and the bow and hull of an enormous ship entered Hell Gate, moving south.

"O.K., yah, O.K.." Ajeet said, smiled, then bowed. "Home now."

And we smiled, and I said, "Bye, Ajeet."

"Bye, Leon," he said. "Tomorrow," he added awkwardly, pointing upward and away, then down. He waved and walked off and down the circular stairs.

The giant ship, streaming golden portholes, flowed quickly abeam of my vantage point. On the starboard flying bridge, ablaze in floodlights, I could see the tiny figure of a sailor looking up and admiring the city lights. I waved my arm back and forth, and though he must only have been able to see my silhouette, he miraculously waved back.

"C'mon, Polly!" I shouted, breaking into a trot alongside the rapidly passing vessel. Soon the name Singapore Star appeared on the three-story-high transom, and I ran faster to keep up with the ship, but she and the waving sailor were pulling away. Making a last burst of effort, I suddenly tripped and fell, skinning my knees and the palms of my hands.

"Hey, are you all right, fella?" a man with a collie said. "Here, let me give you a hand." He reached down and I took his hand. Easily he lifted me up and I brushed off my hands and pants while our dogs sniffed each other.

"Gee, thanks, mister. I'll be O.K.," I said. I took one more glance at the ship as it passed underneath the Queensboro Bridge, then I turned and trotted home.

Three

LIVING IN THE PROMISED LAND

*I may not get there with you,
but we as a people will get to the Promised Land.*

—*MARTIN LUTHER KING, JR.*

The summer of '65, after my sophomore year in high school, I'd been washing dishes at the Everbreeze in Provincetown, Massachusetts. Frank, the boss, said I was the best dishwasher he'd ever had. Jane the cook, a large black woman in her late fifties, who drove from Cleveland every year for the summer season, was fun to work with, and sometimes I'd grab hold of her, dance around the kitchen floor, and exclaim, "Oh, Jane, the divinity of sex is upon us!" and she'd say, "Shew, Leon, git out my face!" We'd laugh, then get back to work in the din of barked orders, clanging pots, and clattering dishes, sweat pouring down our brows.

First I lived with Art Schneider, the 82-year-old bell-ringing town crier, a ruddy, plump tourist icon who roamed the streets in Pilgrim attire, and then I moved to a seventeen-dollar-a-week room in the Captain's House, a dilapidated rooming house set behind the Pushy Tushy curio and sex toy shop on Commercial Street. There I lost my virginity before my sixteenth birthday in late July. The girl Stella, also a dishwasher at a different restaurant, had a room next to mine, and our back-to-back closets were separated by a thin sheet of plywood. After we decided one afternoon to knock out the partition, we immediately jumped into bed.

A couple of weeks later I moved out of the Captain's House and into a barn apartment on Pearl Street with a bunch of Clan MacGregor drinking actresses and actors, one of whom had gone to boarding school with my brother Josh a few years back, and for all of whom I was sort of a wayward mascot. I drank plenty of their scotch, puking profusely between the acts on the Provincetown Playhouse wharf to the disgust of the theatergoers.

Later a classmate of mine, Taylor Randall, came up from New York for a weekend visit. "Hey, man, ya wanna get laid?" I asked him. "Sure!" he answered with wide-eyed enthusiasm. I left him alone with Stella and, sure enough, the two of them indulged themselves. A problem developed when in a few days pus started coming out his dick and he had to inform his steady girl Sheila back in the city he had gonorrhea and that now, she did, too. Probably. That had to be embarrassing.

I hadn't seen my father, who was only twenty miles away, since we'd had that whole episode a few weeks ago with Mr. Bailey, my math teacher from Van Janssen School. That sucked. You see, Bailey, who was about thirty years old and had a questionable bouffant Vitalis hairdo, was a friend to me. During the school year I'd meet him almost everyday for an hour before school at the 79th Street Coffee Shop for coffee and cigarettes and maybe an English muffin. Often my classmate Warren Patton (he taught me to smoke King Sano and later Winston cigarettes), or any other buddy who felt himself in the misfit category, would show up, too. It was cool because it gave us boys some refuge, some steady family-like visiting time with a caring adult when things weren't so easy at home.

Warren had it really bad: one night he invites me and Neil Feinman over to his ground floor apartment in a new 89th and East End Avenue high-rise to spend the night in early ninth grade; we're hanging out in his bedroom, when all of a sudden we hear this bloodcurdling scream coming out of the living room. "Waaaaaarren! Waaaaaaren! Get those FUCKING KIKES out of my house," his mother shrieks. We bailed out the window, all three of us, and walked down East End Avenue over to my house, Warren in tears, his face hidden in the palms of his hands. His mom was a bad alcoholic.

Anyway, I told Bailey over breakfast and a smoke one morning I was going to be working up in Provincetown for the summer and he oughta come visit, which he did about three weeks ago. We're partying at the barn one night, Bailey and I, celebrating Annie Serena's birthday and drinking lots of red wine with a bunch of theater friends, when all of a sudden the double barn doors are thrown open, and there, standing in a black cape with outstretched arms, one held out, the other twisted upward and behind, is my father, who ferociously but playfully growls to great effect, "A-hahhh, Happy Birthday! A-hahhh, the count has arrived!" He spots me and Bailey, comes over, and wraps his cape around each of our shoulders and leads us outside, saying, "Gentlemen, might I have a word with you?" I have a fearful feeling in the pit of my stomach, sensing what he's up to but unable to put it into words. He begins casually, nonchalantly, in that pseudo-cultivated, Hollywood–British theater accent, "Gentlemen, there are certain considerations that, as a father, I am obliged to bring to your attention, certain legal considerations, shall we say, Mr. Bailey, Peter, if I may." He paused, puckered his lips into a sardonic smile, and continued, "Considerations which could be brought to bear in regard to unfair advantages being taken, in a, uh, homosexual manner of speaking."

There! He said it, and I reeled right around and socked him in the stomach, yelling "Fuck off!"

"Striking your own father?" he exclaimed back in exaggerated astonishment.

"Mind your own fuckin' business," I shouted, storming off into the night. I later found Bailey at his rooming house, and in spite of my asking him to stick around, he said forthwith he was clearing out of town and that my father was a bastard. So, that was that.

I don't know what this whole sexual thing is about, but it seems I've had my share of it, like flies to shit or, should I say, bees to a flower. Maybe it comes from my father always parading around naked like a Greek god or something, showing off and doing his Walt Whitman–"Body Electric" thing; or telling me how great it is I "fucked" my next door neighbor Bee Zee when I was eight. Maybe it comes from having two foul-mouthed brothers, or having to choke Robert's chicken or anything else he made me do under threat of having my head bashed in followed by a trip to the hospital, or from being President of the Vagina Junk Club in second grade, where we fiddled with each others' wienies during nap time on our floor blankets and whispered about climbing up Miss Klein's dress. Maybe it comes from the underpants checks we had at Camp Cedar Isles after fourth grade where we had to drop our drawers so the counselors could have a look at our butts and dongs and see if we'd shit in our jockey shorts from the bad water we had to drink, or from being forced in the park to suck that pizza-faced tough guy's dick at knife point and lie face down when I was ten in the snowy late afternoon dark. Maybe it comes from having dirty fingernails and only having to take a bath once a week, unlike the super-rich Park Avenue ethnic German Jews, who took daily baths and went to temple on Saturdays and got free tickets to Madison Square Garden or Yankee Stadium; no, they weren't some dirty East European shtetl Jew, like Adolf and Becky Perlman, my grandparents, scavenging dead fish off the beach for dinner. Maybe it comes from Mr. Tipple, my fifth grade English teacher who'd try to get me to quit bouncing around the class and being disruptive by having me sit on his lap while he rubbed my inner thigh, or from Mr. Bouvier, my seventh grade French teacher asking me in private how many times a week I beat off; or maybe it comes from all those dick-blistering circle jerks with half my classmates I'd never tell him about. How 'bout being able to watch my mother naked, muff, boobs, and all in the bathroom until I was around ten, at which time I remember proudly showing her my first strands of pubic hair and feeling strangely embarrassed a short while later? Hey, you know what? I bet it comes from being felt up when I was eight by some fat creep of an older man in the 86th Street Strand movie theater, who kept dropping quarters in my shirt pocket, while saying, "C'mon, come with me to the bathroom." I suppose it didn't help that it was a matinee, that I was alone, and that the movie was *And God Created Woman*, starring Brigitte Bardot.

Summer was coming to an end and school and football practice would be starting up again soon. I had to be getting back. I hitched a ride up to South Wellfleet to check in with my father and see about a ride to the city. While there the phone rang and it just happened to be my mom. I hadn't spoken with her all summer, but now she informed me that finally after twenty-three years of marriage she was moving out. I whispered this information to my father.

"Tell her you're not going to go with her," my father said, puffing on his cigar while seated in the recently recovered orange paisley wing chair across the wide, sloping floorboards on the other side of the living room. The low plaster ceiling, which seemed to fall down in places every year after being made soggy by rat or raccoon piss or a leaking roof, felt all the more oppressive, though most visitors thought the antique house so charming, so fuckin' romantic, so sou'westerly Olde Cape Cod. The dust and mold were killing me and I could feel an asthma or hay fever attack coming on.

"I'm not going to go with you, Mom," I said into the phone.

"But I've found a lovely apartment three blocks from Van Janssen, 175 West 79th Street. You can walk to school. And your bedroom is very nice."

My father watched me and shook his head, and I said, "I don't care. I'm not going to move. I'm staying at 86th Street." He nodded in agreement.

"But I've had the new phone put in your name."

"I'm not going. Listen, Mom, I've got to go," I said, pushing down a rising lump in my throat.

"All right, my sweet. Don't forget, I'll be at 175 West 79th Street, the northeast corner of Amsterdam. I'll send you a card. When you get back to the city, your room will be waiting. Apartment 6A. And remember—your mother loves you very much," she said, exaggerating the "loves you very much" into a syrupy mush of coercive, enervating baby talk.

"Right. Bye." I hung up the phone.

My father turned his palms upward and shrugged, as if helpless himself. "That's right, well done, my boy." After a moment of silence, he added, "I don't believe it. Can you imagine?"

I could imagine. I had imagined. I'd even encouraged my mother to leave a long time ago, when I was as young as seven years old. I wanted to push her to safety, but at the same time I loved my father, and the thought then of no family was too scary. At best I could try to make my mother happy, like when I was ten and secretly called everyone in her address book, inviting them all to a surprise party for her fiftieth birthday. Now, with my brothers long gone off to college, it was finally over. There was nothing left. I couldn't believe it. I went for a walk and stood alone in the woods.

What's the point, I thought, noticing my feelings—bits of identity, familiar sensations, and comforting associations—fall away and dissolve into a vacuum on top of which my body caved.

I had had a recurring nightmare when I was five or six in bed on the top floor of the 86th street house. In an orange void I'd be in a race with no competitors. Even I, my body, was not present. There was no beginning and no end to this race, just an infinite orange nothingness with a high-pitched, unbroken sound of silence; then some garbage would appear, a floating empty and label-less soup can or two. The cans would drift slowly by and disappear, and the dream would repeat itself, over and over, garbage to distant garbage. I'd waken and listen to the soft brush of pulse rhythmically coursing through my ear against the pillow, and then I'd sit on the edge of my bed, staring out in silence at the steadily burning fifteen watt bulb in the hallway. I would know that if I called out in the night down to my mother or father, whether or not they came, it would make no difference. Maybe that's how I now felt.

Well, fuckin' well. That's that, I thought, bracing myself for whatever lay ahead. Getta fuckin' move on. I made arrangements with my father, who was staying on in Wellfleet through September, to get a ride with his friend John Curtis (a China-born scholar turned furniture salesman after he was run out of the State Department by McCarthyites) down to the city. A week later, after I moved my scant belongings out of Provincetown and spent a couple of nights with my father feeling pathetically wheezy and hay feverish, John Curtis dropped me off in front of 549.

As if performing a ritual by rote, I went down the steps to the basement entrance and spun the metal tab of the mechanical bell set in the door. I waited for my mother to answer. I spun it again. I listened for footsteps. Hearing none, I climbed out of the basement entrance and went up the stoop. Grabbing hold of the brass knocker, I rapped it several times and waited. I took a deep breath, looked up and scanned the fading red bricks, then turned and gazed out across 86th Street and over East End Avenue to Carl Schurz Park.

Gone, I thought. Over.

In a few moments, my small beat-up suitcase in one hand, portable record player in the other, and blue jean cap cocked slightly off the left side of my head, I went down the steps. Heading down East End Avenue for seven blocks, as I had done on my way to Van Janssen School for Boys the previous ten years, first with my brothers, then on my own, I arrived at the 79th Street Crosstown bus and, in shame for the betrayal of my father and in fear of my uncertain future, I took it over to the West Side.

In spite of moving out to her own apartment my mom was still depressed. Though the long war was over and all was now quiet, she still mixed her heaviness with several glasses of Heaven Hill bourbon at night, enough so that she'd fall asleep in the living room at her antique cherry slant-top desk with head in her arms. Each night through the fall I'd notice her as I went to my bedroom, where I'd smoke cigarettes one after the other, save the butts in a fruit-cake tin, and try with minimal success to concentrate on the intensely difficult homework load demanded of Van Janssen students. My attempts to work had the quality of isometric exercise, lots of strain with no movement, and after I was thoroughly exhausted, punishing myself into the wee hours so that my physical suffering countervailed my fruitless efforts and feelings of failure, I'd set my three alarm clocks inside three overturned metal wastepaper baskets next to my bed and go to sleep, for it was only the amplified clatter and clang of the three along with my mother's exasperated and despondent exhortations in the morning that could jar me awake into reluctant movement. I was habitually late for school.

Over the years Van Janssen School for Boys, a small, rigorous independent school founded by the Dutch in 1625 when New York City was New Amsterdam, had superimposed a stable structure onto my life when there was little at home. Monday morning chapel and Tuesday morning assembly, both with a singing of the Doxology and a hymn and a recitation of the Lord's Prayer, cultivated an alternative vision of hope to the nihilistic violence and chaos of home life on 86th street, a bit of light at the end of the tunnel. I was well-liked there and a natural leader, and though I had often brought my family turmoil to school, acting it out in a myriad of mischievous, disruptive ways, my behavior was rarely malicious, and its consequences didn't amount to much more than an excessive number of three-hour Saturday detentions seated in silence with back straight upright and hands folded on the desk.

Academically I rarely did well, often performing near or at the bottom of my class. This reinforced a negative self-image, but it wasn't in fact such a terrible disgrace because classes were very small, held to extremely high standards, and it was almost impossible not to learn something no matter how out to lunch you might be. In addition, the school fostered a magnanimous elitism bred through its three centuries of excellence, such that the humblest scholarship students from Spanish Harlem, Bedford-Stuyvesant, or Chinatown (sons of a janitor, a maid, a curio shop owner) knew alongside fellow students from Park Avenue, Sutton Place, or Fifth Avenue (sons of CEO's, psychoanalysts, world-renowned architects, or conductors of great orchestras) that we were all la crème de la crème, receiving the finest traditional education, designed to carry us to the pinnacles of our chosen careers. We were special; we were privileged; much was expected of us; and, as I said, I was well-liked. Nevertheless, I felt like a turd.

"Mom," I'd often say that fall, "I feel like a failure. I feel like a bum."

"But you're such a good boy, an angel," she'd respond evermore vacuously, as if her energy had been all but wrung out of her and she could not bear one more iota of loss.

Over the previous few years, beginning in seventh grade, I had begun to develop a comforting romantic affiliation with the down and out, drinking booze stolen from liquor closets or acquired from accommodating strangers on the street who'd buy for me and friends. One early April Saturday in 8th grade I walked aimlessly alone in a long, moth-eaten overcoat eighty-six blocks down Third Avenue to the Bowery, lost in dreams of escape, on the road, far out at sea on a freighter or clipper ship, along Cannery Row, on a freight train going west. On the way back uptown I came across an old man sitting on a stoop, his face stubbled with several days growth, eyes cast down and glazed. Sitting next to him on the step, I struck up a conversation. His name was Joe Antenucci.

"You know," he said, "I'm the loneliest man in the world."

"You ever go to church, Joe?"

"No, that's long since passed."

"You ever get out of the city? You know, out into the country, where there are cows, and lots of green, and quiet?"

"No, I don't."

"Well, I'm gonna take you out to the country, Joe. Get some fresh air." I excused myself, went to a corner phone booth, called my mother at home on 86th Street, and told her I had a new friend who needed to get to the country.

"C'mon, Mom! He's the loneliest guy in the world. He needs to get out of here. Drive us up to Warwick." We had an old farm there, a weekend place my father had bought in 1953.

"Curious," she answered.

"C'mon, Mom, just for the day. It'll be good for him."

"Well, I don't see why not. If you think so."

I made arrangements to meet Joe the next day at the entrance to the subway at 86th and Lexington at 10 AM. Sure enough, he showed up. We drove up to Warwick in our Studebaker Lark, ate some lunch, and walked around a bit in a rolling cow pasture with yellow dandelions and tall oak trees. We drove back, dropped him off at the same subway entrance, and that was the last time I saw Joe Antenucci.

Clearly, my mother had a soft spot for the downtrodden, being one herself, I suppose, emotionally speaking anyway. She was game for any good cause. For example, last spring in 10th grade she helped me organize a march in front of the FBI to protest the killing of Viola Liuzzo and Reverend James Reeb in Selma, Alabama, and Goodman, Schwerner, and Chaney in Philadelphia, Mississippi. My mother got us the parade permits and police barricades. Even my father showed up. We had over a hundred kids marching from a few private schools. I must admit I had secret fantasies of going uptown to Harlem to lead the oppressed masses out of slavery and abuse down 5th Avenue alongside Martin Luther King, Jr. into the heart and face of white America, where and when everything would come to a grinding halt and everybody would wake up in liberation and love one another.

Fuck it. It wasn't going to happen.

Football helped me through the first couple of months back in school. Like my brother Robert, I too, had become a valued player, the starting center and a linebacker. I didn't quite live up to my brother's stellar legacy. He'd been a star halfback before dropping out of Van Janssen to join a townie gang in Warwick called the Cam Busters. He roared around in his fifty-dollar '48 Ford with chrome pipes coming out the back window. He smelled like cow shit from living and working on Frank Card's dairy farm, and he hitched up with a poor, brown-toothed girl, Mary McKowky from the neighboring hamlet of Edenville, telling my revolted father he was going to "fix her fuckin' teeth and marry her." Later he became the prodigal bad-ass who'd returned home after a career-changing stint commuting from Warwick to Saunders Trade and Technical School in Yonkers, where he studied auto mechanics and tool making to finish up at Van Janssen and lead its football team to the 1961 League Championship. This was due to the good graces of the headmaster who had some faith in Robert by readmitting him, which is more than my father demonstrated by not going to any of our games. Anyway, that fall our team was clearly headed midseason toward its own championship as well, albeit with questionable determination.

"C'mon you guys!" Warren Patton, defensive captain and middle linebacker, screamed at us, erupting with palpable, red-faced emotion during our game with Poly Prep. He let out a desperate howl, "Hold them!" His cry, so intense that it seemed inordinately out of place, as if emoted from some tortured cauldron of hell deep in his bowels, made me laugh out loud. We had been up through the third quarter twenty-one to nothing, but in the final minutes Poly Prep, having scored two touchdowns with extra points and a field goal, was on a drive toward a possible winning touchdown. He turned and caught me at left linebacker with an uncontrolled grin on my face.

"C'mon you fuckin' KIKE," he roared, "let's go!" He then violently crouched down into his defensive stance facing the offense and presenting his sizeable posterior to me as the ball was snapped. Without thinking I planted my foot into his butt, knocking him over, then pounced headlong over him and, fortunately for both of us, into the path of the ball-carrying fullback, who tumbled down upon us. We stopped the drive and won the game.

For our efforts, Warren, Alan Sterner, John Medoff, and I were named the game's MVP's by the coach and awarded tickets to the Jets game the following weekend at Shea Stadium. There, Alan brought a fifth of Wild Turkey which we passed back and forth amongst ourselves in the bitter cold while reveling in a pounding of the Buffalo Bills by New York. Little did we realize that four rows behind us the coach, Mr. Sears, was sitting with Mr. Appleton, the Headmaster, observing our every swallow of booze. We were all kicked off the team, and the team never made it to the championship.

The punishment did little that fall to discourage our delving into alcohol, pot, and even LSD which was being heavily promoted by Timothy Leary at the time. One early Sunday morning after dropping a tab of what a friend had said was "your kind of drug, Perlman," I spent the hours between midnight and dawn pacing my bedroom, pleading with God to bring me down and remove the spider-infested webs which were forming in every crack on the wall, gazing down out the window to 79th Street six floors below and feeling as if my vantage point was no longer from my somewhat familiar room but rather a place far out in space beyond the moon from where I could never ever return home. Oh, God, if only I were like that milkman down there making deliveries, instead of some hollow alien floating in nothingness.

On another weekend my mother stood outside my bathroom door, knocking. "What are you boys doing in there?"

"Nothing," I said, holding in a deep toke off a joint, my cheeks puffed out and ready to burst with laughter as I looked in alarm at my friend John Medoff's equally shocked blowfish face.

My mother knocked again.

"Oooh, my groin," I groaned in mock pain, believing that a reference to a "private" area of my body might offer an explanation for why John and I were behind the closed bathroom door.

"What's that smell?" she asked, obviously perturbed.

"It's a hernia," John said, breaking out in laughter.

"Arrgggh!" I cried out.

"You boys, really! I don't know what I'm going to do with you!"

John Medoff had quickly become my best friend. I guess, like Warren, there was something quietly desperate and wise beneath his meek and affable exterior which attracted me. Though shy and courteous, he was not afraid to joke or make serious contact. A conscientious student and proficient clarinetist, he had transferred from the Allen-Stevenson School in ninth grade and had won the respect of his classmates for his musical, drama, and academic abilities. He had terrible acne and often I'd accompany him to his dermatologist, where with good humor he'd emerge from painful treatments mimicking and deriding his doctor's German accent and torturous procedures as if he were Mengele himself. We grew accustomed to drinking and smoking dope together on a regular basis. Inviting me up to his Fifth Avenue and 87th Street apartment, John showed me a pork belly he had dangling from a rope like a large bar of soap over his bedroom desk, dripping fat into a grease-filled bowl. He introduced me to his father, a well-known balding psychoanalyst and psychiatrist who treated the rich and famous, including, the doctor told us in inebriated confidence, a world renowned concert pianist who'd made a recent comeback at Carnegie Hall after years in neurotic seclusion. His father, John told me, had also recently lost a terrific amount of money in the stock and commodities markets, including, no doubt, pork bellies, which resulted in him plying scotch into me, John, himself, and John's stepmother Rhona with abandon. On several occasions we drank ourselves into a stupor until dawn, even removing our clothes in a show of all-revealing openness and affection, wherein I tried to convince everyone present I was a miserable bum and a failure, and Dr. Medoff would say, "Don't be silly, Leon. You're an artist! That's what you are, old man!" and Rhona, sitting there in her open terry cloth wrapper with her twat in plain view and big tits hanging out, would slur, "Oh, good god, Leon Perlman, you are so sweet and simply the most adorable, handsomest young man I've ever set my eyes on." John had also told me his biological mother lived in a halfway house for schizophrenics and worked as a maid, and that when she and his father had split up when he was ten years old, he had stayed with her, until one day she locked him in a closet for eight hours. Upon release from his confinement he had run away to find his father, never to return to her care again. How John was able to keep his eye on the ball is beyond me.

Throughout the fall Warren Patton, John Medoff, Taylor Randall, and I, along with various other Van Janssen boys and sometimes girls from Nightingale-Bamford, Spence, Brearley, or Hunter, frequented the Gold Rail Tavern on 110th Street and Broadway up by Columbia, where, posing as college students, we got hammered on Seven and Sevens and were never carded. In fact we had been visiting this small bar ever since ninth grade when we first went there dressed as ruffians with fake moustaches after a school drama club performance of *Abe Lincoln in Illinois* at the nearby Riverside

Church theater. It was also there that I learned from a smooth-operating, condescending senior, Bob Erhenfeld (just destined, it seemed to me, to hustle his way to fortune and fame while making it look easy) about his sexual exploits, exaggerated no doubt, with Sophie Heinz, a lovely girl from Hunter College High School I had met the previous spring at a school dance. I had liked her then with her sweet smile and waist-long Joan Baez hair, but with summer coming on I hadn't pursued her. Now in these dark, short days of late fall with winter rapidly approaching and the brightness of a home life, however dim, all but extinguished (I hadn't visited my father once since returning to the city), an interest in girls took on a new urgency, as if only in the other sex could warmth and comfort be found in this desolate world freezing over.

In early December on a Saturday night I had a party at the 79th Street apartment. Keg beer, scotch, and vodka flowed freely, pot and cigarette smoke hung in the air, and Ray Charles and Jesse Collin Young and the Youngbloods blared from the stereo, as bobbing bodies were buoyed in a sea of rhythmic motion. I had invited Sophie, a few of her girlfriends, many of my classmates and their dates, as well as sophomores and seniors. The apartment was rocking and on the verge of being out of control in a normal, pleasing sort of way. I was flushed, loose, and having fun until I looked out across the living room and saw Erhenfeld laughing and talking with Sophie in the corner. Suddenly beyond my control and much to my surprise a powerful feeling welled up and erupted, like an attack of emotional projectile vomiting.

"Get the fuck away from her, Erhenfeld, you cocksucker!" I bellowed, hurling the command like a sotted cannonball blown from my guts. I was stunned by this eviscerating release, shocked and breathless that some subconscious secret of my heart had been ripped out and publicly exposed. My knees giving out, I gasped and collapsed in a raging howl of tears. Quickly John Medoff and Taylor Randall lifted me by the arms and carried me off to the shower next to my bedroom.

"O.K.! O.K.! Shut the fucking water off," I called up to Randall from the shower floor, where I sat soaking under a cold blast of water, propped up against the tile wall like a limp Raggedy Andy. In a moment we were hooting it up and laughing. "Oh, man, where the fuck did that come from?" I asked, somewhat bewildered and embarrassed.

"You're fuckin' wasted, man."

"Yeah. Tanked with a capital T."

They wandered back out to the party, and while I changed alone into dry clothes I pondered in subdued amazement how the bottom had just fallen out from under me (even though I knew I was not particularly drunk) and how I now felt at the mercy of some new, unfamiliar feeling, something bigger than myself.

A bit sheepishly but determined to acquiesce to this mystery and pursue it, however blindly, I, too, wandered back into the living room and found Sophie.

"May I take you home now?" I asked.

"Yes," she answered. "You may."

We ate Pepperidge Farm Orleans cookies and drank tea in her fifth floor apartment on East 79th Street, talking until two in the morning. To me, she really was beautiful with her glistening long brown hair, dark eyebrows, and creamy complexion. The gaze of her shy but attentive brown eyes sometimes fell to her hands with their delicate, long fingers as she spoke about herself. She played classical piano, had perfect pitch, and had been studying at the Dalcroze School of Music since she was four years old. She told me about her parents, who had kindly remained in their bedroom so as not to disturb us. Her mother was chief buyer for Lord and Taylor department store on 38th Street and had worked there for many years. Her father Mort was a horse photographer, working shows in New York and equestrian events in Vermont, and she said, he drank too much.

"I can relate to that," I said, sharing a little about my father and family. Every word we spoke, it seemed, was carefully chosen, and our breaths felt light, almost held in, so as not to interfere with our intent listening or upset in any way the delicate feeling between us.

When it came time for me to go and we stood in the hallway outside her apartment door, a winter wind whistled in the elevator shaft, and as I looked at Sophie I was overcome with a loneliness and sorrow as deep and long as my whole life, made possible only by the contrasting beauty and hope which she now personified. My eyes searched hers for a moment, then unlike any other time I'd experienced, they flooded with tears, revealing a pain I had hardly been aware of, and I willingly let her see me as I cried and held her warm hands, and then slowly I drew her into my embrace.

Throughout December and into the bitter cold of January we secretly (until my mother got the bill) spoke for literally hours on the phone almost every weeknight, sharing details of our lives and dreams for the future. On Friday evenings for dinner I joined her and her parents, who seemed to take a liking to me right off. Mort would broil a thick steak and serve us plenty of wine. Sophie and I would then go out, see a movie, and top it off with an exotic sweet at Serendipity dessert shop. On Saturday we might go to the Frick Museum on 70th and 5th, then ride the subway down to South Station and ride the ferry over to Staten Island. We bought similar earthy brown leather shoes from Fred Braun, and with her in her long brown hair and blue jean skirt and me in my own torn jeans and a very beat-up leather jacket Mort had given me, together we felt cut from the Village folk music scene, organic and whole earth before the terms became fashionable. On several weekends we tried out different church and synagogue services, but felt most partial to simply seeking out the jeweled warmth and silence of St. Thomas Episcopal Church during non-service hours, where the vaulted ceiling soaring skyward into soft rainbow light took our breaths away and cloaked us peacefully from the bustle of the street and the disturbances of our lives. One Saturday matinee as standees at the Met we were carried away on the music of La Bohème, and soon thereafter I bought Sophie a carved antique ivory whistle in a Third Avenue junk store of two Baroque lovers poised to kiss one another. What a find and a perfect gift! To the degree I had been so despairing only a few weeks before, I had now passionately thrown myself headlong into love with romantic abandon.

But my dark undercurrents were not far away and I had difficulty holding them at bay. With Sophie I had finally summoned the courage to visit with my father at 86th Street. He had returned to the city in October, but it wasn't until late in the afternoon of a snowy Christmas Eve day that we rang the bell to his house. It was an inconsequential get-together, but it broke the ice of our separation. He was polite enough, didn't pry much, and was grateful for the Don Diego cigar I had brought him. I think he approved of Sophie; but still, I imagined he was disgusted with me, and the now strange house felt heavy, dark, and dusty. I was glad when we got out into the crisp night air after a couple of scotches.

We had then walked down to 78th Street between Park and Lexington to where my mother's oldest sister Aunt Eleanor lived with my Uncle George Farnsworth in their five-story townhouse and were hosting their annual black-tie Christmas Eve cocktail party with carols. Despite being embarrassingly underdressed in our jeans, we were let in by Ethel, their tiny Hungarian maid in their employ for fifty years and wearing a white uniform dress. My white-haired and portly Uncle George (Brigadier General, U.S. Army, Retired) greeted us in his red plaid Christmas cummerbund and tuxedo from the top of the stairs, booming in his basso profundo, Harvard Law sort of way, "Merry Christmas, fella! Good to see ya, good to see ya," then drawing on his pipe, followed by "Mmm, mmm." We climbed the stairs, and were then welcomed into the living room by my Aunt Eleanor (Colonel, U.S. Army Retired, physician) in tweed with white pearls from Van Cleef and Arpel, my mother in white poppets from Woolworth's, and Aunt Mimi, seated at the grand piano in a bright green dress and draped with a string of Chinese red enameled beads the size of crabapples, organizing her sheet music. The room was filled with gaily chattering people and fine perfume; partners from my uncle's law firm Harris, Todd, Caldwell, Cumberland, and Farnsworth and their wives; my uncle's cousin and President Eisenhower's Attorney General, Turner Farnsworth; and, of course, the Brewsters, the Pierces, the Dodges, the Prices, the Andrews, the Reeds, etc.; investment bankers, lawyers, corporate board members, physicians, college presidents, etc., etc. Elsie, another Hungarian maid, served white mushroom caps filled with red caviar and black caviar on water crackers with egg and sour cream along with radishes cut in the shape of roses and ribboned carrot florets. There were platters of freshly baked cookies and cut crystal bowls of champagne punch, and Lazlo the Hungarian butler entered with a silver tray of champagne-filled flutes. In a few moments Uncle George, who was in Van Janssen's Class of 1912 before going off to Pomfret and then Harvard, tinkled his glass and called together me and some older Van Janssen alum in attendance for the annual singing of the Van Janssen Song, much to my embarrassment in front of Sophie, who by this time seemed utterly overwhelmed with a frozen smile on her face. Uncle George proposed a toast to Van Janssen, to tradition, to old friends present and deceased, and after Aunt Mimi played a rousing introduction, we men, young and old, broke into

> Our forefathers crossed the Atlantic
> And landed right here on this shore
> They saw this beautiful island
> And said what could we want more
> And then those sturdy Neth'landers
> Decided that they'd come to stay
> And said to the wandering red men
> You've got to get out of our way!
>
> Hoorah for the Orange and Blue
> For Van Janssen will ever be true
> She gives us the knowledge

That sends us to college
Hoorah for the Orange and Blue.

They started the village Manhattan
According to old Holland rule
Along with their homes and their gardens
They builded a church and a school
You may think we're new
But we are not
For that was Van Janssen our school
You may think we're new
But we are not
For that was Van Janssen our school

Soon thereafter Sophie and I slipped out in hot pursuit of reconnecting. Walking arm in arm down Fifth Avenue under lightly falling snow, we entered Central Park at 64th Street, and followed the paths from lamplight to lamplight to Wollman Rink where we rented skates and further attended to the delicate ties which had begun to bind us.

Holding back the encroaching, muddied jungle of ever-pressing high academic, familial, and cultural expectations commensurate with elite breeding, all coupled with confusing and heartbreaking disappointments and violent intrusions resulting in my excess of self-doubt, imbibed tomfoolery, and self-loathing, Sophie and I were forging a sanctuary of tenderness and hope, lovely and youthful beyond words. This was our first true love.

But by the end of the third week in January I knew I had fallen irreversibly behind in my schoolwork, a doomed condition toward which I had begun spiraling by the end of the first week of classes that previous September, even as I had tried to deny its inexorable approach with failing good cheer. Now on this bitterly cold Sunday night with my mother passed out in the living room at her cherry desk in a pool of evaporated tears, I sat at my bedroom desk, surrounded by textbooks and papers, out of cigarettes. I had an open book exam before me, due in the morning, requiring me to discuss *Marbury v. Madison*, its background and consequences for Supreme Court power; I had a test fifth period after lunch in Symbolic Logic on semantic versus syntactic concepts of validity and how they relate to the concept of soundness, about which I could give a shit; I was expected to discuss in spoken French during sixth period the conclusion of Balzac's *Eugenie Grandet* which I hadn't even begun; and in Mr. Sears' History of Emerging Nations class I was supposed to give a talk on Sun Yat Sen, the Koumintang, and the rise of Chinese nationalism on the road to modernity. No fucking way.

I popped open the fruitcake tin of stale butts. With elbow on the desk, and arm and palm propping up my head, I lit and took a couple of drags off a butt, crushed it out in a small brass ashtray, and lit another. I repeated this ritual for the better part of an hour. It was after eleven o'clock and whatever physical motion I now made seemed independent of, unrelated to, and disconnected from whatever, if anything, I may have been thinking.

As if by rote and almost in a trance I went into the narrow kitchen in the back of the apartment, scattering the startled cockroaches, and found my mother's purse. I took out a twenty-dollar bill from her wallet and some change. Throwing on my red watch cap, a yellow wool scarf, and my grandfather's gray herringbone blazer, a hand-me-down with lapels as wide as gangplanks and holes in the elbows, I quietly left the apartment and rode the elevator down to the street. I walked around the corner at Amsterdam and halfway up the block to a Cuban bodega, where I bought a pack of Larks. Just as I was returning, a 79th Street Crosstown bus rounded the corner headed for the East Side and stopped. I climbed aboard, threw fifteen cents into the coin box, which ate and digested my money with a pleasingly rhythmic mechanical sound, and took a seat in the back of the bus.

Passing the green-domed planetarium at 81st Street and the chiseled words "Truth, Knowledge, Vision" over the bronze equestrian sculpture of Teddy Roosevelt on a horse with one raised hoof at the entrance to the Museum of Natural History, the bus entered Central Park. It did not occur to me where I was going, nor did I care.

As the bus proceeded out of the park and rolled passed Fifth Avenue onto East 79th Street, I gazed up Madison Avenue, as it drew closer, toward 80th, and my eye caught the yellow awning of the 79th Street Pub. I reached up and pulled the vinyl exit chord, signaling the driver with a ding of a bell, and the bus pulled over. I stepped off into the cold, empty street, remarkably quiet and free of traffic and pedestrians, most certainly because it was almost midnight on a Sunday evening. I ambled up the block and entered the dimly lit pub.

Sitting at the bar I ordered a scotch and soda without making eye contact with the bartender, and he set me up without a word. The place was empty except for two well-dressed black men sitting a few stools away near the front window. I lit up a smoke, sniffed the fresh tobacco in the new pack, lingering over its coconut smell between sips of my drink. After a few minutes I piggybacked another cigarette off the butt of the first and ordered another drink.

"What are you doing out so late, little boy," one of the men with particularly shining dark skin in a charcoal gray topcoat asked in a smooth, deep voice.

"You talking to me?" I asked.

"I don't see any other little boys in here, do I Harold?" he said, turning to his partner on the other stool.

"You're talking to the wrong person, then," I said with quickly rising discomfort.

"Shit, Moses, you heard the man, you're talking to the wrong person," his partner said.

"Oh, well then, my apologies. But would you allow me to—to redeem myself by buying you another drink? Little boy?"

"I'm not your little boy," I said halfheartedly.

"You heard the man, McHenry," the partner said. "Lay off and buy him a drink."

"Scotch and soda, is it?" he asked, raising his hand at the bartender, snapping a finger, and pointing at my drink. The bartender set another drink before me.

There was something not altogether displeasing about this Moses McHenry calling me "little boy," even if I did partially take it as demeaning. I wasn't sure whether to fight or to smile. After all, it wasn't a completely untrue term about me, "little boy," being sixteen years old next to his forty or so years, and, in fact, the unexpected attention wasn't exactly hostile; and maybe on a cold Sunday night, or rather the very early hours of a Monday morning in late January when I hardly knew where I was or why, his buying me a drink and talking to me felt almost kind or even soothing in a perverse sort of way.

"Thanks," I said, chewing on an ice cube, looking straight ahead at the bottles on the shelf. Catching myself in the mirror between a quart of Old Grand Dad and one of Jim Beam, I snuffed out my butt, lit another, finished off my second drink and picked up the third. "Cheers," I said with awkward, feigned nonchalance.

"And to you the same, little boy," the well-dressed man said, glancing over at me, apparently surprised and pleased at this smidgen of salutatory contact I offered up.

But I was irked at his persistent name-calling and turned my back to him. For at least the next half hour I sat in silence smoking, drinking a fourth and finally a fifth scotch and soda. It was as if my decision-making process, my ability to choose between options had been canceled out. I felt suspended in a pointless medium of thoughtlessness, a fleck of dust, if that, afloat in a beam of orange setting sunlight.

"Let's be gettin' a move on, now, Harold," I heard McHenry say. I raised my head and glanced with heavy eyelids over at the two men now standing at their bar stools. "You take it easy, little boy," he said, and I gave a cursory wave as they walked past me and out the door.

I looked up and down the bar and saw that it was empty and deadeningly silent. Even the bartender had disappeared, perhaps to take a piss. Suddenly my heart began to beat faster.

I jumped off my stool, thrust my pack of smokes into a pocket, and lunged out the door just as Harold and Moses McHenry had entered a yellow Checker cab and were about to slam the door.

"Hey, wait up!" I shouted. "I'm comin', too!" I hurled myself in alongside McHenry who slid over into the middle.

"We'll be stoppin' first at 119th and Lenox," Harold said softly, "then y'all 'll be goin' on."

The cabbie threw the meter flag and steadily caught the Madison Avenue lights as they turned green uptown to Harlem. The ride was quiet except for the meter clicking over ten cents every fifth of a mile and the muted, rumbling hum of snow tires on the empty streets. We turned left onto 116th Street, right onto Lenox, and up to a stop at the corner of 119th. Without speaking Harold pulled a five out of his wallet and gave it to McHenry. Glancing at me with no expression, he exited the cab.

"G'night, Doctor," he said, slamming the door.

"We'll be goin' on to 55 East 135th street, driver."

"Are you a doctor?" I asked.

"No. I am not a medical doctor, little boy. I am a psychologist," he said, placing his hand on my thigh.

"Don't be doin' that," I said, picking up his hand and dropping it back in his lap.

"Oh, come now, little boy, I mean no harm."

"I don't want that."

"Mmm, well, we'll see then." He sighed deeply and added, "Maybe we'll have a little nightcap back at my place."

"Yeah, maybe."

The cab turned right at 125th street and went back over to Madison and headed uptown.

"I've been around here before," I said. "We came up here once. On a Sunday."

"Who's 'we'?"

"My family. We came up here with—a friend. A long time ago. To the Abyssinian Baptist Church."

"Is that right? Now that's a funny thing. For a white boy."

The cab turned left onto 135th Street and pulled over to the curb in front of a fairly new, white-bricked high-rise a block or two down from Harlem Hospital. Pretty nice place, I thought, for Harlem.

"Pretty nice place," I said.

"For Harlem?" he asked.

"Well, yeah."

"Unhunh. Some of us do do all right, little boy, in spite of the obvious disadvantages heaped upon us."

We entered the building and rode the elevator up to his tenth-floor apartment. It was small, clean, and modern with a narrow, carpeted living room, a sofa against one wall, and a dining table at the far end looking out over the Harlem River, a kitchen, one bedroom, and a bath.

McHenry took off his top coat and hung it in a closet by the front door, kicked off his shoes, and walked toward the kitchen, loosening and removing his tie while taking off his suit jacket, and laying them both across one of two armchairs. His skin shone like dark marble against his white dress shirt.

I sat on the sofa, slightly reeling from all I had drunk thus far, both hands stuffed into the side pockets of my grandfather's tweed jacket, collar upturned, yellow scarf dangling from my neck, red watch cap still on my head. It was somewhere after two o'clock.

"Scotch?" he asked, ice cubes clinking into first one, then another glass. A cabinet door clicked open and slammed shut and I heard the booze washing over the ice.

"Yeah, sure. Why not?" I pulled the red pack of Larks out of my pocket and lit one up.

Handing me the drink from the kitchen, he sat down in one of the armchairs with his glass, his belly hanging over his belt. On a coffee table between us lay the business section of the *New York Times* and a new hardbound book, *Manchild in the Promised Land*, next to an ashtray.

We were quiet for a few minutes. We sipped our drinks. I smoked. As the soggy blanket of drunkenness and fatigue grew even heavier over my head, his studious attention became a fulcrum between seesawing discomfort and an absurd giddiness approaching deranged abandon.

"Well, little boy?"

"Nice fuckin' place ya got here." A bubble of sadness rose and belched out in the form of tears from my eyes, followed by a clipped howl of laughter. "Oh, man, I'm so fucked!" I exclaimed, keeling over sideways onto the couch.

In the next moment McHenry was kneeling alongside me, his knees on the carpet, cradling my head in his arms, his thick lips and shining black face inches from mine. "Kiss me, little boy," he whispered, puckering his lips, his whiskey-soured breath wafting over my face like steam from a fat kettle. "Kiss me, you poor, poor little boy," he implored again.

"No!" I howled, lurching away and rolling over into a fetal position, then outstretching my legs and burying my face between the sofa back and seat cushions while tucking both arms straight down underneath my prone body. "That's not what I fuckin' want!" I cried, my words muffled and enveloped in the soft, cushioned darkness. A hand came to rest on my shoulder beneath my jacket, its gentle, radiating warmth penetrating my skin and ushering me into peaceful oblivion. Within moments I slept.

A crescent of orange sun bridged the brown rooftops of old apartments, warehouses, and rusted stacks and rose over the Harlem River, streaming sunlight into the apartment.

McHenry's hand thrust down beneath my underpants and kneading my ass had wakened me, and I rolled over into his round plump face still alongside the sofa, and again he said, "Kiss me, little boy."

I sat up, my head throbbing, my mouth sticky as if stuffed with cotton and white glue. "No, man," I said, pressing my forefingers into each temple while placing my feet on the floor. "Where are my shoes?"

"I took them off to make you comfortable," he said. "They're right here." He placed them before me.

"I need some water."

McHenry stood up, walked into the kitchen, and returned with a glass of water. He sat next to me on the couch and watched me drink. "There now," he said when I finished. "Now will you kiss me, little boy?"

"No, man. Look, I have a girlfriend." I said putting on my shoes and hat and standing up. I tried to recall how my new and special feeling with Sophie fit into all of this, and I meekly added, almost apologetically, "She cares about me." More emphatically I stated, "I care about her. I have to get to school now."

"Just one kiss, then."

"I don't want that."

"Jesus!" he growled. "What the hell do you want? What the fuck are you doing here?"

I shrugged.

"Well, how about just letting me suck on your white-ass, little-boy dick?" he asked in exasperation.

I shook my head no. "I gotta go."

"Well, let's go out to a bar, then. Get some drinks."

"I really gotta get to school," I said, walking to the door, wrapping my scarf around my neck.

"Well, all right then. Hold your god damn horses while I get my shoes and coat. I'll drop you off. I'm goin' downtown anyway."

While waiting, I lit up a smoke, and in a few minutes we went out the apartment, down the elevator, and into the bright, bitterly cold day. The air was clean and a biting wind blew off the river across the salt-stained asphalt of 135th Street.

We hailed a gypsy cab and rode downtown in silence, except when I asked to be dropped off at 79th Street and Broadway, a block from my house so he wouldn't know where I lived.

As I started crossing the street away from the taxi into the rising sun toward Amsterdam, he called after me from his downturned window.

"Hey, son! You watch your backside, now! They're not always decent like me." I waved and he slapped the side of the yellow door with his palm and the cab sped off, losing itself in the flow of traffic down Broadway.

My mother had left for her secretary job at the National Sharecroppers Fund. I showered, brushed my teeth, and gargled, then put on a clean shirt and a very wide brown tie with white polka dots. I stepped into my grandfather's brown pleated pants, baggy and oversized, slipped his tweed jacket back on, and pressed my feet into the ugliest caramel-colored thrift store shoes from Austria I'd been able to find with useless, thick metal toe taps the size of half-moon silver dollars. I made myself a piece of Pepperidge Farm white toast with peanut butter and jelly and a cup of Twinings Orange Pekoe tea with milk and sugar. Then I wrapped my yellow plaid scarf around my neck, threw on my red watch cap, picked up my canvass book bag, lit up a smoke, and headed out, very late, to school where I supposed I had ought to be.

Ambling down Amsterdam to 76th Street, I cut over to between Broadway and West End and entered through the red door of Van Janssen at number 247. No sooner than I'd stepped across the threshold did I see Mr. C. Boynton Cross—Eaton, Oxford, Modern European History scholar, and balding Head of the Upper School—beckoning me from atop the concavely worn stone staircase with an impatient waggle of a finger and a stern gaze down his pronounced British nose.

"I'll see you now in my office, Leon," he said, turning on his wing-tipped heel and heading up a second flight of stairs, as if he were walking with a stone balanced on his head, to his cubicle which appeared to be a converted janitor's closet off the top floor landing.

Just two weeks before, he had called me into his "office" for a confidential conference, as he'd called it. He knew he could always count on me for an honest answer, for honesty was, generally speaking, one of my virtues, or shall we say, one of my charming survival skills, especially in combination with my innocent, endearing smile; he had wanted to know then how serious the pot smoking situation was without revealing any names amongst members of my class of thirty-five, lest my loyalty to friends be compromised. I had said, "Hmmm, now let me see," and counted out on thumb to pinky of first one hand, then the other, then back to the first, and again into the second, informing him that at least two-thirds of the class was getting high on a regular basis. He had seemed terribly aggrieved by, but grateful for this information. But now as I trudged up the stairs, I suspected that our meeting was not about to be as cordial or accommodating as then.

"Leon," Mr. Cross began, face-to-face with our knees cramped about six inches apart from one another in this most intimate of cubicles. "Where were you last night? Your mother called the headmaster, who in turn called me seeking your whereabouts. We called Dr. and Mrs. Medoff, Mr. and Mrs. Patton, Mrs. Randall, Dr. Sterner. Now Leon, tell me truthfully, where were you?"

"Well," I smiled innocently and scrunched up my face. "Uhm, well." I hesitated, then thought, fuck it, and said, "Well, long about eleven o'clock or midnight last night I was out of smokes, so I went out to buy a pack. A bus came along. I took it crosstown, went to a bar, got loaded, and went up to Harlem with this guy."

There was a long, long pause in which Mr. Cross pinched his forehead while squinting his eyes shut and pursing his lips. "Oh, no, Leon, how—how could you?" he finally sighed. "You—you didn't, uh, how shall I say?"

"Fuck him? I mean, have sex with him?" He let out an endless breath from his puffed out cheeks, while I quickly answered, "Oh, no, but he sure wanted to."

There was another long, long pause.

"Leon? I'm going to be quite—quite frank with you. I'm afraid this is an expellable indiscretion, and, at the very least, a matter of grave concern for all of us who care about your future. Now, you've been at Van Janssen for a long, long time, and you are a member of our family, as I am sure we are a family to you. It would, therefore, be heartbreaking for all of us should we be forced to lose you. Instead, Leon, I propose to you a choice, which if you agree to make in the affirmative, will allow me to keep you in school and matriculate in June following next. To remain enrolled, Leon, you must agree to enter some sort of psychotherapy, either with a psychiatrist, an analyst, or some sort of professional counselor." He paused, tilted his head aft to scrutinize my response, then added, "Agreed?"

"Maybe I could see Dr. Medoff, John's father," I said hopefully.

"I don't think that would be appropriate. We'll find someone in consultation with your mother who has no, shall we say, conflict of interest. So then, Leon, once again; agreed?"

"Sure," I said, shrugging my shoulders with a halfhearted smile. "Why not?"

"You've made a wise decision, Leon. I'll call your mother." He scribbled on a pass and handed it to me. "Off you go then. To your classes."

"Thanks," I said.

"It's up to you, Leon," he rejoined.

I wandered off down the hall, lugging my heavy book bag over a shoulder, to face the History of Emerging Nations class which I was despondently sure would prove to be irrelevant and humiliating. It was inevitable!

"Let's see," I thought, "Who was Sun Yat Sen?

Four

THE PLUMBING TRUCK DRIVER MAN

I felt like an infiltrator. I'm sure they noticed that I was conspicuously different, but for the time being they left me alone, and I was able to quietly enjoy my work, increasing my knowledge and strengthening my body. Quickly enough, they had called me "the kid." But I didn't much mind, as long as the ripple of disturbance, which my employment at the shop had caused, subsided and I was accepted in the necessary, albeit demeaned position of truck driver, yardman, and gopher.

Brought in from the field where I had been digging soil pipe ditches by hand, quite anonymously, for the last two sweltering months in a Tustin condominium development, promoted, and given a raise to $4.75 an hour, I saw for the first time the dirty pink and crumbling shop facade of Southland Plumbers, surrounded by a high chain link fence peaked with barbed wire. Here is where the men, the plumbers, returned each day after 3:30 in their own Ford F100, 150 or 250 Camper Special pickups, corresponding to their apprentice, journeyman or master plumber status. Here is where the heavy equipment—the larger utility trucks, the backhoe, the trencher, the forklift, and the flatbed—returned for storage and reloading.

The source of supplies, Southland Plumbers was located south of downtown Los Angeles in Paramount, a municipality part of that amalgam of indistinguishable small cities oozing down the Harbor, Long Beach and 605 Freeways from Bell to Compton, Torrance and the ports of San Pedro and Long Beach. This conglomeration constitutes the greater Port of Los Angeles, one of the world's mightiest industrial and commercial hubs. Southland had jobs going throughout it all.

During the course of my year's employment at Southland Plumbers, I grew quite familiar with the materials of the trade; the blood of the business; the stuff of waste management and flow control; the beneath-the-surface, underground, behind-the-wall, in-the-dirt stuff of plumbing; galvanized, coated, black, concrete, clay, soil, ABS and PVC pipe, and type M and K coils and twenty foot tubes of copper. Fittings of every description, pipe dope, nipples, oakum, solder and lead, stacks of boxed American Standard and Norris toilet bowls, tanks and seats, ball, gate, globe, check, relief, needle, and outside yoke and stem valves, tubs, lavs, Houdi rims and sinks, steel rod, and hangers were all handled by me, counted, stacked, loaded and unloaded daily. I also became familiar with the ways of these men called plumbers. And, perhaps more importantly, I was at twenty-one years of age, quite secretively, obsessed with becoming a man.

My association with Al brought me to the plumbing profession. I rented a small, comfortably run-down apartment chopped out of what was once a fine, Spanish stucco and tile-roofed mansion in the mostly Hispanic, dilapidated but hip district of Silver Lake. I worked at Burrito King, a fast-food stand on the corner of Sunset Boulevard and Alvarado. Here, at my work, I first met Al.

Twice a week he stopped and walked up to the window for a burrito con queso and a Coke. Most striking about him at first was the car he drove, the first of its kind I had ever seen—a white, ferociously sleek, low-lying and monstrously powerful wedge with fourteen-inch-wide, hardly street legal rear tires, a De Tomaso Pantera. Although his toughened, weather-beaten face and the black panther tattoo leaping and growling off his massive left bicep were impressive, what was next most striking about Al was the gentleness and sadness in his eyes.

Almost every visit to the stand Al revealed something new to me. He was visiting his aging mother in a Silver Lake convalescent hospital; he was a pool shark; he had been a plumber since he was seventeen; he was now thirty-eight; he had an intense, almost obsessive relationship with a young woman named Cheryl (he even brought her to the stand once, and she was quite beautiful, blond and full-breasted with a sweet smile); he had seventy-five union plumbers working for him; his partner, he told me, was an asshole, screwed up on cocaine, but his oldest and best friend; Al had been busted for selling marijuana to a narcotics agent, but had beaten the rap by paying a $10,000 bribe to a federal judge through his attorney; he'd been known as Cadillac Al in the sixties when his plumbing company started to take off and he'd bought a new Cadillac every year, until he went really classy and bought a Jaguar XJ6. But it had no balls, he said, and he sank a 427 Corvette engine into it, which threw the precise British machine's body out of whack, so he said the hell with it, and bought the Pantera. He had cared for his mother since his father had left when he was twelve and now he avoided her. He lived in Seal Beach in northern Orange County and had a powerboat with twin 288 horsepower inboards moored outside his living room, and he'd just had a bid accepted on the biggest construction job of his life, a four hundred and forty-unit condominium village complex in Redondo Beach. Feeling like he'd really overextended himself, he was sure this job would either drive his company under and into bankruptcy, or he'd make more money from it than the total from all his previous twenty-two years in plumbing. Al was a volcanic marvel, filled with passion, terror, innocence and dark confusion, and an intriguing, if not endearing, self-revealing manner. Sometimes the thought of his mother would fill his eyes to the brim. Other times the same thought caused his eyes to flash crimson with anger.

"Can I have a job, Al? Anything better than this $2.75 an hour grease trap?" I finally asked one day, somewhat fearful that my request to alter the forum and nature of our four-month relationship might jeopardize what, I thought, might be approaching a real friendship, even if he was eighteen years my senior. If he said yes, I would no longer be that easy listening, fairly anonymous confessor behind the window of the burrito stand on quiet, sunny afternoons. Who'd want to meet their priest out on the street, anyway?

He momentarily reflected, then answered, I thought, with reluctance, "Yeah, I suppose. Not if you mind driving more than an hour away. Do you have a car?"

"Yeah, I do. I have one of those tiny Honda 600cc cars. I can lift both back wheels off the ground."

"Well, I have a job going, down in Tustin in Orange County. It's forty units. They can use a laborer. It's tough work, mostly digging out ditches for soil pipe. Interested?"

"Yeah, It sounds great! Get me out of this cage!"

"I'll start you at $4.25 an hour, and if you make out all right, I can bring you into the shop later, maybe put you on the delivery truck and give you a raise." He wrote down the name of the jobsite supervisor and the address. He drew a map on the back of the paper and handed it to me. "Be there at 6:45 AM," he said with a smile.

"Great!" I answered, and that's how I got into the plumbing business.

Inside the small brass shed I finished counting out fifty half-inch copper elbows, threw a couple dozen gate valves into the cardboard box, and began counting out the last item on the La Verne job site order sheet, fifty brass nipples. My concentration was broken by the bellowing voice of Al's partner Bob.

"Where's that kid!" he yelled into the yard from just inside the back screen door of the front office. Six feet two inches tall, roughly two hundred and thirty-five pounds, Bob worked out daily on a heavy punching bag and ran five miles on the beach. He had a reputation, Al once informed me, for entering nightclubs high on coke and booze with his friend Bradley, a onetime defensive tackle for the Los Angeles Rams, picking fights and tearing the places up for fun. He drove a sickly green Lincoln Continental with an obscenely elongated hood, suggesting that some locomotive engine lay underneath. He wore an oversized handlebar moustache which he twirled nervously when lost in thought and off guard. When giving orders, Bob had the intimidating habit of swinging his Popeyed arms and thrusting his hardened pectorals to within six inches of your nose for authoritative emphasis. Without question he was the gorilla chieftain of the plumbing troop.

"Leon!" he yelled again.

"Yo!" I answered with a fraudulent nonchalance more forceful than the tremulous palpitation pumping weakness into my chest, arms and legs. Oh, to be strong, to be tough, I thought, stepping out of the shed with the box of supplies and walking over toward Bob. I made a conscious effort not to trot.

"Move it!" he barked. "This is a money-making machine! La Verne just called and they're waitin' on that stuff, so get your ass in gear, take the green pickup, and step on it! Double time!"

"Right, no problem," I answered with an easygoing smile meant to convey my lack of intimidation. But how big and dense with muscles he was! I hoisted the box into the bed of the truck.

"And there ain't a damn thing funny about it, is there?"

"Who's laughing? I'm outta here."

"Better be," he said, swinging his arms, his eyes glued on my every movement until I was in the truck and pulling out the driveway.

Fuck you, you son of a bitch, I thought, laying a patch of rubber and feeling the steady, soothing surge of the 400 cubic inch Chevy engine pressing me back against the seat in direct response to the toe-downed pedal, like a narcotic injection. Though I believed such a departure was an expression of righteous indignation, I was secretly relieved by the thought that it might also be viewed as zealous compliance with a direct order.

I raced down Garfield Avenue, hurled out of the on-ramp onto the Artesia Freeway, jockeyed through two lanes of traffic into the passing lane, and wove my way over to and on up the 605 Freeway to the 210 and out to La Verne—a total of 37 miles—in record 29 minute time and with, I thought, my manhood, at least tenuously, restored.

Later that afternoon I returned to the shop. Tired, dirty plumbers had come back from their various job sites and placed orders for the following day's supplies with Joe Piscatelli, the forlorn but competent eleventh-year yard supervisor whose unshaven face and sad eyes were concealed by Roy Orbison wraparound sunglasses. While the plumbers sucked on cold beers and laughed in the front office, out back Joe and I began filling orders and loading them onto the eighteen-foot flatbed truck for the next day's deliveries.

One of the orders called for some inch and a half galvanized vent pipes, which had to be cut, threaded, and assembled with black iron fittings. Joe sent me to the back of the shop for a vent pipe-assembling lesson from the one other yardman, an old-timer named Eli.

Red-faced, gaunt but strong as thick leather, Eli maintained a foul, sexually explicit sense of humor incongruous with his seventy-two years. He was a kind man with a hearty, staccato laugh. Born in Oklahoma with twenty-four years spent in the Navy, he had worked for Al and Bob since they had become partners. Now he lived alone next door in a small trailer, taking loving care of the one surviving mangy Doberman that guarded the shop at night. The other dog had been killed by a burglar's pipe blow to the head, and according to Joe, Eli had wept for three days.

Eli swung the twenty-foot lengths of pipe about, like so many toothpicks, and fed their ends into the Rigid pipe threader. The humming machine effortlessly turned the pipe, bathing the ends in black oil, as metal shavings dropped into the oil pan.

"This here pipe's hard as a morning pecker ready to piss, but don't you be hasty feeding it into this machine, or sure as shit it'll be eatin' your horny flesh faster 'n yer jerked zipper can chew. You got my meaning, son?"

"Sure, Eli."

"Good. Now you try it," he said, watching me feed another length into the machine. "That's it. Nice and easy. Good! I bet you are a horny little bastard! You like to eat pussy, don't you?"

"I beg your pardon?"

"You're a cunt-loppin' little fucker, ain't ya?" he laughed. "Ya like to lick pussy, don't ya?"

"Well, uh, yes, I suppose."

"I knew it. I just knew it! You make any deliveries over to Gardena?"

"Yes. Sure. We've got a couple of jobs goin' in Gardena. How come?"

"Well, they got these card clubs over there, you know, legal gamblin' and poker? And there's a fox over there named Dahlia—biggest tits and sweetest little ass you've ever seen! And the name of the card place where she works is the Eldorado Club on South Vermont. You know what Dahlia and the Eldorado Club have in common?" He paused with a big grin on his face.

"No, what, Eli?"

"Liquor in the front, poker in the rear!" he howled, punching me in the arm and laughing his choppy laugh. "Now you finish up on the rest of this pipe, son, and when ya got it all done, go on back to fillin' the rest of yer orders, then I'll show ya how to assemble all this shit."

Darkness came and the shop was quiet. Eli let the dog out from its corrugated metal and scrap lumber kennel. Joe glanced sadly over the last order sheet on his clipboard, alternately raising a Pall Mall cigarette and a beer can slowly to his lips. Carefully brushing pipe dope around the threads of a length of pipe, as Eli had taught me, and tightening the pipe into its fitting with a large wrench, I finished the last vent pipe assembly, loaded it onto the truck, and with a furtive glance at my biceps lifted the wooden gates into place.

"See ya in the morning," we bid one another, and I drove home up the Long Beach Freeway, feeling tired yet satisfied with my beginning progress.

Months passed, and I grew stronger, more competent. I knew the names of most of the plumbing supplies. I knew all the job site locations and could get to them quickly and unload. I had stopped eating Hershey bars and chocolate milk with every lunch, preferring instead a small can of V8, a few pieces of Leo's sliced turkey and some Rye Crisps. And because of the mobility, solitude, and independence which my powerful flatbed delivery truck afforded me, I was able to view and enjoy many interesting Los Angeles area sights, such as the shower of golden sparks spewed from a hellish blast furnace at American Foundry in the city of Commerce, where manhole covers were made; or, in the City of Industry red clay pipe for sewers or tile roofing baked in ancient kilns shaped like Indian burial mounds; gas flares ferociously burned atop mammoth refineries in Wilmington and Torrance; acre upon acre of Japanese automobiles waited in San Pedro for shipment across America; and on clear days from high in the hills of Palos Verdes, the Pacific Ocean—flecked with white caps and sails, freighters, container ships and tankers—spread beyond San Clemente and Catalina Islands to Hawaii, Polynesia, and the Indies. My work was a part of all these sights, and often I felt the challenge and exhilaration of the discoverer venturing into new lands, the captain of my own vessel, a plumbing truck.

One spoken word, however, like rocks off a lee shore, threatened to stove the young timber of my budding manhood. I had arrived at 7:45 AM at the huge Diamond Street job site in Redondo Beach with a load of thirty-eight toilet bowls and tanks. The short, barrel-chested site supervisor named Walt, the company's finest plumber, sang out his customary, stuttered greeting while vigorously chewing his gum and smiling broadly.

"What kind of b-bullshit do you have for me today, Leon?" Seeing the toilets, he directed me to Building 3. I drove around to the building's subterranean garage, backed in and began unloading. That spoken word then rang out.

"Hey, pussy! Who told you to dump those shitters here, for Christ's sake!" Stepping out of the shadows with a pipe wrench slung over his shoulder and a fat, wet cigar stub stuck out the corner of his mouth, Hubert Brooks, an obese journeyman with particularly enormous, hairy arms, walked over to my truck.

"Walt just told me. And I don't think it's necessary to—"

"What building did he say? We already got our shitters."

"Building 3."

"Well, I don't figure we can expect you drivers to be too smart, can we? This is Building 4!"

"It is?"

"Yeah, it is! Now get this shit outta here!"

Embarrassed by my mistake, intimidated by his size, seniority and gruffness, possessed of too much youthful goodwill and inexperience for a spontaneous, quick-witted response, I loaded the toilets back onto the truck, pulled out of the garage and found the right building. I should have said something like, "Eat shit, fat man, I made a mistake," or "Buzz off, gorilla breath, didn't your mother teach you to brush?" But I had said nothing, and that had made his original epithet bothersomely significant. For the rest of the day I thought about it. What could I have said?

A week passed before I again returned to the Diamond site on a Thursday afternoon, this time carrying a load of galvanized vent pipe assemblies and hauling the large Pettibone forklift for unloading them. Walt directed me to Building 5 with instructions to place the load on the third floor of the framed, but wall-less structure, a delicate, challenging operation. Great care would be required not to upset the half ton of pipe laid across the forks, which had to be raised to their maximum height.

I inched the loaded forklift away from the rear of the truck, systematically eyeing the ground before the path of each of the large tires for any aberration, such as a stone, depression, or mound. Backing slowly around, I now eased closer to the building and slowly raised the lift, my left foot prepared to instantly plunge in the clutch at the slightest teetering. As the forks reached their third-floor apogee, I leaned them forward ever so slightly to the lip of the concrete floor, thereby completing the maneuver. Suddenly a voice from above and behind me in Building 4 shouted out.

"Hey, pussy! You sure those vents ain't for me?" It was Hubert Brooks, calling across from his third-floor perch twenty-five yards away. "After last week you can't be too sure, right kid?"

I thrust my extended middle finger upward in his direction, thinking that perhaps this was the tradesman-like thing to do, yet feeling wary that such a gesture might constitute a dangerous, if not foolhardy, challenge in light of our extreme size difference.

"Hey, hey! The kid's a tough guy! Keep it in your pants, tweety!" He laughed uproariously, blew me a kiss, and disappeared into the building.

Embarking on and keeping an incensed pace oblivious to pain and fatigue, I scampered from my seat up the thirty-foot-extended lift, leapt like a monkey over the load of vent pipes onto the concrete, and in a matter of minutes noisily hurled the load off the forks and into a pile. All the while in a chattering, silent rage, "Make me feel like a wimp, will you? Fat-assed tub of pig shit! I'll kick your rotten teeth in! You have to lift ten layers of fat just to find your mosquito dick!" All the while suffering and treading against a whirling cesspool of emotion which threatened to suck me into a disintegrative void of cowardice, I worked and quickly removed the several tons of pipe down to the bare, splintered and worn wood of the truck's bed. I then re-hitched the forklift and made my way back to the shop.

Darkness and a chill shrouded the yard in the waning hours of the afternoon as I filled orders, and the beer drinking laughter of returning plumbers drifted from the front office. I hate them, I thought. But still I wanted to be in the trade union and become an apprentice. Al had told me he thought he could get me in. I lifted several cases of pipe dope, sixteen twenty-five-pound rows of cubed caulking lead and some oakum onto the bed of the truck. I then hopped up and began moving the supplies forward near the cab. The screen door opened and slammed shut. I stopped working and looked up. It was Brooks.

Not noticing me, he moved in the darkness past the truck, apparently in search of some needed supply. A few moments later he was returning, cigar stub in mouth, with a couple of flat boxes of toilet seats tucked under his arm. I scanned the bed of my truck and picked up one of six two-by-four pieces of wood, about four feet long, used as a load divider to prevent pipe from rolling from one side of the bed to the other. As he approached beneath me along side the truck, I raised the two-by-four above my shoulder like an ax, and with my heart pumping furiously, I bellowed, "BROOKS!"

Startled, he jumped two feet away from the truck and looked up.

I was now blind and ready to die. "Brooks!" I roared again, slowly enunciating each word, "If you ever call me 'pussy' again, I'm going to bash your fuckin' skull in! Do you understand me? I'll kill you!"

"Well, jeez, yeah," he said, his cigar dropping from his mouth to the ground. "Yeah, sure, no problem. I was only kidding. I didn't mean nothin' by it," he said meekly, quickly side-stepping toward the front office. "Sorry." He disappeared inside.

Holy shit, I thought, that was right out of the Old West. Maybe they'll start calling me Billy the Kid. I got down off the truck, gripped the two-by-four once more and set it down. Chuckling at the sight of my shaking fingers, I sighed. The old Doberman trotted up and nuzzled her nose between my legs, her hindquarters wagging. I patted her side, and her warmth felt good.

"Tough little fucker, ain't ya?" Eli said, stepping out of the tool shed with a drill. He made a playful boxing lunge at me, laughed, and headed out back. "Tough little fucker."

The laughter up front gradually subsided, and the silence of night filled the shop. Joe came out of the front office with his can of beer, smiled at me, and checked over the order sheets on his clipboard. I gathered up the last few items and placed them on the truck.

"Well, I guess that's it," I said.

"Yep, that oughta do it," Joe said. "See ya in the morning."

"We'll see ya in the morning," Eli waved, going next door to his trailer.

"We'll see ya in the morning," I said, walking out to my car.

"Hey, tiger!" Al called after me as I was about to slam my car door. "How 'bout a beer and a game of pool?"

"Sure, sounds good."

"Let's take my car," he said, and we got into the Pantera, drove up Garfield and made a right onto Rosecrans Avenue. Al had inconspicuously watched out for me these past few months, taking me out for a beer from time to time, even double-dating at a Mexican restaurant, El Chavo, on Sunset Boulevard with his girlfriend Cheryl and a girl I met from Silver Lake. That had been a fun evening until the very end when suddenly upon my return from the restroom, for no apparent reason, he had gotten very angry, threw down a hundred dollar bill on the table, and dragged Cheryl by the hair out of the restaurant. Later he apologized to me for his abrupt departure and confided that he had found out she had taken more than a therapeutic liking to her West Hollywood psychiatrist. Although that after-dinner episode was unpleasant and, I'm sure, degrading for Cheryl, I was intrigued by, if not in awe of this great potential for violence, as if he were possessed by some San Onofre emotional reactor emanating power not unlike that which now slung us rumbling down the street.

"I heard you had a little go round with Brooks," he said, laughing warmly while turning into the parking lot of Shady Lanes bowling alley and pool hall.

"Oh, it was nothing. He just bugged me one too many times."

"I guess! He sounded scared shitless of you, and now all my men are razzin' the hell out of him, calling him pussy!"

We both laughed. Really I hoped the whole incident would just die down and out.

We parked, walked inside and over to an empty table in the smoke-filled pool area. The place was alive with the sounds of clacking pool balls, laughter, shouts and murmurs, rolling bowling balls, and tumbling pins. While Al ordered us beers and french fries at the bar, I racked up the balls and chalked my stick. Of course I didn't have a prayer of winning, but Al usually spotted me points and bonus turns, and we had fun, playing games for a quarter or another beer.

I'm not sure why Al liked me, sort of taking me under his wing. Maybe it was because I had always listened to him since our meetings at the burrito stand, or maybe because I wasn't a threat to him, someone he had to boss or be tough with. He could be more himself. I did listen to him, and I think he knew that I understood and could feel his pain and loneliness without a lot of words and specifics passing.

One day he had asked me to pick up and deliver a new television set to his mother at the convalescent hospital on my way home. Pulling me aside in the yard, he gave me the directions, and said simply and quietly, "I just can't go there anymore, Leon," his fists clenching at his sides while his eyes watered and the corners of his mouth bent downward, like a child.

And I, too, believed he understood and could feel my own unspoken sorrow, that he sensed that I was somehow a survivor, that he had respect for me. Thus understanding one another, we had fun and could laugh, as we did over pool that early evening.

When he dropped me off back at the shop, he said, "Now you watch yourself out there in the field. Those goons can be real assholes."

"I will, Al. Thanks," I said. "We'll see ya."

"O.K., Leon. See ya," he said.

I backed up the truck through the overgrown weeds to the front of the two-car garage. Rented by Southland Plumbers for use as a small warehouse, the building had stored several hundred of the same boxed Norris toilets bought over a year earlier when their wholesale price had been particularly low. I now loaded and carefully stacked a portion of them one by one onto the flatbed, twenty-five for Downey, twenty-five for Hawthorne, and thirty for Diamond. With arms aching and wet with sweat, I paused to admire the entire snugly stacked package, then climbed into the cab. The pleasant smell of dirt and black pipe oil filled the dusty cab, and the slow groan of the truck in its first gear effortlessly moved the heavy load. We rocked and rolled out through the weeds, following the lead of the great chunky and squared off metal bow of a hood, and proceeded to Downey.

Located on Arnett Street in a quiet residential neighborhood, the Downey site was typical of a small Southland Plumbers job. I waited for a cement truck to pull out, then

backed up to the three-story framed structure while alternately checking each side mirror. Within ten feet of my des-
tination just underneath the first floor concrete slab, first
one, then another, a third, and a fourth voice rang down.

"Hey! Here he is! The pussy!"

"How 'bout that! The pussy kid truck driver!"

"Yeah, the boss's cheek-spreadin' pet pussy!"

"Here, kitty, kitty, kitty! We got some milk for ya!"

They laughed hilariously. Of course they were, as Al had
forewarned, just being razzing assholes, but still, I wished
I had had a gun. Shark-infested, shoal-ridden, tide-ripped,
these polluted waters presented a bizarre, almost comic
(were I not so intimidated), and dangerous challenge to my
composure, my navigation ability, my authority over my
own ship, my manhood.

Should I say, "Kiss my ass?"

I think not, I thought, for, indeed, they might be tempt-
ed to do just that.

What would Gandhi or Martin Luther King do? Passively
resist? How I'd prefer to upwardly slam my boot, like a black-
belt samurai, in their crotches, driving their bb-size balls up
into their lungs, embedding them like cancerous black spots!

However, stopping the truck and climbing directly from
the cab, over the gate and onto the boxed toilets, I decided
not to engage the plumbers. I offered up, instead, an open-
armed, palms-upward gesture with a slight shrug of the
shoulders, conveying, I thought, the message, "What do you

want? What can I do? You got me!" And then I became invisible, ignored their taunts, and unloaded the toilets. And soon enough, they, too, went on with their work. I believe that had any of them physically interfered with me, I would have fought to the death with my two-by-four, with a piece of pipe, with a screwdriver, or pipe wrench. But, although this thought frightened me very much, it seemed, in fact, quite fanciful.

Thus it was the same at Hawthorne and Diamond (although Brooks was not in sight) and most of the other Southland Plumbers job sites over the next couple of weeks. An army of plumbers, I imagined, was having fun at my expense, while I went on about my business in a condition of fearful aloneness, friendlessness, and steeled invisibility. But I would not capitulate to weakness and flee. I wanted to survive and become a man.

Were it not for Al's partner Bob, I might have survived longer. For several months now the teasing and taunting had subsided, but Bob, it seemed to me, picked up where the plumbers in the field had left off. I don't know why this was, such a bullying, physically strong and rather wealthy man sixteen years my senior singling out his lowliest, least paid and most replaceable employee for torment. Did he see in me his own intolerable weakness, masked so effectively by his bulging muscles, rigorous daily workouts, an opulent car, and cocaine put up his nose? Did he sense and was he resentful or jealous of an intimacy too human between Al and me?

Stepping outside from the tool shed with a set of new dies for the pipe threader one day near the end of August, I found Bob standing outside the screen door, Sonny Liston arms swinging and an order sheet in hand. For several minutes he watched my every movement with a smirk on his face. Uncomfortably, I fiddled with the pipe threader as I attempted to quickly replace the worn dies. I wished at that moment I had had a task more demonstrative of physical labor so that the boss could clearly see he was getting his money's worth out of my employment. Then he spoke.

"Well, Leon, I can see you've got your head up your ass again! They need this order right away up in El Monte. Take the white pickup." He laid the order down next to the vice on the workbench and went back inside.

I wanted to kill him. I wanted to tell him to stuff his order, and then I wanted to quit. But then he would be winning, probably getting what he wanted. Without physically threatening him (He could easily demolish me and would delight, I thought, in tossing me out the door) how could I salvage myself? How could I sustain my dignity and appeal to his own which he seemed to have little or no consciousness of possessing?

I would mount an indefensible challenge directly through his exterior, eye to eye, as it were, or man to man, and I would show no fear at which he could scoff, and the great swell of emotion which now quaked and trembled within my body and tingled my limbs had now to be utilized before it began to miserably destroy me once again.

I opened the screen door of the front office and went directly over to Bob who was on the phone. I waited. He hung up.

"I need to talk to you now in private out back," I said into his face, turned, and went out. I heard him open the door behind me and follow as I walked straight ahead, past the brass shed, the tool shed, the pipe threader, the fitting bins, the steel pipe, the plastic pipe, the copper shed, Eli and Joe, to the back of the yard. My heart was pounding wildly, but I could not pay it any attention. I stopped and turned. He stopped, his head atop his bull neck cocked down toward me.

Looking unwaveringly up into his eyes, planted squarely in the ground without pretense, I said, "I want you to treat me like a human being." His cheek began to twitch. "You said I have my head up my ass. You do not need to talk to me that way. You do not have to be rude. I have done a good job for you here at Southland Plumbers, and I don't deserve to be stepped on. So cut it out."

"Oh, yeah?" he smirked, "What are you gonna do 'bout it?" His eyes gleamed demonically and his other cheek twitched. Perhaps he would now strangle me or push my face in with his massive fist, but I did not care.

"I'm not planning on doing anything about it. In the sense that you mean it, I don't stand a chance against you.

But I'm not against you. I'm telling you something right now. I don't like how you've been with me, your disrespectful use of language, lording over me with your arms swinging as if I were a slave you're itching to deck. It's not necessary. I want you to be a human being and treat me like one." I paused. "You do understand me, don't you?" He said nothing but glared into my eyes. Searching into each of his eyes for another silent moment, I then said, "I hope so. I have nothing more to say to you. I'm going back to fill my order now." I slowly walked past him, underneath his right shoulder, and returned to my work, performing it with unrelenting impeccability and heedless of his presence.

Twenty minutes later, while down on my knees counting out twenty-five iron sanitary tees into a burlap bag at the end of a dark aisle in the fitting bin section, he appeared, standing above me.

I stood and faced him. "Yes?" I said.

"I've been thinking about what you said, and I want you to know I appreciate it. It took guts. And I apologize."

Bob extended his hand, and I shook it, saying, "Why, thank you. I accept." That evening I rode home up the Long Beach Freeway singing some crazy, made-up song with just the right Buddy Holly-like intonations. "Well, I'm a— plumbing truck driver man! Ahey-hey-hey!"

Unfortunately, good things don't always last, bad habits are hard to break, and Bob's shining moment of humanity was apparently just a break in the clouds of a stormy life. Anyway, I had been thinking about returning to college, this time to finish. So when for the third or fourth time in so many weeks he again transgressed our brief understanding (He couldn't help it, could he?), I decided it was time to move on, time to abandon this particular ship.

The screen door slammed and from a distance he watched me working down at the bins, first swinging his arms, then folding them across his chest, then twirling his handlebar moustache, then swinging his arms again, now walking slowly toward me.

"Leon, you work slower than shit! I knew I was right when I said you had your head up your ass! Here. Here's three bucks. Make yourself useful and go get my car washed!"

"Bob," I said, "you just can't help yourself, can you? You're one bullying asshole! You know that? You take your three bucks and stick 'em up your fat fuckin' ass!"

"Oh, yeah?"

"Yeah!"

"Well, you just get your ass right on out of this shop, now, boy! You're fired!"

"Fuck you! My pleasure, big man! I quit!"

And thus my year long employment easily ended among the men of Southland Plumbers.

For a short while I remained in touch with Al who had had sympathy for my predicament and understood my decision.

Once or twice we had dinner and played pool. One Saturday he even took me and my new girlfriend Kate to Catalina on his boat for a day of fishing. But once I returned to school, I eventually lost touch with Al.

I graduated from college in a year and spent another at my first desk job as an order clerk at Keenan Pipe and Supply Company which supplied all the Crane valves for the Alaska pipeline and where I had to wear a tie everyday. The tie-less unionized warehousemen out back resented the management scum up front, though I hardly considered myself management and felt only short-lived prestige as such. I soon transitioned out of the company and into the insurance business with a co-worker whose wife worked in the industry. And now I was beginning my fifth year in my own business as a casualty and life insurance agent.

From time to time the thought had entered my mind to solicit Southland Plumbers' insurance, since it would have been a lucrative account, but I had not yet acted upon it because gaining respect and converts in the insurance business requires much confidence. When I was about ready to tackle the plumbers in this new arena, some unfortunate news came to my attention as I carried some old newspapers out to the dumpster behind my apartment.

Glancing at the rarely looked at Orange County section of a two-month old Sunday paper, I casually read the headline, "Seal Beach Plumbing Contractor Kills Fiancé, Attempts Suicide." I was horrified to learn the story was about Al. An unclear photo showed Al treading water along-side his boat while policemen stood on the dock attempting to reach him with boat hooks. I read the story several times, then called Southland Plumbers.

A secretary informed me I could get in touch with Al at Del Amo Psychiatric Hospital. I called him there.

"Al, this is Leon, your old truck driver friend!"

"Oh, yeah, Leon, thanks for calling me, pal! It's great to hear from you!"

"Jesus, Al, you must be in a world of hurt."

"Things are real bad, my friend."

"Can I see you?"

"You sure you want to see me?"

"Yes. I do."

"We could get a bite to eat?"

"Down there you mean?" I asked.

"Well, I could meet you some place?"

"You mean, they'll let you out of there?"

"Yes," he chuckled softly for a brief second. "I checked myself in, and my doctor and lawyer have it arranged so I can go out once in a while as long as there's no booze or drugs. They test me and I have to be real clean for my trial in December."

We arranged to have deep-dish pizza and Cokes at a place on Santa Monica Boulevard near Westwood. He arrived, driving a Toyota Corolla, but I didn't ask him about it. We shook hands and squeezed one another's shoulders and walked slowly into the restaurant. Except for a half-inch deep and wide indentation in the middle of his forehead, he looked remarkably well and robust. We sat in a corner booth.

"The doctor's allowing me to take steroids so I can get big fast before going to prison. I don't want to be fucked in the ass, you know," he said with genuine concern.

"Are you sure you're going?"

"Yeah. I'll know for how long after my trial next month. My lawyer thinks maybe three years, although I might be able to get out after a year."

"Oh, man, Al. What the fuck happened? What happened to your forehead?" I asked, referring to the half-inch indentation.

"I tried to jam a cop's boathook through my head. I wanted to die, Leon. You see, I was all set to marry this girl."

"What was her name?"

"Tammy." His eyes filled with tears. "We were going to be married last month. And we'd gone back to my place and done some magic mushrooms, you know, psilocybin, which we'd done a few times before and had a beautiful time. All I remember is lying down on my bed upstairs. Then after what must have been a few hours, I realized Tammy wasn't with me. I got up and went downstairs to find her." He paused while the waitress set down our pizza and Cokes, then continued.

"At the bottom of the stairs next to some house plants, I found her. She was just sitting there on the floor, her legs spread out a little to hold her up, like a ragdoll, but looking out into space ... and gone. She was no longer there ... like she was brain dead. Just gone. Gone from this world, not here anymore. I couldn't get her back." He took a sip of soda, and his shoulders melted down to the bench, and he seemed the saddest man in the world. "I couldn't bear to see her suffer. And I decided right then and there to end it for her, and for myself, too."

We ate some pizza for a while and didn't talk. I asked for a glass of water, and Al did, too. Then he spoke some more. "I stabbed her with a kitchen knife, and then I sliced my wrists and my arms all the way up to my elbow down to the bone." He stopped and pulled up his sleeves, revealing his multiple wounds. "But there was no blood! And I didn't feel a thing! Then I began to panic. I really wanted it all to end, so I ran out to my boat and got a gas can. I poured it over the side of the house, and set it on fire, and I was burning, too. Pretty soon there were sirens, fire engines and cops, and I jumped into the water, and the cops were reaching for me, and I was screaming, 'I want to die! I want to die!' That's when I got hold of that boathook and punched this hole in my head." He lowered his head downward, turning it slowly to the right, then to the left. I reached over and touched his arm.

"In the hospital," he continued, "I was screaming at the doctor, 'I wanna die! Lemme die!' and the doctor said to me, 'Soon as this shit you're on wears off, you're gonna be one hurtin' motherfucker;' and god almighty, he was right for all the screamin' I put out to stop the pain." We said nothing for a long while.

"What's gonna happen to your business? Bob gonna run it while you're away?" I finally asked.

"Bob? I guess you didn't hear, then. Bob's dead. A year ago he came in from doin' his five-mile morning run on the beach, then had a heart attack while sittin' on the shitter. Forty-two years old."

"Oh, shit, Al. I'm sorry to hear that."

"Well, it was comin', and his lifestyle, you know. I bought out his wife. Now I've just made Mark, my bid man and draftsman, my forty-nine percent partner. Of course, he doesn't know what the hell's hit him, but he's real eager and responsible, and I don't think he'll run it under while I'm away."

We talked a little more, about the trial and the judge's reputation, about Bob, and the plumbing business and what I'd done in the seven years since leaving Southland Plumbers. But the moments of silence were longer, more intimate and important than the talk.

I hoped he would get real big before prison, and I told him so. Still his arms filled out the sleeves of his golf shirt, bigger than ever, and the panther hung in the air, leaping and growling.

We walked to his car in the darkness of night, and I said, "I'm really very sorry, Al." For the last time we bid one another goodbye.

Five

FRAUDING

To be impeccably organized, to account for every minute of the fourteen-hour workday carefully logged in a Day-Timer scheduling book; to present a well-groomed image of professionalism with weekly manicures, thrice-weekly car washes, daily weightlifting sessions at the health club; to frequently study and review the contracts; to recite until flawless the sales tracks or programmed pitches so necessary for a smooth closing; to build enthusiasm by listening to the motivation tapes of the biggest winners such as Joe Gondolpho who flew clients from around the country to his office in his own Learjet 25 or Joe Girard who sold the most cars in history; to never hesitate to ask for business and to always ask for referrals; these were some of the attributes which had made the Leon Perlman Insurance Agency number one. But now it all seemed silly.

How far I had come, I thought, from those aimless hippie days, making burritos in Silver Lake, driving the plumbing truck, struggling through college to sit proudly with a necktie behind the service desk at Keenan Pipe and Supply, circling the block three times with palpitating heart before mustering the courage to make my first auto insurance sales call. Yes, in spite of everything, 1980 would measure up as the most intensely productive year on record. A real winner, as District Sales Leader of the Year, and a standard for excellence. In retrospect, how ironic.

I gazed out the top floor office window of the Barclay's Bank Building over Tarzana, home of Edgar Rice Burroughs. The sun was rising over a yellow haze and the traffic on the Ventura Freeway. The phone rang on the L.A. number of the rotary system, and because neither my secretary nor the other agents sharing the suite of offices (known collectively as the Atkins, Fanning, Perlman, and Dawson Agencies) had yet come in, I answered. The L.A. number and its $400-a-month display ad in the fat Yellow Pages of the Central Los Angeles directory had been a lucrative source of junk business—the assigned risk liability insurance (the minimum required and provided by the state for drivers declined by our preferred parent company because of questionable or poor driving records) and the comprehensive and collision coverage, the minimum required to secure bank loans. The more stable and loss-free homeowner, auto, and life policies were written on the white populace of the suburban west San Fernando Valley through our well-established and industry-respected parent company.

"Hello. Is Herbert Lloyd Dawson deh?" an agitated voice barked as I switched on the tape recorder, licked the pickup suction cup and fumbled to attach it to the receiver.

"I'm sorry, Mr. Dawson isn't in the office, yet."

"That muthafucka, he frauded me!"

"I beg your pardon, Sir—frauding?"

"That muthafucka, he frauded me! He—fraud—me. Less jus say, frauded me outta my money, 'tendin' he's gonna get me inshawnce."

"Have you had a loss, Sir?"

"Loss? Yeah, man, I lost my muthafuckin' diamonds out my glove compartment. Now he told me I got comprehension and collusion, and shit that's stole is covered! And the goddamn claims man says my shit ain't covered!"

"Well, Sir, comprehensive and collision coverage pertains to the loss of or damage to the vehicle, not the contents in the automobile. I can give you Mr. Dawson's home phone, if you'd like to discuss the matter with him there."

"Hey, man, I don't want his muthafuckin' home phone, man. I tell you one thang, I'm not gonna' be hasslin' heem cuz I can win too goddamn much money in court on bo'shit fraud! Now he got my ass on the sore spot, and I'm gonna get even one way or the other!"

"May I have your name, Sir, and I'll have Mr. Dawson give you a call when he comes in."

"Troy Cheney. He betta call, or somebody's gonna be sorry."

"Very good, Mr. Cheney, I'll have Mr. Dawson give you a call. Thank you for calling." I hung up.

"God," I muttered to myself, rewinding the tape recorder for another listen.

I leaned back in the upholstered executive chair against the wall. The wall, covered with official looking certificates and plaques (Order of the Purple Medallion, Life Underwriters Training Council, Commercial Masters Society, District Sales Leader of the Year, Million Dollar Round Table, etc.), served to reinforce for the blank-eyed client sitting opposite that what he or she was purchasing was more than just an insurance policy; rather it was a piece of or a step toward security and success, a responsible achievement like attaining an academic degree. For the agent, acquiring these wall accoutrements was not difficult. Just make your calls, look the part, ask for appointments, recite your sales tracks, and the plaques and certificates would come regularly into your office like mackerel for dolphin jumping through a hoop.

"Frauding," I pondered, putting on the tape.

The central air conditioning kicked on, its white noise whoosh signaling the eight o'clock hour and the start of the business day. The front door clicked open and slammed shut. It was Bill Fanning.

The four agents of the Atkins, Fanning, Perlman and Dawson Agencies had all come into the business at roughly the same time. Each of us had been in our mid to late twenties. Milton Hines, our district manager, had trained us all, dazzling us with his flagrant disregard for underwriting procedures and regulations in pursuit of a prospect's signature and check. With a few strokes of his pen on a homeowners application, for example, he could transform a questionable, never-before-seen old house into a newly painted, rewired, and re-roofed risk of the most favorable kind; or he might advise a commercial insurance prospect that our policy covered absolutely all losses short of nuclear war at the lowest price in the industry. The prospect would sign, and two months later the newly insured client would receive his severely restricted policy and a bill for several hundred dollars in additional premium. Even then, Milton would tell the client, "Don't worry; trust me; after your inspection there's no finer coverage for the money available in the industry." Uncovered losses, Milton always advised his agent trainees, were the problem of claims adjusters, not salesmen.

For Milton, nothing mattered but the sale. His stereotypical green plaid polyester pants, yellow golf shirts, and white patent leather shoes personified the quintessential insurance sleaze bag. At the age of forty he drove a new powder blue Sedan de Ville, worked only four days each week, three hours each day, brought home a steadily rising three hundred thousand dollar a year income, took a month long vacation every year, owned a house high in the hills of Sherman Oaks overlooking the Valley and a thirty-six foot sailing yacht berthed at the California Yacht Club. Yet these facts served to help us forgive his and our own less than honorable and attractive shortcomings while still striving for success.

Of the four agents, Bill Fanning had been the least successful. He had, unfortunately, completely given in to his thirst for alcohol, and perhaps in his consequent and utter failure, there was something honorable.

"Good morning, Bill," I said, as he retreated into his sparsely adorned office. On his wall all that was displayed was a small and defiant certificate of his membership in MENSA, an organization for people with high IQs. There seemed something decidedly stupid and sad about belonging to such an organization. If Bill was intelligent enough to see through the plaque and certificate charade, why play the game and lose? Next to his desk on the floor he kept a jug of wine. Only last week Les Atkins and I had discovered a pint of vodka in his attaché case. We confronted Bill on his problem, but partial as we are to the taste of the stuff, we lacked conviction, and Bill had emphatically told us to mind our own business. Ours was more a relationship of business convenience than committed friendship anyway, and none of our businesses was interdependent, except in paying for the rent and the L.A. Yellow Pages ad and phone number.

"Good morning," he answered.

"Hey, Bill, listen to this!"

"That mothafucka, he frauded me! He—fraud—me. Less jus say, frauded me outta my money 'tendin' he's gonna get me inshawnce!" the tape player boomed.

"Can you believe this guy, Bill? Herbie Lloyd Dawson's gonna shit!"

"I can win too goddamn much money in court on bo'shit fraud!"

I went into Bill's office, where he sat behind his desk in dirty dungarees and a wool lumberman's jacket.

"Holy mackerel! He's really hot under the collar," Bill said, laughing.

"I guess! So, Big Guy, where'd ya sleep last night?" I asked.

"In my cave." This was not some metaphorical statement for his psychic condition. It was an actual fact. Bill had taken to spending the nights away from his family, and, I surmised, in some primal yearning to feel his essential roots, to become reconnected to something as real as earth under his head and body, he had found a cave in Soledad Canyon off Route 14, heading out toward Palmdale, Lancaster, and Mojave. For whatever reason, Bill was out of control, and the smell of dirt and the sound of the scurry of prairie rats under a star strewn desert night was a comfort, a haven real as rocks up the ass, when it appeared one's tenuous existence depended on the sale of insurance abstractions.

"What are these?" I asked, fingering a stack of insurance binder forms on his desk. A binder is that piece of paper given by an agent to a client indicating that coverage is in effect pending issuance of a policy. Atop these binders was printed The William Fanning Insurance Agency. They were not the standard binder issued from the regional office of the parent company we represented, which we all used.

"Oh, I'm doing a lot of outside business," he answered. This, I thought, meant that applications for insurance unacceptable to our parent company were being placed with other companies. But Bill didn't have the authority to bind coverage with other companies.

Within a few months The William Fanning Insurance Agency would be finished. Bill Fanning would be gone. And a warrant for Bill Fanning's arrest would be issued. Collecting insurance premiums made payable to William Fanning, he would hand out scores of William Fanning Insurance Agency binders, saying to his clients, "Don't worry, you're covered." He would pocket the money and no policies would be issued. Were a client to have a loss, he would backdate a parent company application to a date and time prior to the loss. Too many customers would begin to complain about not having their policies. Too many losses would occur without the parent company being in possession of an application. Bill Fanning, eventually, would disappear.

Returning to my desk, I rewound the tape and played it again. "He—fraud—me! Less jus say, frauded me outta my money, 'tendin' he's gonna get me inshawnce!"

Sighing, I put my feet up on my desk. In light of a recent jarring setback in my life, I had lost my desire to sell. I barely could go through the motions of prospecting. I remember an agent once told me when I was first starting out that an insurance agent's license is a license to steal. I felt immobile, comfortably suspended in lethargy while my monthly renewal commissions rolled in.

The front door opened and slammed shut.

"Good morning!" Deborah Strout's voice rang out. Replacing my invaluable former secretary who had left for a romance in Texas, Ms. Strout was a stopgap measure to slow the downslide of my business while I tried to come to terms with my future. I found her bubbly, born-again exuberance disconcerting, her greasy platinum blond hair pulled tightly around one side of her head and off in a protruding pony tail from the other side exceedingly unattractive, and her grammar intolerable. When clients asked to speak with her on the phone, she would answer, "This is her," and from my office I would have to shout, "This is she! This is she!" How easy to kick a person when she's down. How inviting when you're down. Yet she did her job well, deflecting clients' requests to speak with me, informing them that I was "in the field," while adequately handling their problems.

"Ms. Strout, listen to this."

"I'm not gonna be hasslin' heem cuz I can win too goddamn much money in court on bo'shit fraud!"

All I had wanted from this profession, I thought, was normalcy. Clean-cut, competent, honest and respectable normalcy. Honest to god, I tried to be a good insurance agent, and, I think, I was quite good, not just in terms of sales, but in the quality of the service I offered. I did my best to educate my clients about the dangers which threatened their lives, homes, and businesses, and how they could protect themselves. I had wanted to do good and be good. But wanting is one thing; any fool can want. Doing and being good requires something more, something like wisdom, objectivity, self-reliance, and compassion. That's what I had botched up or never even acquired. I sold insurance, but I could never be the insurance man of my dreams. How difficult it is to look back to the time when you thought you were so good, and realize now you were but a fool.

"Now he told me I got comprehension and collusion," the tape played. Then rewound, it blared out again, "He—fraud—me!"

The lobby door clicked open and slammed shut, and by the sound of the quick-paced steps and the clunk of the attaché case on his desk, I knew Lester Atkins had arrived. A gentle soul and an ex-marine Vietnam vet, Les had introduced me to the insurance business when we both worked at Keenan Pipe in downtown Los Angeles. We started selling part-time, then went full-time after a few months. His Cumberland Gap, Virginia upbringing with his single mother lent him a modest, "po' white" humility and authenticity which rang pleasingly true in his appreciation of mundane, middle class values. He liked to go to church; he had a nice wife who worked at the insurance company's home office; he had two cute daughters; and he had just purchased a nice stucco house with a pool in a new development in Northridge. It seems he would have made the perfect insurance man, yet he hated the work, and this made me like him all the more. In two months, only Les and I of the Atkins, Fanning, Perlman, and Dawson Agencies would remain to hold down the fort, and then, not for long. Over coffee we listened to the tape several times, laughing, then we settled down to do our paper work and make some calls for the next hour or so.

The front door clicked open and slammed shut and the sound of Herbie Lloyd Dawson's Irish tenor voice singing "I'm in the Mood for Love" wafted through the office. He, too, now wanted to minimize the pressures of the insurance business by keeping sales production high and claims low, controlling the flow of paper, reassuring distraught clients, and prospecting. Today, as everyday, to avoid these pressures, Herbie would be in and out of the office in less than three hours.

"Good morning, everyone," he then melodiously announced in a syrupy radio announcer's voice, the professional insurance man's voice he had acquired years earlier when working as a commercial lines supervisor in the home office before going into the field as a salesman. The voice could calm any distraught customer and let them know they were in good hands.

"Hello. Is Herbert Lloyd Dawson deh? I'm sorry, Mr. Dawson isn't in the office, yet. That muthafucka, he frauded me!" the tape player roared.

"What in God's name is that?" Herbie asked, standing in the doorway to my office in his olive green three-piece polyester suit and holding an oversized Samsonite attaché case. At six-feet two-inches tall, well-groomed and slightly overweight, he presented an image of unruffled competence which he relished but hardly believed or merited. When Herbie came into sales, our district manager Milton had given him several important commercial accounts from a re-tiring agent's book of business. Whenever an agent left the business, the parent company would retain his accounts, pay him a year's worth of commissions (his contract value), and then the district manager would redistribute the departed agent's accounts among his salesmen for servicing. Milton believed Herbie, with his experience as a former home office supervisor in commercial lines, could best service these commercial accounts. Thus, Herbie was thrust into an income bracket and level of responsibility which had not matched his ability, and, to compensate for this inadequacy, and perhaps others, everything about Herbie Lloyd Dawson was big, powerful appearing, and radio announcer smooth.

"I beg your pardon, Sir—frauding?" the tape player screamed.

"Frauding, Mr. Dawson?" I asked.

"That muthafucka, he frauded me! He—fraud—me."

"Oh, Herbie, really! How could you?" I implored.

"Less jus say, frauded me outta my money 'tendin' he's gonna get me inshawnce!"

"Turn that thing off. For God's sake, who is that?" Herbie cried as I pushed the stop button.

"Mr. Cheney. Mr. Troy Cheney would like you to return his call immediately." I pressed the play button.

"Have you had a loss, sir? Loss? Yeah, man, I lost my muthafuckin' diamonds—"

"Turn that thing off. Give me that tape!"

"—out my glove compartment. Now he told me—"

"You can't have it. It's my tape!"

"—I got comprehension and collusion, and the shit that's stole is covered." I hit the stop button.

"Listen, Herbie," I said calmly, "He says you have his ass on the sore spot and he's going to get even unless you give him a call. So I suggest you get on the horn and take care of it. And good morning to you, too, Ol' Blue Eyes."

"Oh, God, Leon, you're so infantile!" Herbie fumed and walked brusquely into his office to sit beneath his certificate and plaque bedecked wall.

"Squirm, faggot, squirm," I thought. I don't think I'm an innately cruel person, but something about Herbie seemed to bring out this mischievous, if not sadistic and sometimes violent, streak in me. Sure, there's the time I simply tired of his upbeat smoothness, and out of loneliness, I guess, I had put my nose up to his face and said, "C'mon, Herb, let's get real, let's get closer, let's have a drink together and get something down, bro, you know what I mean?" And he had immediately proceeded to confess his homosexuality to me. Now I don't think I'm particularly homophobic. Maybe I am. I like to think of myself as very tolerant of individual differences, but from this initial confession there came a flood of unusual personal revelations from Herbie, which on the one hand he would flaunt around the office and on the other hand he would utterly hide beneath his Mr. Smooth Insurance Man image. There was no regular in-between, just a lonely place with two parenthetical extremes—gay bars, leather, cock rings, glory holes, doggy chains, key chains worn on left or right, butch and nelly guys, bathhouses all together on one side and Mr. Radio Announcer on the other. I hit the rewind, then play buttons. "He—fraud—me."

In one month Herbie Lloyd Dawson would be out of sales and back in the home office from 9 to 5. Les and I would be stuck with two empty offices and forced to rent them to two Iranian "businessmen" who sold diplomas from B.A.'s to Ph.D.'s in the field of your choice. The Iranian connection was made through my insurance ad in *Shahrfarang*, a weekly magazine of the new and burgeoning Iranian community. Since the Shah's fall, there had been a dramatic influx of immigrants, and I wanted to be one of the first to capitalize on the opportunity.

"Less jus say, frauded me outta my money, 'tendin' he's gonna get me inshawnce!"

"Will you please shut that thing off?" Herbie called out.

"Frauding. Frauding. Frauding. Frauding." I chanted.

"Frauding. Frauding. Frauding. Frauding,," Les Atkins chimed in.

"Frauding. Frauding. Frauding. Frauding!" Bill Fanning sang out.

"Frauding! Frauding! Frauding! Frauding! Frauding!" we all chanted in unison.

"STOP! JUST STOP IT! ALL OF YOU!" Herbie screamed.

We laughed and went back to shuffling papers for a while.

Three weeks before, my world, of sorts, had fallen apart. There had been a run on the Sierra Bonita branch of the Security Pacific Bank on Sunset Boulevard. Hundreds of us had lined up on a Friday morning to cash paychecks from, or stop payment on checks to, The Center for Dynamic Living, the front door of which had by now been chained and padlocked. Really, I didn't have much to worry about, financially speaking, because I insured most of the people lined up at the bank, and after five years in the business, I insured a lot more people from the outside. My accounts, as any good risk management advisor would encourage, were well diversified.

Of course there was a cluster of losses which could have aroused suspicion—an odd display of malicious mischief and vandalism losses all along Gardner Street where the founders of The Center lived; broken windshields on their Mercedes; a brick through a plate-glass living room window; deflated tires. Then that embarrassing weeklong news special on Channel 2—*The Cult of Torment!* God! It could dawn in the consciousness of any home office adjuster or underwriting manager watching the tube: a pattern of losses and shoddily underwritten risks exceedingly out of the ordinary exists in the West Hollywood area, such as homeowners policies on dwellings with ten adults cohabitating under one roof or auto policies with twelve unlisted drivers. Not your squeaky clean, no tickets, no accidents, white-in-good-neighborhood, steadily employed, two-car-garaged, *Father Knows Best* type of risk. Then the libel and slander and malpractice mess. Well, it could have happened to any good insurance agent working a lucrative referral network. After all, didn't Mel Levinson work the B'Nai B'rith, or Howie Snelman, The History Teachers Association, or Jeff Frame, the Masons? So I worked a psychotherapeutic community—a cult some would call it. Did it so matter I was a member of that community?

I leaned back in my chair and stared out the window for an hour or so, reviewing in my mind the previous evening's life insurance appointment, Michael and Marsha Farley. At ages 28 and 26 with a baby in the oven, two cars, one new, new house, good location in Chatsworth, they had been perfect prospects. He was a computer programmer at Rockadyne, and she was a teacher. Nice people.

I had left the office around 6:30, drove westbound on the Ventura Freeway to Canoga Avenue, then north up to Chatsworth. Their small cedar shake ranch with rock roof was modest and clean. Typical Valley. I parked my highly polished black Caprice Classic and rang their bell.

After the exchange of a few well-planned niceties I easily maneuvered Michael and Marsha to the living room couch with Mike on my left and Marsha on my right in front of the coffee table.

"Let's just talk about money for a minute, O.K.?" I began. "I imagine like most people today, you are interested in saving and accumulating money, but that's a hard thing to do in today's economy." I paused, nodded my head ever so slightly in the affirmative and looked at the Farleys until their heads also nodded in agreement. "Michael, I recently had the opportunity to study the savings habit of the American people based on a longitudinal study of one hundred men beginning at age 25. Now, this government study says that the average Joe earns his first regular income between the ages of 18 and 25, and his income tends to go up until he reaches 50 or 55. Then his income levels off until Social Security kicks in, then it stops. Now here's the point, Mike, that really startled me. This average guy will earn between his first and last paycheck over $490,000. The man with specialized training will earn over $710,000 during his working years. That is a lot of cash, Michael. And I just bet from a quick glance at your lovely home you've never earned less than $10,000 per year since you started working, agreed?" I paused, nodded affirmatively and looked at Marsha. "But here is the evidence that stunned me. This is how the original one hundred made out after having all this money go through their pockets. One, just one man was well-off. He had money. Four had income. Five were working, but not well-off, fifty didn't have an income and needed to work, and eight were fortunate not to have the kind of job where they pat you on the back, throw you a lunch, hand you a watch and say goodbye at 65. Thirty-two were dead. They couldn't even take what was coming to them from Social Security! That is about average. One out of three will not live to 65. And you know what, Michael—and this is the real shocker—" I paused, then said, "I—can't—do—this—anymore!"

I fumbled like a rookie to pick up the brochure and graphs laid out on the coffee table and repeated, "I just can't do it anymore, Marsha and Michael. I'm sorry. You'll just have to find another agent. I'm sorry. The meaning's gone. It has nothing to do with you."

I stood up, went to the door, and dumbfounded, the Farleys followed.

"Well, gee, would you like a cup of coffee or something?" Mrs. Farley sweetly asked.

"No. No thanks. It's all right, folks. I'll have someone call you. I've got a lot of personal stuff going on right now. So long."

I sat up in my chair from the recollection, stood and stretched. "Wow," I thought, "now that there is one dent in the side of my shiny black car."

I hit the play button on the tape recorder.

"Well, sir, comprehensive and collision coverage pertains to the loss of or damage to the vehicle, not the contents in the automobile."

"Off, Perlman! Shut it off!" Herbie's voice commanded from inside his office.

"Yeah, right," I said, shutting off the machine. I sat back and admiringly studied my plaques and certificates for a while.

That Thursday night before the run on the Security Pacific Bank which handled all the Center's accounts and the accounts of many of its members (and two days before my wedding to one Kate O'Hara, I might add), people in Group 1, including me, and a few of the founding therapists brought Roland Marks (formerly Jack Markowitz) into the conference room of the plush Center building on Sunset Boulevard between La Brea and Fairfax. It was odd as hell seeing this powerful, handsome, and charismatic young man—mastermind of the Center's phenomenal growth over the past nine years, author of four psychology books ("pop" though they were), proponent of a new interpretation of dreams, featured speaker at psychological association conventions, guest on the *Tonight* and *Good Morning, America* shows—now stunned, sitting there like a captured Jim Jones or Mussolini, surrounded by enraged, confused, and frightened interrogators.

"Do you have any Swiss bank accounts?" screamed one lower level group member, and Roland moved his head in the negative. Roland and the other five founders of the Center and their wives had lead increasingly lavish lifestyles in proportion to the success of the therapy business. In 1971 there had been a very small clinic with as few as thirty clients. The therapy offered was intense and radical, a complete breakdown of psychological defense mechanisms in order to experience and live from a "feeling" rather than an "image" reality. Entering members of the community were required to commit "image suicide" or be willing victims of image homicide, depending on your point of view. By 1976 several books had been published, a quest to take over the field of psychology had been formulated, and the now three hundred members of the community were zealously pushing to achieve "excellence" not only in their chosen careers but in their other individual life areas of sex, love, relationships, and play. Excellence would be achieved by regular exercise of the five personality dynamics of expression, activity, clarity, feeling, and contact. Psychological Fitness Training. PFT. By 1980 this packaged-life formula seemed to be working beyond the expectations of most members.

The founders had purchased a fifty-thousand-acre vacation ranch outside of Payson, Arizona along with three hundred and fifty head of Beefmaster cattle (all but twelve of the animals starved to death in a macabre scene of incompetence when the cowboy therapists failed to anticipate high spring flood waters, which prevented the delivery of hay to the animals). The Center had a thousand-client outpatient clinic with a sprinkling of legitimating Hollywood celebrity patients, and four more branch communities in Hawaii, Boston, Montreal, and Munich. Roland—Doctor of Psychology, licensed clinical psychologist, keystone of the structure—was leader of it all.

"What happened to all the money for our gym? The gym fund?" screamed another member who had devoted his life to the Center.

"There never was a gym fund!" exclaimed a frizzy haired young woman from New York who had been the "executive" secretary of the organization for the last six years. "You stole our money and put it into your fucking ranch! That ranch was never for us! We want our money back!" she demanded.

"No! No! The money's still available! We'll return it. That's not embezzlement! I don't want to go to jail!" cried one of the founders who was also a medical doctor. It was his signature that had allowed insurance reimbursement for "services" rendered.

"To hell with embezzlement!" mourned a blonde woman with tears flowing down her cheeks. "My therapist fucked me! Literally fucked me, then made me have an abortion. I can't ever get my baby back!"

Throughout the Center building, like in some bizarre psychiatric ward, people were screaming and shouting at one another. Others cried by themselves. And others sobbed in one another's arms. Couples that had been together for years were breaking up. Friendships were ending. Lawsuits were being threatened, while some people hysterically implored others to remain calm and levelheaded, hoping that the community would survive. Cigarette smoke, which in the psychological and physical fitness model of the Center had been taboo, now drifted through the building and up and down the streets of the West Hollywood neighborhood, like dust rising from the rubble of a collapsed building.

After straightening out a persistent Check-o-matic billing problem for one Mrs. Grimm, who without fail bothered me on a monthly basis, I grew bored and hit the tape player again.

"Now he told me I got comprehension and collusion, and shit that's stole is covered! And the goddamn claims man says my shit ain't covered!"

"Well, Sir," I loudly recited along with the tape player, "comprehensive and collision coverage pertains to the loss of or damage to the vehicle, not the contents in the automobile. I can give you Mr. Dawson's home phone, if you'd like to discuss the matter with him there."

"Hey, man, I don't want his muthafuckin home phone, man. I tell you one thang, I'm not gonna be hasslin' heem cuz I can win too goddamn much money in court on bo'shit fraud. Now he got my ass on the sore spot and I'm gonna get even one way or the other!"

"Whew, Herbie! That dude is bad," I called out, hitting the stop button.

"Perlman, you are an ass," said Herbie. "Why don't you stop your infantile shenanigans and turn that tape over to me?"

"Herbie," I said, getting up from my desk and walking into his office, "I need you. I need to talk. Let's get real." His phone rang.

"Good morning, this is the Dawson Insurance Agency. Herb Dawson speaking... Uhunh, why surely, Mam, if you hold the line for a moment, I'll be happy to check that for you; very good; thank you," he said with a velvety cadence. Pressing the hold button, he snapped, "Will you get out of here, please, and let me do my work, for God's sake?"

"I've got a line for you to hold for a moment, Mr. Dawson," I said in a velour voice.

"What the hell are you talking about?"

I glanced at my crotch where my hand had taken out my limp pecker and was now stirring it in his lukewarm coffee.

"Good god, Perlman! You're insane! And disgusting! Wash my cup!" he screamed, lunging for it across the desk.

"My cup runneth over!" I shouted. Adding, "I'll wash it! I'll wash it!" I ran out of the room. I washed and sort of meekly returned the cup with a sheepish smile and a please-forgive-me-I'm-not-so-bad pat on Herbie's broad shoulder.

Fear, and its inverse, security, had held the community together. Leaning back in my chair, feet up on the desk, I pondered how Roland and the other Center founders had fostered faith and trust by providing companionship, family, and deep connection to those who feared loneliness; inclusion and worth to those feared being ostracized; and praise, reward, and a pat on the head for those who feared being busted.

The bust. That weapon of "image homicide" which, when leveled by a therapist or fellow member, could drop you in your tracks. In my first group session nine years before, when I was having difficulty talking in front of other people, Roland had busted me. He said, "You would rather suck cock and remain a passive faggot than share your guts in any real kind of way." That bust, though not true, had made me less cool, less able to hide behind a mask of composure. To not suffer it again, I had wanted more than ever to reveal my true self.

What true self could that be? The feeling behind the image? I leaned forward, laid my head in my arm on the desk, and remembered.

After my first week at the Center, I had come into the one-on-one session with my therapist, laid on the soft carpet of the dimly lit empty room and dejectedly announced, "This therapy, this 'cure' for neurosis, is not working. I didn't even want to get up to come here today. Why bother? What's the point? Maybe I should get my money back."

Sitting in the room's one chair behind me, the therapist had asked, "Have you ever felt like this before?"

"Of course," I had said. "All the time. The story of my life. Life's a shithouse."

"Be very specific," he had said. "Tell me about a time when you didn't feel like getting up, when you felt, 'why bother.'"

Into my mind, I told the therapist, came my mother, standing over me in high school, and she was saying, "Get up! Get Up! It's time for school. You'll be late." Even the alarm clocks clanging inside the three empty metal wastepaper baskets had not aroused me.

"Talk to your mother," the therapist had said.

"Right now?"

"Don't play stupid," he said gently. "Tell her how you feel."

"Uh, leave me alone. Let me sleep, Mom. Why should I get up? Why bother? What's the fucking point, Mom?" I had asked awkwardly and somewhat angrily.

"Don't act angry. Just tell her how you feel. What makes it so hard, Leon, to get up?" he had asked.

"There's no point in getting up."

"Why is there no point in getting up, Leon?"

"Because there's nothing left anymore. My brothers have gone away. Pop is gone. Our family has died. You're unhappy, Mom. Why should I get up?"

"Tell your mother. Ask her why?"

"Why should I get up, Mom, why the fuck should I get up?"

"Speak to her without getting angry. Just talk to her, Leon."

"Why should I get up, Mom? Why should I get up and leave you? There's nothing left of us anymore, Mom, there's nothing left anymore! Oh, Mom, I don't want to leave you, too." Tears had begun to well in my eyes, then flowed freely down my face. "Mom, there's no point in me going to school. What's the point, Mom, you're all I have left, and now you want me to leave for school? Oh, Mama, what's the point? There's no point anymore!" I sobbed deeply. My arms had tingled with feeling and my fingers had knotted together with hands uncontrollably buckling inward at the wrists. And the sobs had doubled me over and became interspersed with dry heaves.

Then the therapist, in a smooth close of the session and nailing shut the lid on my allegiance, leaned forward from his chair and over me and had whispered, "Now I know you are a good person."

I sat up and hit the play button for one final listen of the day before Herbie and the other agents would take off for home, cave, or appointments.

"Hello. Is Herbert Lloyd Dawson deh?" Mr. Cheney barked. I found the tape almost soothing.

"I'm sorry, Mr. Dawson isn't in the office, yet."

"That muthafucka, he frauded me!"

"Right on, Troy," I thought.

"I beg your pardon, Sir—frauding?"

"That muthafucka, he frauded me! He—fraud—me. Less jus say, frauded me outta my money, 'tendin' he's gonna get me inshawnce."

"NOW ENOUGH IS ENOUGH!" Herbie thundered, barging into my office. "GIVE ME THAT TAPE!"

"Have you had a loss, sir?"

"Loss? Yeah, man, I lost my muthafuckin' diamonds out my glove compartment. Now he told me I got com-prehension and collusion, and shit that's stole is cov-ered! And the goddamn claims man says my shit ain't covered!"

Herbie circled around my desk and tried to reach in front of me across to the tape player. "You can't have it. It's mine, you big moose!" I shouted.

"Well, sir, comprehensive and collision coverage pertains to the loss of or damage to the vehicle, not the contents in the automobile. I can give you Mr. Dawson's home phone, if you'd like to discuss the matter with him there."

"I'LL HAVE THAT TAPE AND I'LL HAVE IT NOW!" He declared.

We struggled momentarily, and I had to use all my strength to hold him at bay. "It's mine. It's a great historical record! You'll destroy it!"

"Hey, man, I don't want his muthafuckin' home phone, man. I tell you one thang, I'm not gonna' be hasslin' heem cuz I can win too goddamn much money in court on bo'shit fraud! Now he got my ass on the sore spot, and I'm gonna get even one way or the other!"

Suddenly, Herbie, who was immensely bigger and surprisingly stronger than I, gained some significant leverage and momentum and was able to hurl me out of my executive chair, across my desk, and onto the floor.

"AHA! NOW I'VE GOT IT!" he bellowed triumphantly.

"Shit, Herbie! I guess. And you got my ass on the sore spot, too!"

"Which you deserve after a day of torture!" he said with a look of maniacal glee, crumpling the plastic cassette in his raised fist.

"Yeah, I guess. You're right," I said, clutching my bruised left buttock. "I had it coming. But shit, Herbie, that tape was a classic in the annals of insurance lore! I'll tell you one thing, er, thang, Herbie; you can destroy a tape, but you can't hide the truth."

"Now what in God's name are you talking about?"

"Frauding. You—fraud—me. Less jus say, frauded me outta my money, 'tendin' you gonna get me inshawnce! Isn't that right, Les? Isn't that right, Bill?" I called out to the other agents. "Frauding, Herbie. Plain and simple frauding. Frauding! Frauding! Frauding! Frauding!"

"Frauding! Frauding! Frauding!" Les chimed in.

"Frauding! Frauding! Frauding!" Bill sang out.

"Frauding! Frauding! Frauding!" we chanted in chorus.

And then Herbie, too, joined in, and the office rocked with the joyous homophony of "FRAUDING! FRAUDING! FRAUDING! FRAUDING!"

Six

THE BLACKFISH INHERITANCE

Our land, or should I say my father's land, looks out over a marsh, green in summer, amber in fall, sometimes white in winter, brown in spring to Loagy Bay, Lieutenant's Island, Wellfleet Bay, Great Island and Cape Cod Bay beyond. Three hundred and sixty-four years ago a small group of white men, including Myles Standish and William Bradford, rounded Jeremy Point, the southern tip of Great Island just north of Billingsgate Island and entered Wellfleet Bay in their small wooden shallop for the first time. Coming from the north where they had found Indian corn at what is now called Corn Hill in Truro, Standish and his men explored the Wellfleet shore, then continued south where they first encountered Nauset Indians at what is now called First Encounter Beach in Eastham. These pilgrim Separatists found the Indians, the soil and climate of the Outer Cape inhospitable and thus continued their exploration inside the long, crooked arm of the great glacial peninsula around to what would shortly become their first New World home, the protected bay of Plymouth. It is a long view, well-earned through the limbs of some strategically untouched pitch pine, rustling scrub oak and beach plum to where the blue fish jump the foaming crests, and still the oil rich blackfish ply the depths to their all too frequent stranded deaths on the ebb tide. It is a long view into the past. And my connection to this land and sea is primordial.

The vantage point of the view is from the deck of my father's boxy beach bungalow, which he bought at auction for $1,700.00 from the Town of Wellfleet and had moved from the new National Seashore park on a truck in the early hours before dawn and placed on this hill. Since arriving, it has officially been called "the studio" to avoid the higher taxes that would be levied with a second dwelling on the twenty-four acre property. Running the length of the deck, in front of it, is a moat-like lap pool, which you cross by means of a small bridge. Around the pool and on the deck sit cement cast urns of fruit, powerful busts, and relief sculptures made by my father. Next to the bridge and at one end of the pool stand two lengths of four-inch white P.V.C. pipe eight feet high, topped with portulaca and cascading white petunias, suggesting the entrance to a Grecian temple. In the aquamarine water a charming yellow duck, a child's plastic swim float, still swims, catching every breath, gliding here and there with its steady smile. Parked to the right of the pool as you look out, partially hidden by a tall poplar and broad pine tree, a 1961 faded white Chrysler Newport with a 383 cubic inch, semi-hemi engine and a space-age, push-button, emerald dash sits with deflated tires. Ever since my father had the handicapped gas pedal added to the left side and had first tried to drive after his amputation, roaring up the driveway at fifty miles an hour with a rare look of terror in his eyes and skidding to a stop just before careening into the pool, the car has served merely to ward off intruders in the off-season, like a scarecrow. Across from the deck and pool, beyond the sandy parking area and just behind a low-lying bayberry bush stands an eight-foot tall bearded man in a fishnet toga, pointing to the view, inviting you to look.

Wind chimes tinkle in the breeze, their sound sometimes drifting down the path through twisted, churning locust trees into the hollow where stands the original 1709 Cape with light blue shutters and tiger lilies, six-foot ceilings, attic-nesting raccoons, sloping floors and powdered sills. A damp mustiness hangs in each room. It goes away only with the frequent summer banging and rusty door-spring twang of the front screen door. Here, hungry, cavernous memories of childhood laughter and distant family happiness, cucumber sandwiches on white bread, beach bonfires, playing in the sand with an ancient cast metal truck and a rounded brick eroded by the surf, holes dug through sedimentary layers of tan, orange, and brown sand deep toward China, the distant morning bugle and protective, drone-shooting guns from Camp Wellfleet artillery training base, now part of the National Seashore, echo from the infant wellspring of my consciousness or before beneath the surface of the ever passing present. And always the safe and endless sandy road with grass growing in the middle, beckoning me to follow its magical course. Here I returned for a longed-for reunion with my father, grateful for the reprieve granted his life. Here, I returned to start anew. And here, I returned to take care of business.

Leaving behind thirteen years of California life and a one hundred and five-degree heat wave across the Panhandle and Oklahoma with panting, drooling dog and uncomfortable pregnant wife, traveling against the flow of many westward bound dreamers in our giant yellow Ryder truck with tiny orange car in tow, up through Arkansas, Kentucky and West Virginia into the Northeast, we swam through the soft sand at the foot of our driveway and arrived.

"They arrived in this enormous truck pulling a tiny mosquito," my father excitedly told everyone, delighted with his metaphor, but mostly delighted at our return. Somewhere in my mind I thought this return was my defeat and his victory. Hadn't he always said, "Frank Lloyd Wright once told me, 'If you were to hold the United States up by Maine like a jigsaw puzzle, everything loose would end up in California?'" The packaged, sunny, superficial West Coast lifestyle revolted him. He found that even the word "lifestyle" trampled on the very notion of authenticity, as if one could simply turn one's self in for another like a car at the end of three years. But there was genuine joy in our reunion and my greater purpose, I thought, would enable me to tolerate any cutting criticisms. Now, you see, I felt it necessary to stake my claim to that least unhappy portion of inheritable geography, which, if I did not play the man, I stood to lose.

A year and a half earlier in March my brother Josh and I had stood outside the hospital bedroom of my then dying father.

"Does Pop even have a will?" I asked Josh.

"Christ, the old man's probably got one scribbled on some piece of paper buried beneath fifty, nineteen-forties vintage, unmatched shoes in the bottom of his closet."

"Yeah, and another one hidden in the back of the refrigerator or liquor cabinet."

"The taxes will kill us."

"You're right. He's never been big on 'estate planning'," I said, with these favorite insurance industry words now impregnated with new and real meaning not previously understood in my seven-year career reciting sales tracks designed to help victims choose against economic destitution and for security and independence with the stroke of a pen and a Check-o-matic bleed on their bank account.

"Really, if he lives, we should try to do something," we agreed, making a decision of deep consequence, not as children or brothers, but as men set on a course of survival.

Moving to protect our rightful lairs led to animal-like conflict, like the clacking of ibex horns in spring.

My father gave Josh, the manager, power of attorney to handle his affairs while he passed through the critical ordeal of his seventy-third year. Two aortic aneurysms, one inoperable on the aortic arch and the other in the diaphragm, spewing sclerotic material into the veins and arteries of his right leg before being clamped, pushed my father to the brink. He lost his leg beneath the knee.

Calling me soon thereafter in California from his office at a management consulting firm, my brother said, "I have had a new will prepared by my firm's attorney with safeguards to assure incontestability. We need to protect ourselves from our brother's ex-wives. Mention of Pop's art collection has been eliminated and the words 'items of decor' have replaced 'works of art.' We'll have to get the statues and paintings out fast, particularly the David Smith, Noguchi, and Pollock. It's essentially the same will that he showed us before. New York, Warwick, Cape Cod to the three of us equally and no mention of Puerto Rico. Incidentally, I have consolidated all of Pop's accounts, about a hundred and forty thousand bucks, into one money market fund and prepared comprehensive worksheets analyzing his expenses and net worth, including dividend, royalty, and real estate earnings. It's a major job, and while he's laid up I'm charging him $500 a month to manage his financial affairs, which he's agreed to. I need your help in getting him to sign the new will."

I did not "help" in getting the will signed because my brother would not at first send it to me. "Why should I trust you?" I then said.

"You piss me off!" he told me. When a copy of the will did finally arrive, I read that my brother was "literary executor" of the estate with all rights to my father's published and unpublished writings and artwork bequeathed to him. Whether or not this bequest was precisely my father's intention, I nevertheless felt it was evidence of my brother's treachery. And when, a few months later, I borrowed $1,500.00 from my slowly recovering father who instructed me to obtain the money through Josh, and a money market check arrived with the names of both Josh and my father printed on the top "As Joint Tenants," knowing from my insurance work that joint tenancy means equal ownership with full ownership passing from one to the other tenant automatically upon the death of either one and bypassing any probate or the dictates of a will, I now felt, "Aha! Now I know the bastard is cheating me!"

"You untrusting scumbag! You're drunk," Josh shouted at me over the phone and hung up.

"Dear Josh," I wrote,

Contrary to your belief, I do not question your integrity, your goodwill and purpose in handling Pop's affairs. I do not, however, trust anybody, especially in business affairs, or where matters of faith and legality vie for dominance. Perhaps to say that I don't trust anybody is too blatant and all encompassing a statement. More appropriately, I trust some people with some things and others with other things. Ultimately, I am most responsible for my well-being by relying not through faith on the good intentions of my neighbors, but on knowledge comprised of mutually agreed upon contracts, commitments, and/or other tenets of reality.

This is not to say that I adhere to a pompous, George Farnsworthian (my tweedy, bow-tied Harvard Law uncle) philosophy of life. Rather, I am merely watching out for my interests in a non-poetic way, based upon a reality which I do know and which has been nurtured these past few California years in the bitter betrayal of my most naive, idealistic, trusting, and loving intentions.

Again, your integrity as manager of Pop's affairs is not even in question. Your work is appreciated. My poetic sense is touched by your devotion to the old man and our mutual rallying around him in his time of need. My more businesslike, functional sense as a contributing member of society respects and appreciates your expenditure of time in boring, tedious details.

It is this functional sense that to me says let's do things right in accordance with the wishes of

Pop and with established legal procedure, playing by the rules which most facilitate the execution of his desires and which protect each of our own interests.

Therefore, to reiterate the essence of our conversation today on the phone, I want the following request to be taken in a spirit of mutual respect and attentiveness to detail as pertains to the entire estate of our father. As one who has power of attorney and can sign for Pop, remove your name from the money market account, leaving ownership of the funds to our father alone. As a joint tenant with your name included as it is now, you are an equal owner of those funds, and they will bypass probate and go directly to you upon Pop's death.

I do not enjoy playing politics around the life of Pop. I do not hold you responsible for this, but I suppose it results from an essential disharmony and chaos which has always characterized our family. Nevertheless, rather than being insulted by my request and thinking me a "scum bag," or a negligent, drunken, lazy, and tactless Californian, please merely comply with it and know that I remain with underlying love

Your Brother

And to my father, who was now recuperating beautifully with remarkable will, courage and humor, writing a new one act play about greed and the destruction of a New York City landmark, and learning to walk with a prosthetic leg while in residence at Burke Rehabilitation Center in White Plains, I wrote and advised of the need to correct the money market account situation. I also "reminded" him in passing of Josh's $500.00 monthly fee.

"The outrage! Charging your own father to care for him!" he later shouted at Josh. "I, who've provided you with everything, sent you to school and camp and college! No more power of attorney! Your five thousand dollars taken from me is deducted by codicil! You're not to have it!"

"You were on your ass, for Christ's sake, with scribbled wills hidden everywhere and fifty different accounts and bills pouring in for the last eight months. My fee, which you agreed to, was cheap for the goddamn mess of things!"

"Out!" he ordered my brother from the house. After a visit in Warwick with his lawyer, with new swim leg tucked under his arm, my father was driven by Tel Aviv Limousine Service from his townhouse on a snowy East End Avenue to Kennedy Airport, and from there he was off to Puerto Rico to resume his life.

"I can't tell you how pleased I am that you've returned. This is your home," my father said, sipping my orange juice, bourbon and bitters cocktail creation and admiring the view from the deck to the bay. "And my God! This drink is terrific!"

"Thank you. From now on we'll call it our 'Cape Cod Special.'"

"I've been working on a new head, very powerful, modeled from a picture of William Loeb. You know, that ghastly New Hampshire reactionary."

"Yes."

"But I'm tired of cement casts. Maybe we could try something different."

"How about bronze?" I asked.

"Bronze? How am I, Toulouse-Lautrec, legless and dying, supposed to pour molten bronze when I can barely pour myself a drink? God, you're as stupid as ever," he playfully chided. "Thirteen years in California and you learn nothing? Did I ever tell you what Frank Lloyd Wright once said to me?"

"Yes. You did. But I haven't ended up there, have I? How about resin? I could buy some at the boat shop in town? It's easy to work with and light weight."

"Ah, yes. I forgot you know a lot about boats. Do it! We'll pour it tomorrow. And you should stop trying to sell your boat in California. Bring it back here. This is the perfect place for a boat."

"It would cost a fortune to truck it here. I should have sailed it here," I lamented.

"Are you mad? And have my future grandchild sunk off the coast of Nicaragua? Not on your life! No, you got out of there as best as you could. When is our baby due?"

"The end of February, the first of us to be born on Cape Cod."

"You were all raised here, for God's sake. I dunked you in Loagy Bay when you were a month old, what, twenty-five, no, could it be … thirty-five years ago?"

"Yes … Pop?" I asked after a momentary silence.

"What? Speak!"

"You've always asked for our input about what's going to happen to all your properties."

"Of course. Speak. I could be dead any moment. It happened to my father. He just finished his sentence, quietly laughed, looked away, and boom, gone. So, speak."

"I don't like the idea of all of us getting everything. It means maybe selling off land and—"

"No land is to be sold off!" he declared vehemently.

"Well, I don't want that, either. But I'm thinking that with all of us getting everything, it will be very hard to work it out. Suppose Josh wants to sell and move to San Francisco? Suppose Robert gets a fourth wife and leaves another angry mother demanding a share of his wealth? Suppose I want to live here and raise my family? Can they come and visit whenever they want? Will my home be put up for sale as my brother's alimony payment? I want you to leave each of us our own separate property. I want you to leave Josh Warwick because he's always loved the country and farming; I want you to leave Robert the New York City house because he's a city doctor; and I want Cape Cod because I love this land and the sea, and this is where my firstborn will come into the world."

Momentarily reflecting while puffing on his cigar, my father then said with deep seriousness, "I couldn't agree with you more. Consider it done."

During the final three weeks of our reunion, my father was most welcoming and generous. He took me and my wife to Sweet Seasons for dinner, praised the dinners we made for him and neighbors, complimented us on our appearances, and thanked us for our help.

In return, allowing him all the necessary leeway for his eccentricities and old age, we shopped for him, did his dishes and laundry, cleaned up the relentless daily mess of his scattered clothes, newspapers, crumpled notes to himself, plaster of Paris and cement drippings on the living room floor and deck. We took him to A.I.M. Thrift Shop on Main Street in Wellfleet for more clothes. When he walked down the street, limping with his cane, white hair flying, dark glasses set on his prominent nose above his cigar, a dashing red kerchief tied round his neck in contrast to his torn blue work shirt, greeting and chatting with this and that old-timer and his new, fifty-cent blue-and-red-striped seersucker pants slipped down to the forever exposed crack of his tiny Russian ass, I felt proud and happy to again be walking with him.

Even the uncomfortable task of letting him know I wanted the Cape property had produced no tension. I felt that as much as we loved one another as father and son, so, too, did our spirits commune as men in mutual love of the land.

So when it came time for his departure, I felt welcome on the land and eager to begin my life on it anew. And he, too, was pleased.

Bidding me, "Enjoy, my son, don't worry about me," my father left in mid-September for New York's fall season of opera and theater with occasional museum visits, cocktail parties, intimate dinners with a few remaining old friends at Casa Brazil and breakfasts alone at the Mansion Restaurant, a favorite of many taxi drivers. I knew, that for as long as he lived, he, too, would enjoy his life.

In December when again the winter snows would fly, he would head for the warmth and beaches of Puerto Rico. Then in spring he would return to New York until he would hear from me that the sweet purple lilac were again in bloom, and he would come back to Wellfleet.

Thus our Cape Cod life began. Throughout the fall I did my student teaching at the Nathaniel Wixom Middle School and Dennis–Yarmouth Regional High School in preparation for my teacher certification and new career, and we stayed on down in the old house in the hollow late into November, warmed by fires in the shallow fireplace and a kerosene heater. We lasted longer, I thought, into the darker, colder days of the year than anyone had in this century, or at least since 1930 when my father had bought the house for $600.00 at the age of twenty-one. But as the northeast winds blew atop the locusts and the temperature dropped daily, as surely as the life inside Kate's belly grew, we moved up the hill with the first flurries to the furnaced warmth of the studio, and from there we noticed for the first time new winter companions, two Great Blue Heron nesting in the marsh below.

The exposed, wind-whipped hill more than compensates for the studio's smallness, and for the most part, we felt cozy. Still, we each needed to get out regardless of weather conditions or time of day or night, to relish our final days of freedom and intimacy with each other and ourselves, to transform our growing excitement into resolve before the new life would irrevocably alter our own. Therefore, we walked intensely, daily, together and alone.

There is no better place for walking than the Outer Cape in winter. Many night walks were taken, dog by side, layered in long johns, sweats, sweater, pants and oilskins, bent into the snow and biting wind which played the eerily singing wires like a bow across a saw, holding fast to the pitching asphalt deck with seasoned sea legs, beating through the wild darkness to Lieutenant's Island and back, and occasionally passing in the night a familiar homeward-bound Peugeot's headlights and rusted-out muffler roar, one of the islands few winter residents.

One crisp January morning at first light, we awoke to an unfamiliar distant roar and deduced that the sound must be the ocean. We excitedly arrived at the edge of the Maguire's Landing Beach parking lot excited and ready to investigate. Looking down the sixty to one hundred-foot-high, steeply sloping dune which runs the length of the Outer Cape from Nauset Beach in Orleans to North Truro, we were stunned to see that the beach below, where only a few months earlier gaily colored umbrellas, mothers and babies, surf-riding teenagers and dads had basked in the summer sun, was now awash in a hissing, foaming cauldron of angry waves chewing off great hunks of snow patched dune. It is a pitched battle every year with the Cape losing more land than it gains.

In the quiet, chilly solitude of winter, the Outer Cape's natural beauty is still able to surmount the painful encroachment of growth and development, which has assaulted the land in the seventies and eighties. One can remember how it once was; the bustling, precarious imbalance so evident in summer is less intrusive.

When you walk out Lieutenant's Island Road toward the bay, much has changed. Old Mrs. Boland's driveway is now overgrown and barely discernible. When she died, her land was subdivided and sold off, and now a sign, TIDE WATCH— RESIDENTS ONLY, proclaims the entrance to a twelve-lot development. Across from the entrance on the right three new houses, all marsh view, are squeezed on half and three-quarter-acre lots. Further along and off in the bushes you can see a remnant of the old road I used to follow on my way to Aunt Tanya's twenty-five years ago to help her make beach plum jelly. Part of it is now a driveway to another new house built tall to grab the view from a second story living room. Keep on walking and you come to Tom Kennedy's road, which used to be sandy with grass growing in the middle. Once old Mr. Kennedy let me shoot his 4-10 shotgun. Now the paved road, Bayberry Lane, leads to Dick Butterworth's ten-house development. On down the road on left and right the story is the same. Where in my childhood there were only three or four houses, more than twenty-five now stand. But the air is organically sweet and rich, especially at low tide.

The marsh between Lieutenant's Island and the mainland is exquisite and unchanged, since Joe Shuldice left it to the Audubon Society. Only the narrow road which crosses it and a small bridge, and sometimes the stranded carcass of an old boat, mark an inoffensive human presence. The grass and road are covered with water at high tide, making the island inaccessible. In winter a jagged blanket of white ice spreads endlessly out to the bay like an arctic landscape. At low tide crying gulls circle high above the road, dropping oysters and clams, cracking them open. The birds swoop down and eat. They chase each other. In summer one-armed fiddler crabs, the oldest in the world, scurry along the road and in the mud and grass. There are also horseshoe crabs, and turtles. Wild salt hay, used by early settlers as fodder and mulch, is left on the upland shores at high tide, partly surrounding the marsh like a great nest.

On February 25th I walked quickly across the marsh toward the island, uneasy about being away from Kate for too long. Something caught my eye out in the marsh, a mound of blackness against the white. Carefully making my way across the ice, I came upon one of many tidal inlets or ditch-like channels, and saw there, draped half in and half out of the channel, stranded on ice, a twelve-foot, roughly one ton, pilot whale or blackfish. Its kindly, wide-open eyes led me to believe it was still alive, and I knelt down and stroked its smooth head and back. Though its body was still soft, not frozen nor at all very cold, it did not breathe, and I concluded that it was dead, suffocated by its own weight.

Nearby in another ditch I discovered a much smaller whale, maybe eight feet long, in the same condition. And thirty feet away a third whale, ten to twelve feet, also lay dead.

There is something poignant about the life of pilot whales which is part of the soul of Cape Cod. Individual and mass beachings, like so many shipwrecks on the outer shore, have occurred in Wellfleet Bay and Eastham throughout their recorded histories. The first form of whaling by white men in the New World, drift whaling, was practiced by the Pilgrims who took advantage of this proclivity for stranding. They herded pods onto the beach by slapping their oars in the water and shouting. For every blackfish cast ashore, one barrel of oil had to go as a tax to Plymouth, the capital of the Old Colony, with the remaining oil used for barter and lamplight.

In 1982 one of the largest unintended mass beachings in recent Cape history occurred when seventy-one whales washed up on Lieutenant's Island. Though volunteers struggled to keep them alive by trying to push them back out into the water, talking softly to them and gently stroking their backs to calm them, none was saved, and their carcasses were buried on the beach. Among all seventy-eight species of whales and porpoises, single animals will occasionally beach themselves, but mass strandings are common only to a very few species, including the pilot whale or blackfish. Some scientists believe the whales are responding to innate, age-old migratory patterns. According to this theory, the mammals are retracing ancient paths but run into the geologically recent Cape Cod land mass. Another theory proposes that the whale's system is in chemical imbalance caused by either malnutrition or water pollution, which makes the whales sick or damages their echo-location systems. The lemming theory suggests that the lead whale in a pod becomes lost during stormy weather and ends up on the beach. The pod follows. Although there are many theories, Cape Cod mass strandings remain a mystery.

The day following my discovery, after we had gone to bed, Kate went into labor. Leaving the studio around midnight, we drove the thirty-one miles to Cape Cod Hospital in Hyannis. Fifteen hours later, on February 27th, a much wanted, healthy, seven and three-quarter pound baby girl was born, and we named her Grace.

If winter walks and the birth of my daughter further strengthened an already existing bond of appreciation for Wellfleet's beauty, they also fostered a functional commitment to the preservation of that beauty. In the spring, when not substitute teaching as a now certified social studies teacher, I volunteered some time to help create an organization, the Wellfleet Planning Committee, and write its newsletter, whose purpose was to limit growth by proposing articles for the town meeting's warrant and educating the voters. We advocated increasing the minimum building lot size requirement from half to one acre in residential districts, having a building moratorium (especially to stop a proposed mall with post office outside the town's center), creating a solid waste disposal alternative to the dump which was polluting the water table, and toughening zoning requirements to protect the town's ecologically fragile marshes.

One day I was at the South Wellfleet post office tacking up a WPC flyer announcing a meeting. A scruffy, thin old-timer with stooped shoulders, Joshua Nickerson, who ran a junkyard down in Paine Hollow, glanced up at the announcement as he was leaving the building. He shook his head and laughed.

"It's too late, sonny," he said. "Ain't no goin' back. We're finished." He chuckled and sauntered off to his car.

Even still, wanting to give back to the town and land some of the fullness I felt had been given to me, I worked enthusiastically for the WPC. Further deepening my relationship with the town, I also lined up a summer service job as its recreation program director.

To our delight, the crocuses, daffodils and tulips pushed up through the sandy soil, and the marsh below turned from muddy brown to green. When the plump blooms of moist and perfumed lilac hung once again from their branches, we opened up the old house down in the hollow, and soon thereafter my father returned.

He stood, cigar in mouth, in the doorway of the PBA plane at Hyannis Municipal Airport, waving his cane at me, Kate, and his new granddaughter, while an airport employee dashed out the fifty yards from the terminal across the tarmac, pushing a wheel chair. The image of MacArthur wading through the surf flashed through my mind. To claim yet one more summer of life, my father had returned.

"Here! Here!" my father shouted from the deck, as I drove up the driveway with Kate and the baby on our way to the beach in late July. We were finding it increasingly impossible to get past the studio without him flagging us down with another list.

"I've got to have these things," he said. "Milk, Carbona Spot Remover, more Jim Beam, the *Cape Cod Times*, and something sweet. I need a piece of candy. Maybe some non-pareils, or orange slices, or black licorice?" He waved the list at me, and I got out of the car, climbed the steps, walked over the pool, and took it. "This humidity is awful, isn't it?" he asked.

"We'll take you to the bay for a swim when we get back."

"That would be great. I feel so stranded on this deck, like a blackfish, stuck with this ghastly view. Isn't that awful? Whoever would have thought it would come to this?"

"Is your leg hurting you today?" Kate called up from the car window while nursing Grace.

"Naturally. So what else is new?" and he grimaced with an apparently sharp, stabbing pain in his stump, lasting only a moment. "Ah, that was my nonexistent little toe." He gave a short, sardonic laugh, and added, "Fascinating, is it not?"

"You know, Pop, you really ought to have someone— a boy, a housekeeper, a chauffeur—someone to drive you around, shop, cook, clean, fix stuff. You know, just to make your life easier? I mean, you should be able to afford it now, don't you think?"

"Are you mad? I have absolutely no … what do the money creeps call it? Cash flow! Anyway, I have that Bruegel, Donny Snow, to fix things," he said, referring to a heavyset, local boy, really a young man, of enormous physical strength and foul mouth who had in the past drained the pipes for winter, primed the pumps in summer, chased out the raccoons, and appeared to be a reincarnation of one of the

Flemish painter's portly peasants. "And his wife brings me cookies. So get out of here! Go to wherever you're going, and pick me up some club soda on your way home."

"O.K., Pop. What's that smell?"

"My lunch. I'm cooking a leftover cutlet and kasha varnishkes. I never forget. Now go!"

"Barf. See ya later," I said, bounding off the deck and into the car.

After eating our cucumber sandwiches on Cahoon Hollow beach, napping, then playing in the sand and surf, we rinsed in the fresh water of Great Pond, stopped at the liquor and general stores, and returned home three hours later.

"You know, you don't have to drink to be with him," Kate quietly admonished me before walking with Grace down to the old house.

"Right. I'll see ya in a while."

I prepared a shaker full of Cape Cod Special, and together, my father and I drove out across the marsh and followed the sandy road around the north side of Lieutenant's Island to the deserted beach at Loagy Bay. Sometimes even against my will, I felt irresistibly drawn to him.

With a self-made paisley sash wrapped around his waist, towel draped over his shoulders and cane in each hand, he walked slowly up the sand path through the beach grass, pausing every five steps to allow the discomfort inside the plastic swim leg to subside while a cloud of cigar smoke drifted away from his head in the slight breeze. Carrying beach chairs, plastic cups, and the shaker, I followed.

At the crest of the small dune, the broad mouth of Blackfish Creek near high tide lay flat before us and a long ribbon of empty white beach stretched out a half mile toward Wellfleet Bay and thinned out of sight around the western shore of the island. Across the water the steep dunes of Indian Neck plunged to the shore. Within a stone's throw a halyard on a small sailboat swinging on its anchor melodically clinked against an aluminum mast. We walked down to the wet sand. Here in 1949, '44 and '43 my father had ceremoniously splashed each of his baby boys in these joyous waters, welcoming them into life.

One month earlier while standing with Kate, Grace, and my father on this same beach, attempting to carry on the family baptismal tradition, I had been forced to say to my father in a rare demonstration of unheeded assertiveness, "It's my goddamned baptism, and I'm the father, and I'll do it the way I want. Now please be quiet!"

"Yes, but why ruin it with religion?" he interrupted.

"They that go down to the sea in ships," I more loudly re-read from the 107th Psalm while Grace wriggled in the arms of her mother, "that do business in great water—"

"Oh, God! I didn't do it this way!"

"—these see the works of the Lord, and his wonders in the deep. For he commandeth, and raiseth the stormy wind, which lifteth up the waves thereof—"

"Ruined. You've got it all wrong!"

"Quiet! 'They mount up to the heaven—'"

"This should be about the joy of life in the here and now. There's nothing else!"

"They go down again to the depths: their soul is melted because of trouble—"

"They think they've got trouble. They should go without a leg and have to stand here as long as I am!"

"They reel to and fro, and stagger like a drunken man—"

"I could use a drink!"

"—and are at their wits end. Then they cry unto the Lord in their trouble—"

"What good has religion ever done for the world? It's only another crutch placating and anesthetizing the soul!"

"Now shut the fuck up! Sweet Jesus! '—and he bringeth them out of their distresses. He maketh the storm a calm, so that the waves thereof are still. Then are they glad because they be quiet.'"

"Thank god for quiet."

"'So he bringeth them unto their desired haven.' May you have a good life, Grace, and enjoy these waters as much as I have," I concluded, splashing a little water on her forehead, making her cry.

"There. That's all you needed to say. Now let's go home and have a drink."

"Listen, Pop. I'm the father. Am I not entitled to baptize the way I want?"

"And I'm the grandfather who made this whole mess."

"Right. Let's go."

"I knew we shouldn't have had him come," Kate said later.

"You were right. Another memorable event with him at center stage, consuming all the oxygen," I said, regretting that the moment had not been entirely Grace's and feeling somewhat awash in shame.

Now my father waded out into the water, let float his canes, and swam. I, too, swam along side him. Then, gathering up the canes, I led him out of the water as he held fast to my arm for balance. We sat in our chairs and I poured drinks from the shaker. The ribbon of sand slowly widened with the receding tide, and we listened to the gulls cry in the late afternoon sun.

Several weeks later a neighbor, Abe Gotlieb, joined my young family and father down in the hollow for a dinner not unlike others that summer. A tall, lumbering, sixty-two-year-old retired physicist from General Dynamics, turbo-fan designer for the F16 tactical jet fighter, son of a founder of the American Communist Party and possessor of John Reed's pocket watch, Abe was often anti-liberal, sometimes reactionary, and fiercely anti-Soviet. Living just down the road in the Whispering Pines development, he had watched over us during the winter, been a good friend, and worked with me on the Wellfleet Planning Committee. He was an unrestrained drinker, whose brooding, volcanic quietness, and mumbled words failed to disguise a gentle kindness, and he had a voracious appetite. Sitting on my right across from Kate, Abe now shoveled down his third portion of charcoal broiled bluefish and pasta.

"Guess what I heard at last night's Planning Board meeting?" he asked, washing down his food with a great swill of René Junot table wine.

"Ach, you're such a bullvon, Abe. You eat with a vengeance!" my father, ignoring the question, interjected from his end of the table opposite me, either the foot or the head of the table, depending in our minds on whose house, his or mine, we were in that evening.

"Mind your own business, you old hen," Abe retorted. "Old lady Bouchard has sold out to a developer, Hans Wolfe, and he just filed a twenty-two lot subdivision plan abutting your northern boundary."

"No! I don't believe it! That's outrageous!" my father shouted in exasperation. "That obese, greedy Nazi, the Chairman of the Planning Board no less, is utterly raping the land! He disgusts me! This is his, what, fourth development since he's been chairman of that so-called planning board? The conflict of interest alone is staggering!"

"What conflict of interest?" Abe asked. "There's no conflict. You can't exclude someone from serving on a town board or committee because of his profession. Should we have no fishermen on the Marina Advisory Committee? No conservationists on the Conservation Commission?"

"Don't give me that falsely fair, free-market reactionism! That bastard is an exploitive rapist! He's raping my land to fill his greedy pockets, cashing in my birds, my trees, my beach plums, my clean air and water, my peace of mind for his packaged Tide Watches, Ebb Tides, and Sunny Acre Estates! He is ruining my Cape Cod! Is there no stopping him?"

"Pop, watch your blood 'pleasure,'" I said, using the malapropism created by him to lessen the anxiety posed by the real threat of his high blood pressure. "We are trying to stop him and his kind. Abe and I and the Planning Committee are trying to get zoning changes to limit density and preserve open space, wildlife, and the quality of life here."

"Ach, the son of a bitch won't get me! I tell you, my children, life is nothing short of war to be waged with courage, grace, and dignity. It is a pitched battle between the creative, boldly loving, liberating forces of life and beauty and the fearful, acquisitive, self-stockading forces of death and ugliness. It is war between Man in the highest, most universal and capable sense and man, the base, self-serving, narrowminded, animalistic survivor. It is a war which, I am afraid, we are losing."

"Thank you, doctor, for the diagnosis," Abe commented, "but I find your prognosis unacceptable. I have unflappable faith in man's technological ability to surmount any obstacle in the way of his growth and development."

"Oh, yes, I have faith, too. In the final detonation. We are becoming very worthy of your technological gifts," my father added wryly.

"I don't know, Abe, sometimes I don't know which side you're on," I said. "You seem to have these giant tectonic plates grinding away at each other somewhere deep inside you, one for preservation, one for growth and development. You know the old labor song, don't you, 'Which Side Are You On, Boy?' Which side, Abe?"

"Both."

"Well, Abe," Kate spoke out of courtesy to our dinner guest, "Did you know we've been thinking of trucking our boat back here? We've had no acceptable offers this past year, and of course it will cost us a fortune, a hundred and thirty dollars a foot or four thousand dollars to do it. That'll wipe out our savings from Leon's insurance contract value," she added, glancing at me, "But hopefully Leon will get a full-time teaching position, and with my work at Barnstable Human Services we should be able to afford it. The boat is like a second home to us; she'd be great in these waters; we really miss her."

"New England winters can be tough and expensive on a boat, but it sounds like a delightful idea," Abe said supportively. "Have you thought about where you might store it? Bay Sails Marine, I hear, tends to be expensive, but Wellfleet

Marine caters more to the fishermen and the less well-endowed. They'd be your cheapest bet for winter storage."

"Well, actually, I thought we might put Intrinsic near the foot of our driveway for the winter," I responded.

"You're not putting that boat on my land!" my father exploded.

"I thought you said this was my home as well."

"It is your home, but it is my land, and I won't have it fucked up by any nautical sculptures. I'm ready for coffee and brandy on my deck. Kate, not a bad dinner for a low, Bayonne, Jersey dame."

Kate's eyes watered from the cutting remark.

"And don't get all teary-eyed and bitter from my joking. You have to be bigger than that. I have been called a Jew, a Shylock and a kike, but we must rise above that on the ancient, angry ether of humor unfamiliar to the spiritually shallow, yes? Good night. Abe? Drive me up the hill. And my son, I'll see you on my deck for a cigar."

In the brief aftermath of dinner Kate wept on my shoulder, saying "I can't stand him anymore. It just is no good with him here anymore." I comforted her with an intermittent rub on her now thin, almost bony back. When distressed, she didn't eat much. Talking quietly, we finished the dishes. The baby woke crying. Then I had to go, and I walked up the dark path to the deck where the wind chimes tinkled and his red ash glowed in the starry blackness of night.

Toward the end of August, Kate and I were still hopeful about establishing our lives on the Cape. I was, however, beginning to feel quite discouraged in my efforts to obtain a permanent teaching position. Jobs, like land, were at a premium. The only opening that appeared in the paper was for a combination Ancient History–English teacher at Harwich High School, and though I was weak in Ancient History and not certified in English, I applied without success. Nevertheless, I visited every middle and high school principal and school district superintendent from Provincetown to Bourne to let them know I was eager to work. We also began to think about my father's departure and the necessary move back up the hill to the studio.

While checking the classifieds one evening in the Wellfleet edition of The Advocate, I noticed a For Sale ad in the real estate section: "Small Cape W/ FP, Cheap. Will move onto your lot." Kate and I talked about how nice it would be to have our very own place on the land and not have to shuffle back and forth between my father's houses. I mentioned the house to my father, and though the notion of us needing our very own place did not seem to make sense to him, the convenience of not having to move did. Also, I thought, another winterized quarters would make it possible for him to stay on in his studio under our care should he become more acutely incapacitated by old age, and so he said, "Do it. Don't gabble."

The house was located in Eastham next to the Best Motel and was scheduled for demolition to make room for an office complex to be called Eastham Commons. It was cute enough. I drove with the owner–developer to our land to walk over and consider possible sites for placing the house.

"Twenty-four acres?" he said in disbelief. "Do you have any idea how much money you're sitting on?"

"Yes," I answered. I then gave him a low offer of $18,000, including the move, to think about, and we parted.

That evening on the deck my father and I discussed the new house.

"Do you think we could survey off a half-acre lot around the house, Pop?" I asked, thinking that with our potential equity residing in the structure only, it would be more secure and wise for us to own the land underneath the house as well. More importantly, I thought, the house would more simply and truly be ours and not subject to the politically precarious impulses of a father-son relationship. It could be a home for my family.

"I don't see the need for that," my father answered, puffing on his cigar. "This is all yours."

"Well, still, I'd feel better if the land underneath the house I'm putting all my money into were in my name. The house isn't a boat after all."

"You can have your lot, then, for $40,000. That's cheap for the Cape!"

"C'mon, Pop. I thought you said this is all mine?"

"And I'm not dead yet!"

"Well, what do you mean this is all mine?"

"Ach, you're so stupid! It's all going to you! It's your inheritance! You're an heir, for God's sake!"

"What exactly do you mean by it's all going to me?" I persisted, sensing something hidden.

"When I die, you get it all. That is, you have the right, and Grace has the right to live here as long as you both live."

"What do you mean I have the right? What the hell does that mean?"

"It means that upon the death of Grace, it all goes back to the birds. I have willed it all to the Audubon Society! Isn't it a heroic, noble statement?"

I sat in stunned silence, unable to answer his question.

"Well?" he asked after a minute through smoke, which lazily drifted up around his head and away.

"And what about my grandchildren? And Kate's grandchildren? You have made it so this is no longer family land and Grace and I will only be custodians of what was once your land and now belongs to Audubon. We will have no ownership."

"Ownership is only a destructive Western notion. Think of the Indian conception of land ownership. Their relationship was far more custodial, reverential, and non-exploitive. For them, land was like air and sea and the stars to which they had rights and a spiritual relationship, but they did not feel a need to own nature. Land did not belong to them."

"And look what happened to their land," I responded. "I am not an Indian and this is a greedy, white, capitalistic society. I want what goes with ownership."

"And what is that?"

"Power. Power to determine my own life."

"You can't have it and I won't give it to you. That you'll have to find on your own."

We finished our Scotch. Then I fixed him another for his bedside while he unstrapped his leg and sighed. We kissed goodnight, and I walked down the dark path with waves of anger, hurt, and confusion clashing against one another, feeling as if a portion of my being was washing away, like sand on a winter beach.

Clearly I was not going to be a landowner. Had I lost simply power, or the hope of ever acquiring it? In either case I felt it even more necessary to obtain a permanent teaching position, and I decided to extend my search off Cape and to go anywhere for work. Boston had no openings. Millinocket, Maine, possible. Maine Indian Education? A romantic ring to it, but remote. New Jersey, no. Oklahoma, maybe, but hot and no water. I called my former professor in Los Angeles.

"L.A. is desperate for teachers. They're hiring anybody. With your certification, you're in, and the pay is great," he said.

I flew to Los Angeles the following morning.

That evening before going to bed, Kate called to tell me that my father had just phoned her down in the old house.

"I can not fathom why he's back in Los Angeles of all places!" my father had said.

"He wants to teach. There are jobs there," she answered.

"He should be here. This is where he belongs, by the sea which he loves, helping the town's children in that recreation program, saving the town, saving the land! I'm stranded without him, for God's sake!"

"He wants to teach."

"Don't just keep saying that! You, who have no vision! You're the one who's pushed him in this direction, wanting him to be some puny little public school teacher like your dead father! All you really want is your low father! And that's a low vision! Low!"

Kate hung up.

The following morning, as Kate later described to me, while I had been standing in the sweltering heat on a massive motley line of humanity outside the Department of Education in downtown Los Angeles, she had bathed Grace, eaten breakfast, and driven up the driveway on her way to the beach with the baby cooing in the back seat.

"Here, Kate!" my father shouted from the deck, waving his cane with one hand and flapping a list in the other. She stopped and rolled down the window.

"You and I, we had a good talk last night, didn't we? But don't tell Leon," he said conspiratorially, his words slightly garbled around a large Partagas morning cigar.

"Oh, no. I will tell Leon. We have no secrets."

"You, woman! You low, sick bitch! You're so psychologically unfit!" he had bellowed, hurling his cane across the pool and bouncing it off the side of the quickly departing car.

I returned from L.A. the following day with a job secured, if I wanted it. But I did not. The heat, smog, congestion, and the past were too much. I had, after all, wanted to start anew. And, therefore, I would leave for an interview in Millinocket, and then check out Maine Indian Education in Calais on the Canadian border.

On the ride from Provincetown Airport, when Kate told me of the altercation, I did not feel anger over this typical tirade, only pain, sorrow, and a steeled determination to preserve my family's well-being and whatever positive feelings remained within the previously longed-for reconciliation and reunion with my father.

I left again the next day and flew to Bangor. It was September 10th and many schools had already opened. Renting a car, I drove to Millinocket, interviewed, then continued on over to Washington County, the easternmost, Down East area of the United States most opposite Southern California, to meet with the Director of Maine Indian Education. I took the job he offered as tutor for marginal Passamaquoddy Indian students bussed to the white Calais High School from Indian Township. I was to start September 21st. I located and rented a decent $275 a month house outside of Robinston seventeen miles south of Calais, and then I returned to the Cape.

In our final days together, my father and I visited on the deck, watching sunsets and drinking Cape Cod Specials. I took him a few more times to Loagy Bay, and we swam side by side. And sitting atop the dunes at White Crest Beach, we watched and listened to the combers roll in and break upon the shore while the gulls soared and hung on the wind. I helped him pack his things, and I, too, boxed my belongings, so that when September 15th came, we were ready for our departures.

Abe arrived, looking like a sad old Saint Bernard dog, to take my father to the Hyannis airport. I helped my father cross the bridge where he stopped, raised both arms, cigar in one hand, cane in other, in a loving hail to the long view. Holding fast to my arm, he then stepped down onto the sand next to the car, stopped again, and we embraced.

He then said, "Go off, my son, as you must, and claim your life. It is all one can ever have."

Thinking you terrible, awful, wonderful old man, I said, "Good-bye, Pop, I love you so very much," and we kissed, and he kissed Kate and his granddaughter Grace, then eased himself into the car and slammed the door.

"Thanks, old friend," I said to Abe, squeezing his shoulder, and together they drove away down the sandy road.

Late that afternoon, with rented Ryder truck packed and full, and our little car hitched onto its towed dolly behind, we had covered the old house windows with newspapers, rolled up the carpets, scattered camphor balls about, shut off the propane tanks and power main, made arrangements with Donny to drain the pipes, slammed the door, and hid the key. Then we, too, hailed farewell to the house, and the four of us crammed into the truck's front seat—Kate, Grace, Brutus the dog, and I—and drove up from the hollow and paused briefly at the hilltop in front of the studio. With the chimes tinkling behind us, we gazed out across the marsh to the bay beyond, breathed deeply the sea air, and then, feeling somewhat like wayward pilgrims in search of a new land, we drove off to find my Indian pupils to the north.

Outside the cold drizzle glistened on the few remaining orange, yellow, and brown leaves as I looked up from my October 24th newspaper and stared out at the view from the kitchen table. In the distance, beyond the tops of the down-wardly sloping, moss-draped conifers, the St. Croix River—in the middle of which Samuel de Champlain had wintered on a tiny island three hundred and seventy-nine years ago—flowed into the great, gray and desolate Passamaquoddy Bay, stretching north, it seemed, to some unknown arctic tundra. I turned to page 17 of my paper and was startled by the head-line: "94 Whales Stranded On Cape Cod Beach." I read the first paragraph.

In one of the largest mass strandings of the late 20th Century, 94 pilot whales or blackfish beached themselves early yesterday morning on Eastham's

First Encounter Beach on Cape Cod. Despite heroic efforts of rescue workers to revive the whales on the flood tide, all but three of them succumbed. The three surviving whales were rushed to Brewster Aquarium, where they are reported to be in fair condition.

Through glassy eyes I looked up from the paper and out at the now liquid landscape. How cold Champlain and his men must have been, I thought.

Seven

THE LETTER

Leon Perlman
RR 1, Box 27
HILL, NH 03243

November 3, 1988

Dear Pop,

This is business and other. In the matter of your sizable estate, I am left with considerable anxiety about your offspring's ability to pay the inheritance taxes without selling off assets which are dear to all of us, especially the land and houses. The government could demand over a million dollars in cash. You say, "Don't worry, there'll be plenty of money.

Your mother is as liquid as the Nile." But Mom in her seventy-ninth year is in excellent physical condition and could, like her father, live well into her nineties. Furthermore, her liquidity is quite limited. She lives off the dividends and is unable to touch the principal of a generation-skipping trust, which ends on her children. And even if she could, she might not want to preserve the assets of her ex-husband.

You on the other hand in your eightieth year drink heavily, smoke several Partagas cigars a day, have had your right leg amputated, whet your appetite daily with marijuana cigarettes, have a cancerous condition in your bowels and an inoperable aneurysm on your aortic arch, and you carouse almost nightly at the Tavern with your youthful and adoring entourage. Were it not for your defying, implacable will, any reasonable person would characterize your demise as imminent and the consequent need for minimal estate planning critical.

Unfortunately, when it comes to meeting the real needs of your children, you have rarely been able to escape the bounds of self-centeredness. Instead, you have forged ahead in pursuit of your romantic, theatrical vision of life with you writing, directing, and acting the leading role, changing sets, creating characters, shaping them, casting them aside, adding a prop for the desired effect, building steadily up to the Final Curtain. But will there be thunderous applause and cries for "Author! Author!" which you will not hear, or will the audience flee for the exits as the flats of our lives cave in and the gold leaf cornices crumble and shower down upon us?

Perhaps these two alternative questions are too extreme, but for us, your children, the show will be over, the theater closed. For us who have spent so much time on your stage and in your audience, the time to go home will at last have arrived.

Please do not misunderstand me. I do not want you to die. I admire and am proud of your achievements—your Emmy Award for the Churchill series, your face on the cover of *Saturday Review*, your friendships with the rich and famous, your incredibly shrewd or lucky real estate and art acquisitions. You raised yourself up from Brighton Beach poverty and married into one of Boston's most distinguished Protestant families. You sent your children to the best schools. You have overcome illness and physical handicaps, and you continue to swim, write, paint, and sculpt to this day. You have presented a virtuoso performance demonstrating a remarkable talent for living.

Even your eccentricities are a source of pride for me. Your lifelong knitting of a colorful death shroud, your color-clashing, ill-fitting, thrift store wardrobe, the dirty shambles of your living quarters out of which rise self-created sculptures, your productivity in spite of many drinks and pills to ease the phantom pain all proclaim a "I don't give a fuck what you think" defiance and determination. Your carefully crafted, self-centered, outrageous image allows you unfettered movement in the world. By shocking people you keep them at bay and remain in control as le grand artiste ou metteur en scène.

I have said I am disturbed by the possibility of unpayable inheritance taxes. They will undeniably intrude into our lives like termites, eating up half of everything. I trust, however, and perhaps naively, that just as you have acquired shrewdly, so you will have sought wisely to preserve your legacy. The lawyer (Crockett) has given his warning. As your confounding whirlwind swirls madly about those who have loved or been impressed by you, calling us to faithful action or throwing us into confusion or anger, I expect that underneath your beguiling image some competent measures on a par with your genuine life achievements will have been taken in our best interests, that is, something other than an impulsively concocted holographic testament yet again altered in a moment of inebriated passion and hidden under some desk top. I must say that I hardly trust your invitation to give our advice in the matter of your estate planning. Frankly, I suspect it is a ploy to surmise which son is most greedy and least worthy, or an opportunity to divine the unfolding sibling scenario after your departure (how will the final act play out?), or a means of projecting yourself into the future thereby extending your life. Please instruct in your will that the estate taxes paid by each son should be in proportion to his taxable inherited assets.

Incidentally, I don't think we should do any major repairs to the old Cape house. The powdered sills, the raccoon holes in the roof, the chipped paint all add perfectly to its decrepitude and will lessen its value when the estate assessors come snooping around. What should I do with all those broken-down chairs in the garage?

You know, in that small field to the left of the old house as you look out over the marsh, I'd like someday to build a studio barn with high doors to bring in and out canvasses and a raku kiln and southern skylights. And off to the left of your bungalow down in the pine grove with the long view to the bay I'd like to build a boathouse with a caretaker's quarters. You really should have had someone living there for you, you know, a housekeeper, a chauffeur, a handyman, a follower for Christ's sake. What a load of horseshit that you couldn't stand having someone around in a subservient, demeaning position. But I think now I understand that it is you who would be demeaned and feel subservient, dependent on another in the weakness and vulnerability of old age. Just look at yourself stranded on your deck like a beached blackfish surveying the land and the years of your life. Who is buying you your Entenmann's crumb cake?

You know, when I came back from my twelve year collapsed quest for California salvation from my confused and at times turbulent past (Need I remind you of my sadistic, sociopathic older brother? A "sunny, silly, packaged and programmed life" middle brother, as you so disdainfully labeled him? Weepy, passive and guilty mother asleep alone at the kitchen table abused by an egomaniacal, flamboyant, alcoholic father too often absent from the family? The prolonged breakdown of our family throughout childhood, culminating in final separation when I turned sixteen? The blood and stitches, smashed vases and eyes blackened by thrown candlesticks; the expulsions, banishments; and the hope?), I looked forward to reconnecting with my oldest, preverbal memory with Gertha, our black maid, holding me to her breast as I looked out over her shoulder to the sandy road with grass growing in the middle, heard the gentle sough of the wind in the pitch pines, and breathed in the fragrance of the sand. No words have ever seemed able to describe this road but that it is the feeling of my connection to life.

The memory of the smell of the sea, the beacon of Highland Light, the rundown vessels of the Wellfleet fishing fleet, and above all, the memory of that sandy road drew me home again. I returned to that haven from my strange career as an insurance agent and the endeavor to salvage my life in the Primal Therapy cult. Would I find that shopping malls and greed had devastated the Cape as much as California?

Well, Pop, our first winter in Wellfleet was delightful. Kate and I felt wrapped in the blanket of our beautiful surroundings and warm, long-ago summer memories. We watched the marsh turn from green to gold, then fill with winter tides and later snow. A pair of blue heron nested within sight of our binoculars. And Kate, so enormous with child and glowing with excitement, gave birth to Grace in late February. The three of us now slept cozily under our blanket as the winter storms howled about.

My student teaching had gone well. Although I couldn't get a permanent position, substituting was satisfying enough, and all was fine until late May when you returned for the summer.

You had said that the Cape was ours. "This is your land," you said one minute. Then the next moment, in front of our old, mutual friends, the Gotliebs, who had treated us so tenderly through the winter, you roared to impress them with your authority, loosened by more than enough Scotch, "You're not storing your boat on my land!" You became threatened by my involvement in town affairs and attempts to save the town from over-development, hammering home the superiority of your connections to the old-timers and people of influence. You ran us silly on errands more so that you could feel some power against your growing helplessness. You began to train Grace to fetch. And when you felt our resistance, you let your psychoanalytical buzz saw whir, probing and cutting into my asthmatic past or Kate's lower class breeding. I had forgotten the effect of your power and my weakness in dealing with it.

I need not go into all the painful details which disrupted our attempt to start a new life once again. But I want you to know that when we left so suddenly in early September, it was not because I could not find a permanent teaching job on the Cape, as I then indicated. I wouldn't have minded continued substitute teaching. We left because I felt driven off the land by you. That's why I wound up on that desolate New Brunswick border teaching Passamaquoddy Indians.

I left to preserve whatever feelings of self-worth I could retain. I left to protect Grace and Kate and to protect the fragile rapprochement you and I had achieved. A stronger man might have stayed and fought. I had lost too many times to be struck again.

My leaving you also explains how I came to be in New Hampshire. I did want a genuine classroom teaching job with a group of students, not a Maine Indian Education, Chapter 1 tutorial position. Teaching 8th grade social studies in Bristol, New Hampshire provided me with that regular classroom opportunity.

We also bought the house here with Mom's help because my family needed a home. You considered the house to be an investment, just a place to live while I gained enough teaching experience to be more eligible for a Cape position. I'm just trying to live. Two weekends ago when I last saw you, you tried to zing me when you said, "Where did you get the money for the down payment on your house?" You knew where I got the money. I said Mom had given it to me, and you said, "Well, then, it's not your house. It's a family house." I responded, "No, it is my house." Enough of that.

It is true that I have enjoyed our latest visit. I still play second fiddle to you, but perhaps that is the way most father and son relationships are. Is a son supposed to feel on guard most of the time with his father?

We drink too much together. On short visits scotch or my Cape Cod Specials along with inhaled cigars settles my emotional churning. I love being with you, talking about my studies, or philosophical topics like wisdom and aging. Driving to the top of the dunes at White Crest for cocktail hour on garden chairs is very pleasurable. You are to me such a handsome, noble man, sitting there without a leg, the wind blowing through your white hair, enjoying your cigar, surveying the wild horses of the sea foaming and fretting. I love you so much, Pop.

Now if we are to return to the Cape to live, as you know we are now contemplating, this is what I want. The gift of seventeen acres to the Audubon is fine with me, setting aside 7 acres and the houses for my sole, unencumbered ownership. The gift to the birds is a marvelous statement to the land rapists, a noble legacy, and an excellent means of substantially reducing estate taxes. However, I want it made clear that payment of taxes will be in proportion to assets received. Josh, after all, is receiving the New York City brownstone which after the Audubon gift will be far more valuable than the Cape property. I don't want to squabble with him about paying his higher taxes. Robert, you say, is now getting the one hundred and sixty-eight acre farm in

Warwick. With his two angry ex-wives and five children there'll be nothing left of it.

Before coming back and taking care of you as needed and as I want to do, I want you to have the seven acres formally surveyed and divided from the rest of the land. I know you will say, "You do it!" With your go ahead I will.

I want you to have a new deed drawn up on the seven acres with you and me as owners in joint tenancy. Hopefully you will live a long time. My name on the deed now will assure that you don't play power politics with my home and family should we fight.

Relinquish some control now, and relinquish it right. You are, after all, as I am, too, moving toward the inevitable relinquishment. Make your ascension easier with less material baggage.

I hold you in my heart

Always,
    Leon

Eight

A VIEW EASEMENT

My father is dying. That much I can see. Oh, he's not collapsed on his deathbed or anything. He gets himself up in the morning. Very slowly. He puts on his leg. Then with two canes he walks into the bathroom, empties or changes his colostomy bag and cleans around his stoma. He Water Piks his teeth and gums. Then he'll make a cup of coffee and cut a piece of Entenmann's coffee cake or some cake made by Donny Snow's wife. He'll pick up the *Cape Cod Times* thrown up on the deck against the slider, settle into his rocker, and look out through the window over the marsh. When he is done sipping his coffee and eating, he'll light up a hefty Partagas and read the paper. This is his usual morning. He is slowing way down, and he's dying.

This morning I made him breakfast. A soft-boiled egg with pieces of toast broken up into it. He enjoyed it very much because it is not often someone is there with the dexterity to peel off the egg's shell; his hands are now quite gnarled with arthritis.

After breakfast, despite his initial resistance, we decided to journey down the hill to the yard behind the old house in the hollow where I have been clearing out some locust and cherry trees and brush to reveal a view of the marsh. It was terribly overgrown, and for the last three weekends in a row I have traveled alone down from New Hampshire with my saw and gloves to cut, drag, stack, and burn. Some of this clearing has been on the seventeen acres of land being donated to the Audubon; the Boston lawyer helping us with the donation said that although we've retained a view easement, it would be prudent to create the view now to avoid future resistance from the sanctuary custodians who might deem any extensive pruning activity a disturbance to wildlife. So I have been hacking away relentlessly.

My father is dying, I sometimes have to repeat to myself. It was a great effort for him to walk out the door, across the deck, and into my car. He has to pee all the time. His prosthetic leg is never comfortable. His bag is for him a stinking chore. He suspects every new ache is cancer spreading. At night he has to take two Halcion to sleep, and his dosage of painkillers during the day has been increased. His liver's in trouble, and if he drinks too much the night before, he's jaundiced in the morning. Yet he keeps his sense of humor.

On the way out of his studio onto the deck, we passed a pillow tossed on a chair, embroidered by a friend with my father's motto, the words "Do It!"

"No one will ever be able to say this one-legged colostomy didn't do it!" he said grasping my arm as we walked slowly away from the car around to the back of the old house. The view is beautiful, and my father was pleased.

I am moving back to Cape Cod with Grace and Kate. I have taken care that things have been done right. When I told him again in the letter that I thought the gift of all the land was a lousy idea, he had a change of heart, changed his will, and left me for the time being with seven of the twenty-four acres, the studio, and the old house.

Well, I must say such a bequeathal was all very nice for me, but hardly written in stone; he retained complete control with the historically whimsical instrument of his will. The only way, it seemed to me, to move this bequeathal along toward actualization was to do it.

"Do it now, Pop," I had told my father. "Give Audubon the land now. Have them pay for all the survey and legal work. And while you're alive, you'll be able to enjoy the recognition for having taken a heroic stance against the developers who have come damn close to ruining the Cape." This was true. I felt this way. I also believed that if my father did it now, his action might establish some credibility, reliability, and predictability to a life which for me had hitherto been incredible, unreliable, and unpredictable. I also wanted to see my father relinquish power and actually give—a giving of the land to wildlife, a giving to a son of a lesser estate tax burden, a giving of one's own life as sure as the rising and setting sun. So, do it, Rasputin, I thought.

Thus, we've moved on this course, and the Audubon donation is all but complete. My father has been written up in the local papers. He's even received letters of thanks from complete strangers for his generous gift. The new survey has been filed at the Land Court in Boston and the quitclaim deed initialed by the chief surveyor there; all that remains is the recording of the deed in Barnstable, and the gift will be consummated.

Equal to the donation in terms of implications for my future have been changes implemented in my father's will. Up until three weeks ago his will was an estate planning catastrophe. The allotment of property to me and my brothers was very unequal. The inheritor of the New York City house perhaps stood to receive a net inheritance one million dollars greater than his brothers. Furthermore, it appeared that even after the Audubon donation, all three properties—New York City, Warwick, and Cape Cod—would have to be sold in order to pay estate taxes and probate fees.

After we discussed three or four different estate settlement scenarios, my father concluded that in the interest of equality and land preservation with each son receiving real and liquid property, the New York City house must be sold. Josh and

Robert should receive the one hundred and sixty-eight acre Warwick property equally with the recipient of the farmhouse there receiving a commensurately lesser quantity of acreage equal in value to the farmhouse structure; also, conservation restrictions should be placed on a substantial portion of the acreage to reduce taxes and to preserve wildlife and open space. As I have requested all along, I reiterated my desire for the now seven-acre Cape Cod property with conservation restrictions placed on five of those seven acres to prevent development, to preserve wildlife and open space, and to reduce estate taxes. After an appraisal of the Warwick and Wellfleet properties, I stated the proceeds from the sale of the New York City house should be apportioned to each son such that each of their sum net inheritances—liquid and real—is equal.

I shared these conclusions in writing with my brothers, my father, and my father's lawyer. Because my father's decent but young, untested, and unsophisticated country lawyer in Warwick had been notoriously inept at bringing the importance of genuine estate planning to my father's attention and had often been swayed by my father's fickle approach, I advised him that it appeared my father had only thirty days to live (not an implausible event). His failure to make a concerted, legitimate effort to bring my father's estate under control would have disastrous consequences not only for land loved by the Perlman family but also, I intimated as subtly as possible, his legal practice as well should malpractice emerge as an issue.

My father announced that it was "Will Time!" and requested input from my brothers. They were to inform the lawyer of their notions of a fair estate settlement, which I believe they did.

Under a pretext of visiting an aunt in Orleans twelve miles away from Wellfleet, the lawyer arrived by plane within a week, carrying a new will. My father would have been uncomfortable had he known the lawyer's trip was for the sole purpose of changing his will. My father signed the document, and it is in accordance with the principle of equality.

"Now all we need to complete the package," my father said the other day, "is for me to die! I can't wait!"

My father is dying. He asked me, "What do you think about all day while you burn brush down there?"

"That this is a momentous time, Pop," I answer.

The seventeen acres, a part of me, are almost gone, like some sort of constructive, positive amputation, some portion of childhood cut away, embalmed in perpetuity, wildlife preserved, pickled forever in the formaldehyde of my father's will. Oh, I know it's good, even noble, and he has followed through. There will be a dozen or more fewer house lots. The taxes will be less. The foxes, owls, raccoons, and herons will be happy. The endangered broom crowberry will flourish. And his name will be preserved. What will remain of this gifted land beyond memories, held in my white man's construct of illusory, time-bound mortal ownership, is a view easement now being created or re-created by me. So cut, slash and burn now for all your worth, Perlman. Take this long view of the golden marsh, where the waters of Loagy Bay at high tide sparkle in the distance! Take it now without rest, for time is running out. This is it.

This is a time of power transference, I think while building up the fire in the wind and rain. There's a new view opening up behind the old house, one I faintly recollect from a childhood long ago. I can smell the sea and smoke and hear the gulls cry overhead. From her nest in the marsh now so closely visible a great heron ascends. This is a time of responsibility and new life, I think. This land—this mortgage free, Land-Courted, precious land as good as gold—is your land, Pop, and this land, at least a goodly portion of it, is almost mine.

I have a pain in my right side; I must ease up on my drinking. I have tried to be a good son, Pop, and I have tried to save myself. I am coming back to the Cape, Pop. I will be with you. Could this be … suicide? There seem to be no words to explain how I feel, Pop—I love you forever you must know, and I am proud of you—but there is a stance I am now taking which says, "I'm here! I am here!"

Nine

POP GOES TO HIS LONG HOME

I knew my father kept a paper bag full of drugs next to his bed—Halcion, Tylenol 3, Percodan, some very old phenobarbital, Dalmane, pot—all hoarded over the years in preparation for difficult times which were now without question upon him. Furthermore, he had said to me while sitting on his deck, "If you think this cancer's going to get me, this one-legged walking colostomy," he paused, then jabbed with his gnarled hand thrusting into the air with a finessed twist of the wrist while declaring with fire in his eyes, "Watch!"

Back home in New Hampshire, his dramatic pronouncement had lingered with me. It surely was his right to take his own life, but I was uncomfortable being an accomplice. I didn't want him to go. I wanted him to stay as long as life would have him, which I knew with a conflicting mélange of welling excitement and grief would not be long. Should I hide his drugs? I struggled with the question and resolved to put myself face to face with it by driving down to the Cape and stealing into his studio while he was away on a doctor's appointment with Abe Gotlieb. Perhaps I longed to be near him one more time before he was gone.

After the three and a half-hour drive from Bristol, I arrived late morning at his small studio house overlooking the splendid marsh below with Lieutenant's Island in the distance, the ebb and flood of the tide there still reminding me of life's natural evanescence and rebirth, something hopeful and greater than the drone of my tiresome, oft-recurring negative thoughts. I entered his bedroom and picked up the paper bag filled with vials of pills. Clutching it to my chest with sadness and self-loathing at my comparative weakness and treachery in the face of his death, I quickly reentered the car and drove down into the hollow to the old house. I wanted to catch a glimpse of the view out back so laboriously created over the past many months. It was now spacious and pleasing through limbed locust trees, which churned like gyrating dancers on the long carpet of rough spring lawn rolling down to the greening marsh. Cardinals and chickadees flitted from branch to branch, their spring songs of celebration echoing in the woods while robins hopped on the ground here and there in search of insects or an occasional worm.

On the distant knoll, areas of blackened earth were now covered by new growth. The previous year on weekend visits down from New Hampshire, when I had first begun the long task of clearing, a brush fire had gotten out of hand and spread wildly down into the marsh, consuming dry winter grasses.

"Down there in the marsh, boys!" my father had commanded the firemen as their noisy, exhaust spewing trucks with sirens and crackly radios blaring, passed before his deck. "He's destroying the only thing I ever loved!" he wryly added, nonchalantly puffing on his cigar. Kate, who reported his reaction, had just brought him a sandwich. "I'll have my lunch now," he calmly said, dismissing the smoky commotion below. "And a little whiskey in my milk." From that moment on he never mentioned the fire and only silently shrugged his shoulders with a what-can-you-do lift when I emerged from the hollow an hour later obviously shaken but relieved the fire fighters had quickly extinguished the blaze.

Now a half a mile up Route 6 heading back to New Hampshire, I passed the Wellfleet Cinemas and Drive-In, the paper bag on the seat next to me.

"Shit, I can't do this," I thought. "It's his fuckin' life, for chris' sake!" I turned around.

Swaying through the soft sand at the foot of the driveway, the Corolla quickly bounced over roots and jostled up the hill, hugging the side of the road to protect the tail pipe and muffler from the crown of grass and bearberry growing in the middle. I ran into the studio and returned the bag to his bedroom. Glancing over the mess of his unmade bed and scattered clothes, I resigned myself to a sigh and once again headed back to New Hampshire.

The following week Abe Gotlieb called to press for round the clock nursing and to request that I come back down to take my father to Cape Cod Hospital for a bone scan the following Friday, the 29th of May. He had been complaining of pain in his pelvis. With my father's health deteriorating more each day Abe was clearly letting me know it was time for a more immediate family presence.

Abe had not been alone in caring for my father. Dennis Conlin, an affable, empathetic local nurse who was also a writer and actor, had helped my father over the past few years care for his colostomy, prosthetic leg, and stump with its "phantom" pain and irritation. Also, Dennis was not one to decline a scotch or two, a cigar, or a puff on a joint with my father. They had become friends, and it was Dennis's home phone that was first to be called if my father ever pressed the Lifeline emergency beacon button which he reluctantly wore around his neck; he had been befuddled by the technology of the device and considered it an insulting reminder of growing infirmity.

Other disciples of sorts also helped care for my father in his final days. Rose Kilpatrick, a Pillsbury heiress, and Marcel Beauvien, a pony-tailed, beautiful young Frenchman, both artists who had constructed their house entirely of discarded materials salvaged at the town dump, stopped by frequently to visit, cook, and clean up. Often they brought a gift from the dump. My father's favorite evening chair was actually a discarded wrought iron rocker painted white with old throw pillows for a cushion.

Daphne Disalvio collected and washed his laundry once a week. Of questionable stability she kept her rather alarming, jowly, middle-aged visage coated with a clown-like greasy white pearlescent base. Painted, oily black, raccoon-like shadows above and below her sweeping false eyelashes hid the cautious, dark eyes of a child. Hot red lipstick haphazardly smeared her lips. Her look suggested an open burned marshmallow, gooey with overwhelming pain and sweetness. The motion of her body and gaze was agitated and jerky, as if in the early stages of Parkinson's disease perhaps brought on by too much drug abuse, and God knows what other horrific influences in a previous life. She looked part homeless bag lady, part street hooker, a true psychic disaster, from whom most people recoiled in horror but for whom my father took a gentle, respectful liking. She responded by serving him with childlike loyalty, gladly doing his wash.

Donny Snow, the heavyset fellow and volunteer firefighter, my father's Bruegel, still came by on occasion, though reluctantly. He had finally rebelled against too many unmannerly intrusions and humiliations suffered under the blade of my father's psychoanalytical buzz saw while illegally building, without a permit, a small bedroom addition onto the studio. Not to mention, my father slyly chiseled away at his wages through unwarranted criticism of his work. Donny had angrily thrown some requested firewood out of the "crippled bastard's" reach alongside the studio and had left a mess of empty paint cans and soggy cuttings of drywall scattered about. There were rumors he had even tossed cans of turpentine and paint thinner into the well pit in a failed attempt to contaminate the water supply. Nevertheless he still yearned for and received a few morsels of paternal affection on occasional visits, a few rough but friendly exchanges of "You fucker!" tossed about; and with my father's end now in sight, he had softened a bit.

I arrived Friday morning for a scheduling meeting with a VNA (Visiting Nurses Association) Hospice nurse to arrange for more frequent, regular visits. While she and I quietly talked inside the studio, my father smoked his cigar out on the deck.

"And please, don't let him smoke in the house without supervision," I whispered to the nurse. "He's been burning holes in his pants and skirt thing, his sarong, when he dozes off."

We spent a few minutes filling out a weekly calendar and writing down the phone numbers of the various caregivers. I wrote out a "No Unsupervised Smoking" note and tacked it to his bedroom door.

"We have to leave now for his bone scan at the hospital in Hyannis. Thank you for coming by," I said, feeling more secure medical people would be checking on him more often. "Ready, Pop?" I called out to the deck.

We crossed slowly over the lap pool bridge, arm in arm, and I helped him step with his aluminum walker to the Corolla.

"'Man goes to his long home,'" my father said, sinking into the car's passenger seat with a grimace, his words garbled around his cigar "'and the mourners go about in the street.' Isn't that great?" He pulled his paisley sarong and thrift store robe into the car with great effort and slammed the door with a sigh. "Ecclesiastes," he added, spitting out a bit of tobacco with a flick of his tongue.

We drove slowly down the driveway and out to Route 6.

"Strawberries! Strawberries and chocolate. That's what I want," he softly exclaimed with a rasp as we approached the Orleans rotary. We rounded the circle and pulled into Stop and Shop where I bought a half pint of the berries and a bar of dark Lindt chocolate. He slowly ate one berry and a square of the chocolate, savoring the mix of flavors and textures as if they were the finest wine. After a few minutes he relit his cigar with the Bic lighter encased in blue suede and worn around his neck on a leather thong. He smoked quietly, then slept as we drove along the two-lane stretch of highway known as Suicide Alley for its numerous head-on fatalities and on up to the hospital in Hyannis. I removed the cigar from his fingers, tamped it out in the ashtray, and placed it on the dash.

The hospital x-ray technician, a burly young man, bored and humorless, ordered my father on the table in the sterile white room, positioning him with indifference, if not roughness, for a look at the pelvic bones of this gaunt old man. The exam was pointless, not worth the time and discomfort, and the three of us seemed to know it. Had he been stronger Pop would have created a row, maybe even socked the technician; but clearly his life was slipping away and he seemed resigned, albeit grudgingly.

"My bag is full," he said after the exam. I escorted him alongside his walker into the bathroom where with contempt he emptied the contents of his colostomy bag into the sink and splattered the shit onto the floor with a long blast from the faucet. As we left the bathroom he noticed a hospital blanket on a chair in the hallway. "Take it!" he ordered. "Take the blanket! These fuckers have gotten enough of my money." We made our way to the lobby, blanket under my arm, to await the arrival of Rose and Marcel with whom I had made arrangements to drive my father home so that I could leave Hyannis and head directly back to New Hampshire.

We sat for half an hour, chatting a little, comfortably present with one another in the long silences.

"I love Portuguese women," I said quietly, nodding my head toward an olive skinned mother with long black hair across the room. "Look over there, Pop."

Opening his eyes, he said softly in agreement, "She's a beauty."

Rose entered the building and went up to the front desk. She had a scarf tied around her head and was speckled with white ceiling paint on her face, plaid shirt, and jeans. Her no-nonsense hands were strong and large, indicative of the command she seemed to have over her free-form artist's life.

"They're here, Pop." I gently nudged his shoulder and he opened his eyes.

"Fuckers. Let's get out of here."

We slowly made our way across the lobby and out the door, exchanging greetings and pleasantries with Rose. Marcel, with his long blond ponytail protruding pertly off the back of his head like the mane of a spry colt, sat behind the wheel of an old, rusted-out Chevy van parked at the curb in front of the hospital entrance. Rose and I helped my father into the front seat.

"Let's go, you fuckquerre!" Marcel said with gentle play-fulness to my father. "How did it go?"

"Don't ask. Finito."

I slowly closed his door and Rose climbed in back with the walker.

"Thank you, my boy," my father said to me through the rolled down window, looking exhausted by the unnecessary medical expedition.

"O.K., Pop. I'll call you tonight when I get home." I leaned in the window and kissed him on one cheek. Then evermore aware that this could be our final moment, I kissed him on his other cheek. I tenderly kissed his forehead, holding the back of his neck with my hand, and, finally, for the first and last time I kissed him on the lips.

"See ya later, Pop!" I said, and he waved, as they pulled away from the curb.

After dinner that evening in New Hampshire I called my father to let him know I had safely returned. We chatted briefly and he finished by saying, "I want to thank you for everything you've done for me." I told him I loved him and he, too, said, "I love you." Kate read Grace a bedtime story and soon thereafter the three of us slept soundly.

I later learned from Abe Gotlieb that after we had spoken my father had struggled out of bed to the bathroom. He walked with thigh dangling between the arms of his aluminum walker across the room, fighting pain and waning life, all the while forcefully asserting, "It's a matter of will! Will!" After peeing, he collapsed back in bed triumphant and exhausted, and one after the other my brothers had phoned. To Josh he had commanded, "Find your soul!" and to Robert he had pronounced, "You! You have no soul!"

At 5:20 the next morning the phone rang, jarring us awake.

"Is Vincent with you?" Donny Snow urgently asked.

"No, I left him yesterday afternoon with Rose and Marcel at the hospital."

"Oh, shit. There's been a bad fire at the studio. The place is totaled. I was hoping he's with you."

After a moment's silence I answered, "Nope, he's in there, Donny. He's back in there." I took a deep breath and blew it slowly out my puffed out cheeks. "Yeh, he's in there … I'll be down in a few hours. I'm leaving now.'

After dropping Grace off with her best friend's mother, Kate and I drove, mostly in silence, down 3A through Hill, Franklin, and Boscawan. An expanding basketball of feeling in my belly pushing up to my throat was capped by sharp attentiveness. From the dash of the Corolla I picked up and lit the partially smoked cigar placed there yesterday, putting the still soggy end in my mouth, mouthing it and inhaling the smoke deeply.

Before Pennacook we pulled over to a phone booth outside a gas station. I called Donny back. "We found him, Leon, and the dog. I'm sorry. It's really awful."

I then called the lawyer, Ansel Crockett, who only a few days earlier had deeded 17 acres (12 buildable upland and 5 marsh) to the Massachusetts Audubon Society, leaving the remaining 7 acres, old house, and studio to me in a trust specifically created to bypass probate and avoid conflict with my two brothers in New York State. The trust also included instructions to place 5 of the 7 inherited acres into conservation with a restriction to be held by the newly formed Wellfleet Conservation Trust. The legal work and surveying, put off until the very end, had been initiated by me in consultation and negotiation with my father who had, predictably enough, said, "You, you do it! I give up. You take over!" It was certainly an outcome more within reason and grounded in reality than his once grand proclamation, "I'm leaving it all to the birds!" Yes, I had had to convince him of my love of the property and him and to demonstrate that love by committing to moving back to Cape Cod from New Hampshire and relinquishing my life there, up there in those "scary" mountains, as he had once chidingly said. Whatever leverage I felt I had with him had been created only when Kate, Grace, and I had left the Cape in dismay six years earlier. So perhaps ruminating alone for five or six years inclined him to reconsider giving it all to the Audubon, though such a gift would have been the most dramatic and grand public statement to a greedy, land-raping world. The love of a son, it seems, did hold some sway after all, and he was able to give me some bequeathable property, while saving the rest from development and providing an undisturbed home for wildlife. It was indeed a very noble statement.

"'It is Accomplished,'" I told the lawyer over the phone. "The king has died in a fire this morning along with his dog; the studio has burned down." Smoking the cigar down to a stub, I got back in the car and proceeded from Exit 17 down I93 through Boston and to the Cape.

The last of the fire engines sat in the driveway, its radio crackling intermittently with scratchy, unintelligible voices. A blue and gray state police car's engine quietly idled. A small body bag containing his little Portuguese water dog

Sushi lay on the ground. Pop's body had already been taken away. The facade of the studio remained mostly intact. His bedroom, now exposed and gaping under the blue morning sky, was gone and his bare bedspring, the padding and ticking burned away, lay on the ground over which had been the floor and a ceiling. Two walls no longer stood. A Charles Despiau pewter head on his bureau had melted and vanished into the ash below. The bureau was gone. A colorful oil pastel of a horse I had drawn for him many years before had been consumed. In the living room a soggy six-inch bed of muddy ash covered the floor and the exposed wood framing was black and charred, resembling alligator skin. A pungent smell, like an un-bathed, wet armpit, hung in the air. In the adjoining kitchen the metal cabinets had pulled away from the wall. The sink was entirely filled with ash. On one blackened counter a bright red strawberry sat in contrast, protected from fire and heat by its succulence. Just outside the tiny kitchen area the once white metal rocking chair acquired from the dump by Rose and Marcel, now cradled a melted telephone. The living room drywall, adjoining Donny Snow's illegal office and bedroom addition, had pulled away from the wall and slumped to the floor, revealing the interior drywall of the undamaged new room. Spray-painted on this newer inner wall in big, black, scrawling letters were the words BLOW ME YOU FUCKER! Beneath what had been a large Melissa Meyers abstract oil painting and underneath what remained of a built-in sofa I found an unopened charred box from JR's of Partagas cigars, each encased in pearlescently blackened metal humidors. I removed the cap from one, lit up the undamaged cigar, and stepped over to the once white, now blackened, metal liquor cabinet on which sat a large charred and cracked solid wooden head, sculpted by my father's long-ago lover Sonya Little. With my foot I dug away the thick ash blocking its doors and opened it. All the bottles were without labels and black. I opened one, smelled it, and took a long swill of scotch. I puffed on the cigar, deeply inhaling its smoke, then raised it and the bottle overhead, toasting my father: "Now you've done it, Pop. You've really fuckin' done it."

I stepped outside the darkness through the shattered slider and yellow police tape onto the deck. The lap pool sparkled in the morning sun and the inflatable duck glided about here and there on gentle puffs of breeze, parting the ashy surface, its bill seemingly sniffing floating bits of debris. While standing on the pool bridge looking out at the view, I noticed Daphne Disalvio—her shining face painted pearl white, lips blazing red, and thick, black eyelashes swept up and reaching for the moon—waddling up the driveway with a big, white sack thrown over her shoulder. With eyes filled with hopeful anticipation and dread, she called out, childlike, "Where's Vincent? I have his laundry!"

"He's gone, passed away," I told her. With a spastic shudder and gasp she dropped the bag, let out a bewildered wail, and fled back down the driveway.

The next day I received a call from Nickerson's Funeral Home in Wellfleet. The gentleman expressed condolences and offered an array of goods and services—caskets, urns, and cremation. "$1,200 for cremation? He's quite well done, I would think! Any discount?"

I made arrangements with another service. The body was picked up at the hospital mortuary after an autopsy was performed and shipped off to McHoul's crematorium. $900.00. A week later he arrived in a cardboard box at the post office. A week or two after that a state trooper dropped by with some personal effects and the autopsy report.

"How come the autopsy?" I asked.

"To rule out anything suspicious that might have caused the death. We found white powder on the couch. Turned out to be baking powder." Asphyxiation by smoke, the report read.

It had been about 4:00 in the morning when Dennis Conlin received a call from the service monitoring the Lifeline alert medallion my father wore round his neck. The alarm had been activated and Dennis immediately drove to the studio, finding it totally engulfed in flames. With no access to a phone, he drove 100 mph to the fire department in town. Had my father pressed the medallion in a conscious state of terror, legless and unable to escape? Or had he already succumbed, his dead body falling onto the medallion? Maybe a short circuit had triggered the device. I remembered a suicide by fire on a Los Angeles street I had once witnessed where the charred body had shriveled into a fetal position. I pictured that Buddhist Vietnamese monk protesting the war in the 60's. One of the firemen had told me that the point of ignition, the spot with highest heat intensity, was underneath the right hand side of his bed. Perhaps a lit cigar or joint dropped from his hand. I later recalled I had hurriedly plugged a foot-warming heating pad into an extension cord which already had an electric blanket plugged into it under the right-hand side of the bed. It could have been subconscious murder, couldn't it? Or manslaughter to say the least? Or, more intentionally, Donny Blow-Me-You-Fucker Snow might have mis-wired the new addition to create a fire hazard. Regardless of a specific cause, his fiery death could simply have been his fate, a purification of sorts. That he may have sensed long ago. My father had, after all, written a book in 1945 called *The Lonely Hill* in which a jilted lover takes her revenge by murderous fire.

Nor was this the only sign of Hephaistos at work in my father's Ancient Grecophile life. A few years after the fire I reflected on the life and passing of a family friend in my childhood. Robert Rushmore, mustached and lean, also known as Iggy, was an aspiring opera singer who intermittently lived with us throughout much of the 50's decade. Serving as a surrogate parent for me and my brothers, he often supplanted, according to my father, my often depressed and overworked mother in her family duties. He cooked for us, made a delicious icebox cake, organized Easter egg hunts and 4th of July fireworks, greatly exceeded the speed limit in his '55 Ford, much to our boisterous delight, and often sang lovely tenor arias while accompanying himself on the piano. We boys loved him.

Because of Iggy's increasingly central role in our family, which collided with my mother or father's authority or in some way had created some untenable imbalance, my father violently and permanently ejected him from the household late one night. "OUT! I want you OUT of my house!" he roared amidst a living room melee. He smashed a hand-painted, antique porcelain vase jardinière over Iggy's head. I witnessed this event from the top the stairs. I was ten years old. It took forty years after this incident to deduce that Iggy and my father had been secret lovers. I should say here that homosexual friends and relationships were not uncommon in my father's life and I recall many couples—Sonny and Toby, Gordon and Stanley, Bob and Roger—who mingled in and out of our family. Even my first cousin Franklin, a representative of the genteel New England side of the family, recently reported to me that Uncle Vincent, liquored up in a usual manner, had sodomized him at the age of 19, a liberty taken, no doubt, with a degree of long-smoldering resentment of unearned class privilege. This particular deduction of his propensity for men (or in the case of my cousin, boys), however, was cemented upon my reading soon after the fire of a novel written by Iggy in the late 60's in which the protagonist is bitterly rendered with an uncanny resemblance to my father involved in a secret affair with a female much in the role Iggy had played within our family.

His protagonist's life ends in a house fire, and the book, written more than two decades before my father's actual death, is titled *Who'll Burn Down the House?*. Were this not true, I'd say my reasoning, in order to make sense of it all, was beginning to lean toward magical thinking.

Grace had to finish up nursery school, and Kate and I began to think about moving permanently down to the Cape in fulfillment of that enervating condition Pop had verbally imposed (and to which I had agreed) before bequeathing the property. Once again I felt under a soggy blanket of lifelong subservience and shame compensated by adoration and loyalty, distorted at times into some sort of bipolar teeter-tottering of self-aggrandizement and self-loathing, the tiresome extremes of which were often tempered by an excess of drink. Our New Hampshire house was put up for sale at a financial loss, which I experienced as a diminishment of independence and self-worth. A month later we moved into the charming, un-insulated, and decrepit old house down in the hollow, the house where lingered happy dreams of distant childhood.

Now digging through the studio's ash with a shovel, sifting for buried items. I found a pair of blackened brass candlesticks, a male bronze head by Sonya Little, various plates and silverware, a two-foot tall, now blackened bronze statue of Quan Yin with gold leaf melted away. I needed to find the keys to the 1961 Chrysler Newport which sat outside with rusting frame and deflated tires. The car was to be the lead vehicle in the memorial parade to the South Wellfleet Cemetery planned a few weeks away. I recalled my father saying the key was on the shelf above the kitchen sink. Without hesitation I plunged the shovel into the ash-filled sink, turned over the still moist muck, and immediately, as if guided by an unseen hand, plucked out the key. "Aha! Thanks, Pop!"

There had never really been much of anything in the small studio; it had been very modest with white linoleum tile floors and dump-salvaged fixtures and furnishings and thrift store clothes. Continuing to sift and salvage, I went into the structurally undamaged bedroom and office addition where only smoke and heat had left their mark. There were blackened papers and photographs with curled up edges on the table and a soot-covered bed penetrated with particulates and the thiolic smell of smoke. I went through an open box of photos and letters and found one sheet of paper with blackened edges and obscured lettering:

> No matter where; of comfort no man speak:
> Let's talk of graves, of worms, and epitaphs
> Make dust our paper with rainy eyes
> Write sorrow on the bosum of the earth,
> Let's choose executors and talk of wills:
> And yet not so, for what can we bequeath
> Save our deposed bodies to the ground?
> Our lands, our lives and all are Bolingbroke's,
> And nothing can we call our own but death

And that small model of the barren earth
Which serves as paste and cover to our bones.
For God's sake, let us sit upon the ground
And tell sad stories of the death of kings;
How some have been deposed; some slain in war,
Some haunted by the ghosts they have deposed;
Some poison'd by their wives: some sleeping kill'd;
All murder'd: for within the hollow crown
That rounds the mortal temples of a king
Keeps Death his court and there the antic sits,
Scoffing his state and grinning at his pomp
Allowing him a breath, a little scene,
To monarchize, be fear'd and kill with looks,
Infusing him with self and vain conceit,
As if this flesh which walls about our life,
Were brass impregnable, and humour'd thus
Comes at the last and with a little pin
Bores through his castle wall, and farewell king!
Cover your heads and mock not flesh and blood
With solemn reverence: throw away respect,
Tradition, form and ceremonious duty,
For you have mistook me all this while
I live with bread like you, feel want,
Taste grief, need friends: subjected thus,
How can you say to me, I am a king?

Richard II

The absurd grandiosity, the laughably unbelievable synchronicity of this find shocked me into exclaiming, "Oh, c'mon, Pop! Fuck you! Blow *me*, you fucker!"

Down in the old house two weeks later we held a memorial supper which my father, according to the six youthful friends present, had meant to be a Socratic farewell dinner party of his own design with him in attendance after which he was to consume his pills, like Hemlock, before permanently retiring to bed. His more untimely departure, however, required that we leave an empty chair and place setting for the old Elijah at the head of the table. It was a joyful yet dignified affair. Among those in attendance was a woman, Cheryl Little, whom I had only briefly met once before. Cheryl, my father told me, was the daughter of my father's illegitimate and now deceased son Victor Little whom he had sired with his long ago lover Sonya Little of Bound Brook Island north of downtown. This made her my half-niece and earned her the invitation to the table. She was a drummer in a rock 'n roll band called Jalopenia that sometimes played at The Tavern, a Wellfleet establishment owned and operated by my father's friends Reed and Florence Maynard, also at the table, and where my father regularly caroused and was served rare "Steak Vincenté." Suffice it to say the rest of the guests, Dennis Conlin, Reed's's brother Dick, Rose and Marcel, and the Tavern chef/waiter clad in black, were all, loosely speaking and without condemnation, intelligent and loyal free-spirited Wellfleetians, most of them so psychologically dissected by my father with great charm and ferocity, so coddled and maneuvered into the relationship as to have no choice but to be enamored of the vigorous old goat with his flashing eyes and floating hair in his Pleasure Dome studio. It had been his unconventional, boundary-crashing, vocalized insights and behavior often infused with drink and a lifetime of examining human behavior through his writing which enabled an unleashing, a liberation of pent-up feeling and restrained behavior in those people who chose to be in his circle. For this small cadre the resultant friendship had been real.

The morning sun shone brightly over the marsh which stretched out toward Lieutenant's Island and the bay beyond, broad and flat like the verdant deck of a great aircraft carrier in port, nestled between pitch pine woods and my hilltop vantage point. It was teeming with activity. The incoming tide was beginning to fill the channels cut into the marsh's surface and overflow their banks. Screeching heron, hungry, squawking ducks, and gulls soared in broad arcs and swept in for landings, either to swim on the widening glass or to alight on remaining drier island tufts of grass. Atop a ladder leaning against the gray facade of the studio carcass above the sliders, I finished painting in large, uneven yellow letters, "MAN GOES TO HIS LONG HOME AND THE MOURNERS GO ABOUT IN THE STREET. BON VOYAGE, POP."

My brother Josh walked up the sandy road from the old house, carrying my father in the cardboard box with Sushi in a plastic jar atop it. Grace, now six, followed, dressed in a pretty funeral dress sprinkled with lavender violets. Kate walked a few steps behind with a boom box. Grace climbed into the front seat of the old white Chrysler and sat between me and Josh. The car with recently inflated tires and a new battery installed, smelled of mold and dust. Streams of red, yellow, blue, orange, and green crepe paper adorned the fenders and antenna. Kate settled into the back. Josh offered me a toke on a joint, and I declined. He was happily higher than a kite, yet seemingly in full control. A staved-in muffler rumbled with the twist of the key and I pressed the drive button on the futuristic emerald green dashboard, which at the slightest touch shed sun-baked vinyl flakes like scabs, and we rolled down the drive to Lieutenant's Island Road. Other decorated cars and trucks were lined up for a half mile up and down the road. We proceeded to the head of the line at Route 6, passing a pickup, manned by Marty White, one of my father's mentees who had been under the paternal wing, put through college, fondled in bed, and placed in a successful lobster-in-the-rough business. He was ultimately alienated by my father's alcohol-fueled, narcissistically domineering and possessive intrusiveness. The truck's cargo bed contained a large emblazoned banner held up by Marty's partner: BY THE CIGARS THEY SMOKE, AND THE COMPOSERS THEY LOVE, YE SHALL

KNOW THE TEXTURE OF MEN'S SOULS. JOHN GALSWORTHY. Pavrotti sang "La Donne Mobile" from a loudspeaker mounted on the truck's roof, and the parade of vehicles slowly eased out onto Route 6, where a Wellfleet police officer stopped traffic for us in both directions. A half mile toward town we entered the South Wellfleet Cemetery.

I had called Ken Cole, the keeper of the cemetery records, and asked him to mark out the boundaries of the plot my father was to share with his deceased sister Tanya, a respected labor economist with whom he had always claimed with relish to have had an incestuous relationship. Alas, he also had to share the ground with Tanya's second husband Wendell, a closeted consumer of vast quantities of cheap sherry, an uncomfortable retired psychology professor with hidden lust for young girls. My father had despised Wendell no less than the first husband Iago, another "intolerable narcissist of the highest order," he had said, calling the kettle black.

Old family friends gathered around the grave site, my father's first cousin Myron Lipschitz, a Wellfleet painter, and his wife Anne; Max and Sheila Bronstein, friends who had rented the old house in the early 60's and then moved to Wellfleet; the Gotliebs, Abe and Evelyn; my cousins Nathan Haberman, son of my father's sister Tanya, and his wife Pam from down Lieutenant's Island Road and their sons Sam and Zach, and daughters, Rachael, Ruth, and Nina, and my cousin Sasha, daughter of Tanya and sister of Nathan, and her two sons Levi and Ezra all stood in a circle surrounding the space. As my brother Josh and I ambled to our place at the top of the burial plot, Cousin Nathan, a child psychiatrist, stopped us to offer good-humored condolences, saying, "I don't know how you boys survived him; it's a miracle." We laughed. Nearby stood my friend Paul and his son Ben from Maine, friends Chris and Gini and their son Chip from New Hampshire, Stan and Deirdre, both therapist friends from Brewster, and Chuck Meyer who was a high school classmate of Robert's and who had been guided through late adolescent turmoil by my father. Even my mother had flown in for the day. My oldest brother Robert, however, had been too compulsively consumed with work as a psychiatrist down at Roosevelt Hospital in Manhattan and perhaps too awkward, defended, or simply indifferent to stop, make the trip, and feel anything, though his first of now three wives, Irene and my niece Melanie, did drive up from New York to pay their respects and maintain a tenuous fragment of needed family connection. Many other people whom I did not know gathered around. Barefoot children scurried here and there, watched over by unidentified mothers in long swirling skirts and flowers in their hair. Shaggy young men with beards and beads meandered about.

Josh and I took turns digging a three-foot deep hole through the bearberry down into the soft sand. We placed the cardboard box of my father and the plastic jar of Sushi in the hole. I then thanked the gathered friends and family for coming to say goodbye and took a half pint bottle of Courvoisier out of my back jean pocket, raised it high, and proposed a toast of thanks and farewell to my father. Little Grace, who stood at my side, looked up at me with wondering, serious eyes while Kate held us in her gaze nearby. Josh and I took lusty swigs of the cognac and poured the remaining libation into the hole. Old Abe Gotlieb played a mournful jazz improvisation on his tarnished ancient saxophone after which Rose's rotund sister Pauline stepped forward and belted out an off-key rendition of the Negro spiritual "Oh Freedom". She then placed a small package of pot brownies in the hole. Josh and I each shook out a shovelful of sand into the hole, and I invited the assembly to step forward, if they wished, one by one and do the same. As the hole filled with sand, Pavrotti sang out "Nessun Dorma" from the boom box, and it was done.

Two days later I received a phone call. "Hello, Mr. Perlman? This is Glenn Mason. I believe you buried your father in my plot."

"Really?"

"Yes."

"But it was marked off."

"Incorrectly, I'm afraid."

"May I buy it from you?"

"I'm afraid not. I'm very fond of the bearberry there."

That same day I returned to the cemetery with my boom box, dug up Sushi and my father and placed them with the brownies in a new hole much closer to my Aunt Tanya and Uncle Wendell. I made one more libation, filled in the hole, and polished off the remaining cognac. Now it was done ... so I thought.

Ten

MOURNING ABOUT
IN THE STREET

Murmurations of snow dipped and swirled outside the old, un-insulated house. Built in the early 18th Century, the summer Cape cottage had had few upgrades through the years. Inside, the plank floors sloped; the refrigerator was prevented from falling through the floor by a piece of plywood; the kitchen sink drained into a drywell a few feet off the back; plaster fell down onto the living room floor from the lath. Plastic over the rotting, small living room window billowed, then quietly snapped back as frigid night air gusted up from the marsh through the cracks. On my knees I plunged a small shovel into the scuttle, tossed another layer of coal into the stove, and took a long drag of smoke off one of my father's remaining Partagas cigars. He had been dead for seven months.

My breathing was constricted, asthmatic. I tossed the soggy cigar stub onto the small orange flames beginning to lick up through the bed of soft black rock, closed the stove door, and opened the vents. Taking an esophagus burning swill from an Old Smuggler bottle, I then lay in front of the stove, waited for warmth to fill the room, and fell deeply asleep.

Some time later I was enveloped by a blanket of penetrating heat. When I opened my eyes the steel plating of the stove glowed an alarming orange. Closing the vents, I got up and sat in the wing chair and waited to see if the dry, brittle-boned house would burst into flames from the overheated chimney.

Drinking had become dangerous. The absurdity of another possible death by fire amused me in a dark sort of fashion, as did the dramatic absurdity of my father's death and his oxygen consuming, impressive life.

With a clipped, sardonic snort I chuckled. Sitting in his living room in his chair in his rotting old house in that dark hollow with brow damp from the subsiding heat, I pondered how this finally inherited property could ever honestly be mine. I was ruminating and building upon an already established case of blame against him for most, if not all, of my perceived shortcomings and feelings of failure, unwittingly fortifying a wall between me and the inherited land upon which I had now brought my wife and six–year-old daughter to live. Ungrateful shithead, I thought of myself. Fuck him, I thought of my father.

In this ongoing struggle I gave him too much—too much love, admiration, deference, and self-abasement—as I always had from my earliest days in hope of some elusive, ever receding communion, a stupid torture too deep and familiar to let go. And from this insufferability I had acquired any number of avenues of escape.

So on it went, into our new life on Cape Cod.

However, all was not droning misery and drink. Before long I did do some time with a changing cast of Cannery Row characters in a small AA group down the road which met in the back of a dark heavy equipment garage. On snowy Tuesday evenings a small group of us—a truck driver, the garage owner whose specialty was building rock sea walls, a fisherman, an unemployed man recently released from jail—would gather, seated in a semi-circle around a log fire built in a stove fabricated out of two welded together fifty-five-gallon drums opposite the towering presence of a massive, ten-wheel Kenworth dump truck hood. The men in the ghostly dancing shadows were welcoming and nonjudgmental. They shared their tales of devastating disaster and loss far worse, I thought, than my experience, and I found identifying with their falls from grace difficult. Coming from privilege I didn't really think I was one of them. My brother

Josh had often said, "Our family is a strange mix of English aristocracy and field nigger." I'm not sure if it were the former, the latter, or the confusing mixture of the two, which most made me feel outcast, but as an outcast I did feel I had something in common with the other men. And the theatricality of the setting and my longtime romanticizing of the down and out, the "tempest-tost" and "wretched of the earth," helped ease me into their company. Any which way, I felt shame and embarrassment, and I didn't share that.

After settling up with my father's insurance company, claiming not only the total loss of his "studio" house but also every conceivable content item including two prosthetic legs and a walker, Kate and I made plans in late spring for a new house on the hill to replace the burned-out carcass, which had been carted away not long after the fire. It would be located about seventy-five yards from the studio's previous location, leaving his undamaged lap pool and adjacent deck intact.

Two years after the fire and following another harsh winter in which we burned five tons of coal to heat the old house down in the hollow, we moved into a small, stout Cape house with heavy beam ceilings, nine-over-six-pane cottage windows to echo the ones in the hollow, cedar trim and siding, a red cedar shake roof, and a porch with a long view of the marsh below extending out to Lieutenant's Island, Wellfleet Bay, Great Island, and Cape Cod Bay in the distance. It had the look of an old farmhouse with the feel of a wooden ship.

While working on our house as a laborer with limited carpentry skills, I had become friends with our builder Jan Holzmann and his convivial crew, including Dick Maynard and David Knight, both of whom had been friends with my father. Because of that prior friendship, I unfortunately felt the disturbances in my relationship with my father transferred onto and inhibiting my interactions with these and other men, an isolating loss for me which kept me lonely. My father kept lingering around my consciousness, not quite allowing me to fully appreciate the beauty and bounty of my new circumstances. Whether he was doing the lingering or I was choosing to allow for the lingering was a distinction I found increasingly more difficult to discern. The ongoing agitation made me feel weak and uncomfortable, a victim of a chronic illness. Still, Kate, Grace, and I continued to move forward with our lives.

In September I took a job as a school bus driver for Lower Cape Bus and Taxi in North Truro. Also, Jan and I built a small writing shed, eight by ten feet with insulation and electric heat, in a grove of pine trees not far from the house. There I was able to write, or at least try, between morning and afternoon school bus runs.

Kate, who had worked as a school guidance counselor in New Hampshire and was also licensed as a family therapist, now took a psychotherapist job working for a social service agency. Grace was ensconced at Wellfleet Elementary, and mostly for her benefit we joined the UU Church, first in

Provincetown, then in Brewster. First Parish Brewster had a well-attended progressive Sunday school, religious in a sort of pagan UU way. We were pleased to find that the church also had a kind, unassuming minister, the Reverend Jim Robinson, whose gentle qualities of maleness I was unaccustomed to. He was also shy. I felt drawn to him and his eclectic approach to a spiritual life grounded in love without dogma or strict adherence to any particular narrative. We began to attend services regularly and participate in the "paraministry" service work of the church. I visited the elderly, delivered lunches for the Provincetown AIDS Support Group, and for a time I visited a stranger doing time in Barnstable County Jail.

Community theater also became an avocation for me. When in New Hampshire working as a teacher, I had been recruited to perform several roles in school musicals, such as King Arthur in *Camelot* and Horace Vandergelder in *Hello Dolly*. I rekindled my interest in performing and regained some confidence in my ability. In each of my own four high school years I had been in plays and been President of the Drama Club in my senior year. My father, who was a playwright of some note and a one-time actor, attended none of my performances then, except my last. When I asked what he thought of my performance, he replied, "Not much. You'll never be an actor."

Nevertheless, once settled into our new house, I began to pursue acting roles again, and I landed a number of leading roles in the ensuing years. My acting was not only relief from recurrent bouts of negative thinking and depression; it was strong push back against my father's hardwired critical voice in my head. I was able to experience freedom from his domination. The better my performances, often in well-received, gritty and powerful male roles, including Eddie Carbone and Joe Keller, the more I felt I was sticking it to him. After all, hadn't he referred to me at one time or another as a weak person? "This one's for you, Pop," I often said to myself before making my first entrances onto the stage. Still, if acting gave me feelings of competence and power, its ability to extricate me from the burden of this tiresome father–son dance was short-lived.

How I would resolve, shed, or finally outgrow my obsessive attachment to the paternal shadow I did not know. I had been in and out of therapy for many years hashing out my issues since high school. I had drunk and tried drugs to escape them; I had meditated beginning with my $35 Transcendental Meditation mantra purchased from the Cornelia Street TM center in Greenwich Village; I had run away from college in Madison, Wisconsin, which was in anti-war upheaval in the late 60's, to a Vermont hippie commune from which I soon thereafter fled after being repeatedly propositioned for anal sex by a grizzly former Hell's Angel twenty years my senior. I had then lived unhappily with a girl in a cheap apartment on Union Street in Brooklyn, better, I reasoned, than unwanted rear-end penetration; I worked the overnight shift for M and S Maintenance Corporation on Bergen and 4th driving taxi and would walk home at four in the morning along the dark and silent street, anxiety-ridden and desolate with no direction, passing 19th Century abandoned one and two story brick workshops, warehouses, and pocket-sized factories long out of business. Suddenly my loneliness might be broken by the fang-bearing growl and bark of a vicious junkyard dog guarding a scrap metal establishment alongside the oil-slicked Gowanis Canal.

When driving a cab became too stressful and I found myself getting lost and panicked in neighborhoods I knew, I switched jobs to the less hectic position of hansom cab driver across from the Plaza Hotel. The work was expressive of my lost condition, far beneath the expectations of my elite private school breeding, fancifully romantic in my ragged top hat with protruding plastic yellow flowers. I drank Old Crow with the homeless residing in the park or with the other drivers, while watching the parade of both the mentally ill panhandling or proclaiming the end of the world and the rich in mink stoles spilling out of the hotel into limousines. This job, I dreamed, my father would approve of and find amusing for its originality and eccentricity, plus I benefitted from moments more intimate with my horse than were shared with my girlfriend in Brooklyn. Finally, in midsummer of 1971 when I read Arthur Janov's *The Primal Scream: The Cure for Neurosis*, I left my girlfriend and headed to California for the cure. There I wound up meeting and living with my future wife and spending nine years in my twenties in what evolved into a calamitous psychotherapy cult, The Center for Dynamic Living, founded by former Janov followers. The day after the cult collapsed in 1980 (amidst that slew of sensational *Live on Eyewitness News* reports spewing "Cult of Torment" headliners, followed by the most litigious case of psychotherapy malpractice in California history) I married Kate in a ceremony preplanned months before. I became certified as a public school social studies teacher. I took Prozac, canceling its effectiveness with alcohol. I pursued teaching Passamaquoddy Indians in remote Calais, Maine on the New Brunswick border for a year and then moved to New Hampshire where I taught 8th grade social studies and obtained a master's degree from Dartmouth College in an inexpensive program for public school teachers. I also worked part-time as a waiter and a Dead River oil truck driver; back in my new life on Cape Cod I spent five years writing a novella to work out my obsession with a seventeen-year-old girl who had played Guinevere opposite me as Arthur in *Camelot*. I did several Vipassana Buddhists retreats to counter my agitation; I nurtured a long, infatuated friendship, infused with rich but restrained sexual fantasies and a genuine underlying love with another young, wounded and at times seriously depressed woman, a former 8th grade student of mine, and with whom my most fervent hope was to heal her suffering in some heroic and well-meaning manner, paternal and Arthurian. Thus I would transmit to her what

I most needed, redemption and rescue from a floundering morass of dead-end searching concurrent with a bolstering of ego and a tamping down of rising libidinous impulses. Beneath my rationalizations to the contrary, I knew in the long run I was a mishmash of failed attempts at mature and well-individuated identity formation. The ever-changing variety of my experiences lent my competing, narcissistic self-images an air of artistic, over-the-hill Bildungsroman-esque questing and eccentricity, not unlike my father in some respects, I hopefully imagined, but without the merit of his widely-recognized, remunerative, and substantial achievements. Hadn't he always pontificated, "Achievement is the measure of man"? Fending off defeat with every passing year, I felt more hollow, less able to carry the weight of my wandering delusions. A true descendentalist, a wallower in my own shit, I labeled myself with a smirk, disdainful of ever transcending my misery.

Eleven

SEVEN EAGLE FEATHERS
(PART I)
INITIATION

One Sunday morning in our fourth year back on the Cape our U.U church hosted a service by a Lakota Sioux couple, Sonny and Elayne Reyna. They were Sun Dancers, practitioners of a traditional healing and devotional ceremony with sacred drumming, praying with the sacred pipe and its kinnikinic smoke, fasting, and ceremonial piercing of the skin. This was offered in the spirit of personal sacrifice as one prayer for the benefit of one's family, community, and Mother Earth. The Sun Dance, preceded by a long fast, purifying sweat lodges, and a Vision Quest or Hembleciya (the Lakota word for "Crying for a Dream"), resonated with the particular extremist tendencies within my psyche and its perceived needs and fantasies.

Sonny and Elayne had been invited to the church by a parishioner, Mark Schofield, who was a successful massage therapist and proponent of earth-based, cosmically aligned, and energy-oriented New Age remedies laced with Wicca and white wannabe-Native outlooks particularly prevalent in the 90's.

In their Sunday service Sonny and Elayne shared the purpose of their visit, saying that just as the genocide of Native peoples had spread across Turtle Island from the East to the West, now, in this moment of the prophesized Earth Changes, was the time for healing and reconciliation to begin with the People of the First Light, the Wampanoag of Cape Cod and for that healing and reconciliation to spread westward to other indigenous peoples across the land to the West. They charged the church, a predominantly white congregation, with initiating this process. In support of their charge they shared the One Earth One People Peace Vision, a prayer which had come to Elayne, also known as Bluebird, by Great Spirit:

We are One people on One Earth.
All life is sacred. The Earth is sacred.
We cherish and protect
Our Mother Earth, Father Sky, and Sacred Waters.
The Generations of Humankind from the Four Directions

Must live in harmony and balance
With each other and all living things.
We are all related.
We respect and honor the Sacredness of all Life and all
Creation
So Seven Generations from each Generation,
Unborn future Generations, will live.
Seven Eagle Feathers represent future Generations and
Sacred Ceremonies.
They carry our Prayer to Creator.
We pray that Mother Earth and all of her Children will
live.
It is One Prayer:
Peace

After the service I walked with Sonny along with four or five other willing male parishioners through the woods to the bank of a very large, open cranberry bog. Here on the ground beneath the warm sun and blue sky we sat in a circle. Reaching into his satchel, Sonny removed a pearlescent abalone shell with a handful of dried white sage cradled in it. He set the sage afire, extinguished the flames with a breath and gently blew on the embers, making clouds of fragrant smoke. He told us the smoke was the awakening doorway into the world of Great Spirit and our ancestors who are always with us, that it cleansed our bodies and spirit, and helped clarify our prayerful intentions. He passed the shell around the circle, allowing the smoke to wash over each of us. When the shell came back around to him, he placed it on the ground. "It is a good day," he said. He then instructed each of us use our hands to dig our own individual holes in the sandy ground. With the help of Great Spirit we were to pour our suffering and grievances into our holes while asking Mother Earth to heal us. After raking away pine needles with my fingers and digging with a stick, I listened with some discomfort while Sonny cried out to Great Spirit in his native tongue. Leaning over their openings to the earth, other members of our circle began to cry out as well. Reluctantly I followed suit, but I was secretly embarrassed and toyed with leaving.

The moment was not unlike when I was twelve years old and a friend had dared me to go to confession at St. Ignatius Loyola Catholic Church in New York City. Not being Catholic, I hadn't a clue what to say in the confessional, but my friend instructed me with the "Bless me, Father, for I have sinned" part. I went into the confessional booth and listed some innocuous, fabricated sins for the priest behind the screen who then instructed me to say the Confiteor, Hail Marys, or some such things I didn't know. I mumbled my way through with some gibberish, then fled the booth and the church, laughing with my friend outside on the street. Even so, beneath my silliness there was a yearning.

Now in this circle with Sonny I felt that old, long hunger, and I wanted to participate with respect. His generous welcome into the animistic realm required, like most religions, a suspension of my reasonable skepticism, and it offered an inviting spiritual connection with the earth sifting through my fingers, the insects therein, the birds flying overhead, the wind soughing through the trees, the salty moist fragrance of the ocean in the air. The unfamiliar action of ritual held out the possibility of supplanting the all-too-familiar run of my dark thoughts with an unfolding consciousness of Great Spirit or God manifest in the mysterious yet tangible reality of nature. In spite of its awkwardness, the moment felt worthwhile, even exciting. Sonny was, after all, the real thing, a Sun Dancer no less, not some character in a cowboy and Indian western movie or TV show. Who better than he could teach and advise me? "The earth and all of nature are so obviously more vast and mysterious than myself," I thought. "No doubt about that." When we concluded our ceremony a hawk circled above and cried out repeatedly, and Sonny said, "The hawk, he approves."

Not long after Sonny and Elayne's visit, a few of us UU parishioners formed the One Earth One People Committee and eagerly had one of our representatives contact the Mashpee Wampanoag Tribal Council to see how we might achieve some reconciliation and be of help for all the injustices laid down by the white people. It was reported back to us that rather than offer some patronizing white liberal excuse for alleviating our own guilt, it would do us well to look at our own racism for at least a year before beginning a conversation with the tribe. Maybe that would prevent us from inevitably crossing the boundary of wanting to be Indian ourselves out there on the Plains, living in teepees, stealing their prayers, ceremonies, and culture while shopping for dreamcatchers and moccasins at Walmart and scouring our ancestry for a smidgen of native blood.

A bit humbled by this, our first encounter almost four hundred years after that initial encounter with "savages" on a bay beach in Eastham, we went to Reverend Robinson to discuss what to do. Over the next year we and many members of the congregation would begin an in-depth process in study circles and workshops of learning about personal and institutional racism, white privilege, and their manifestations in history. Acknowledging my own racism, which of course I thought I was free of, reminded me at times of Chairman Mao's ordering of self-criticism, confession, and reeducation during the Cultural Revolution. I was defensive and sensitive from the thought reform and abuse I had experienced as a former psychotherapy cult member. Some of our best friends were people of color, many of us said or felt. Nevertheless, we realized there is no escaping the poison of racism intrinsic to our culture and in which we white Americans are so steeped. I acknowledged my own and dubbed myself a recovering racist.

In the meantime back in the privacy of my writing shed, before going to bed I began to regularly say out loud the One Earth One People Peace Prayer by candlelight. I bought a Native American hand drum and sometimes beat it while I said the prayer. I bought a bag full of dried California white sage and smudged myself and the shed with smoke every night before vocalizing my prayers.

After a snowstorm one morning several months later, I awoke and gazed out through our bedroom sliders down into the marsh below. On a not-too-distant snow-covered knoll, rising slightly above the surrounding expanse of white, I noticed a large bird. At first glance I thought it was a red-tailed hawk, eating and pulling away at something. I then noticed what appeared to be a white head on a black body. With pounding heart I quickly grabbed my binoculars and looked through them.

"My god!" I shouted, "I think it's a bald eagle! Kate, call Audubon! Ask them! I see its boots! It is! It is! It's a bald eagle!" I had never in my almost fifty years in Wellfleet seen a bald eagle here.

Kate came into the bedroom. I passed her the binoculars and she, too, bubbled over with exclamations of joy. She hustled out to the kitchen phone.

Crows circled wildly above the knoll and I could hear their raucous cries through the glass. "Audubon says it's an eagle!" Kate called out from the kitchen. "It's here with its immature offspring!"

At that moment a grayish brown eagle swooped down from a tree at the marsh's edge and joined its parent. Together they tore at something with their talons and beaks, indifferent to the cawing cacophony above them. In a few moments they spread their wings, and beating them as if in slow motion, they rose through the crows and majestically wheeled up over the marsh and passed out of sight.

I dressed quickly and went outside down to the marsh. A strong, cold wind was blowing in off the bay. Trudging across the snow, I arrived at the knoll where still a few crows circled overhead. I raised my arms and jumped up and down around the knoll, crying out grateful yelps and howls of praise to the eagles and the crows and Mother Earth for the visitation of these great raptors.

I noticed that all around the knoll and downwind of it small black feathers were strewn. Thinking the eagle must have killed a black duck or possibly a crow, I began picking the feathers up and stuffing them into my pockets. "May your prayers be as prey of the eagle and be carried to Creator," I mumbled, recalling the One Earth One People prayer. Adding to my excitement, I happily fantasized giving away these black feathers to friends.

"It'd be incredible if I found an eagle feather," I thought as I scanned the knoll from side to side. I stepped up to the knoll's most elevated spot. Directly below me and before my feet, I came upon a large fish head within a blood-soaked, shallow depression of snow. While gazing upon the head, trying to intuit its meaning, something slowly came into focus through the translucent layer of thin, crimson snow and ice surrounding the head—the faint outline of a white feather. I knelt down and pawed away the snow with my fingers, revealing not one or two more white feathers, but five in all.

"Whoa!" I softly gasped. "Great Eagle, you have left five feathers!" I lay them in the palm of my hand, carefully tucking them under my thumb. Once again, I cried out, "Thank you, Great Eagle! Thank you, Father Sky and Mother Earth and Crow!"

That evening in my writing shed, while again giving thanks, praying, and enthusiastically pounding away on my hand drum amidst clouds of sage smoke, I paused at the words "Seven Eagle Feathers represent future Generations and Sacred Ceremonies. They carry our prayer to Creator."

"Seven eagle feathers," I repeated to myself. "There must be two more."

The following morning under a gleaming sun I walked back across the snow to the knoll. Within seconds I found the two missing white feathers. Seven feathers had come to me. Back in my shed I placed them in a leaded glass box on a bed of cedar sprigs and sage to which I would later add kernels of corn, tobacco, and rose quartz. From this point on when I said the One Earth One People Prayer I would open and hold the box aloft when mentioning Seven Eagle Feathers.

My immersion into the magic of creation and all things Native was just beginning, and my eight by ten foot writing shed became a focal point for transforming and deepening my relationship with the natural world. I began to refer to it as my hut. Shingled in white and red cedar, it is very conducive to prayer, meditation, or anything else of a private or intimate nature. A formidable building with electric heat and insulation in the walls, floor, and above the low beamed ceiling, it also has a built-in bed with a cot-size mattress covered in sage green velvet, book shelves, a yellow pine board floor, and three windows. One of the windows is an antique American stained and jeweled glass depiction of a wild rose, passed down to me from my maternal grandfather whose ancestors are all Massachusetts descendants of 17th Century Puritan colonists. The window casts a soft rainbow hue during the day.

Initially I felt the building had a magical, Hansel and Gretel quality to it, as if you had just happened upon it in a dark mossy forest of towering trees. Soon the Brothers Grimm quality was subsumed within a Black Elk Native American aura, and eventually the space would draw on the mystical aspects of all the world's religions, becoming a cross-cultural shamanic spirit lodge. But for now the Native American quality prevailed and became even more pronounced, as the building began to acquire the characteristics of a prayer lodge—permeated with the scent of sage, tobacco, lavender and rose oil; festooned around its upper walls with colorful bittersweet vine; filled with the pleasing strains of Carlos Nakai's flute and the soft piano of Peter Kater; adorned with feathers, rocks, minerals, crystals, animal bones, pelts and fetishes each with their own vibrational energy and medicine; and imbued with the presence of spirit guides of an animal, human, angel, Ascended Master, or something of an amorphous nature. With a slowly emerging consciousness I was realizing that all life is mystery, that it is something which I did not create; it is within me as well as around me, and inseparable.

Other people, events, and books such as *Animal Speak*, *The Way of the Shaman*, and *Black Elk Speaks* drew me further into the Native American spiritual way of understanding and communing with nature, its spirit manifestations, and its Creator. A friend invited me to participate in a Wednesday evening prayer circle, attended primarily by women, around a fire pit on a small herb farm in Harwich owned by a woman named Patti Devereaux. There I learned to call in the Four Directions of the Native American Medicine Wheel and received my power animal from one of the participants.

A power animal is a mammal, bird, insect, or any creature whose spirit and character traits act as a protective guide for a person. The power animal given to me was Dolphin, and it wasn't long before I had a leaping dolphin tattooed on my bicep within a hoop from which hung seven eagle feathers. I placed dolphin bones and a dolphin skull found on the beach in my hut. I recalled once walking naked on the deserted Maguire's Landing Beach in October in my twenty-first year and finding a young dolphin rolling lifeless and spinning round and round in the curling Atlantic combers. I waded then into the water, laid the animal across my extended forearms, and carried it a half mile along the beach, the surf hissing around my ankles, before gently placing it back in the water. Due to this small act of honoring the life of the dolphin, I imagined its spirit had returned and was offering to be my power animal. I bought tiny glass dolphins from a shop in Provincetown and gave them to friends and visitors after sharing the One Earth One People Peace Prayer with them.

On a number of occasions the owner of the herb farm and leader of the prayer circle invited another Sun Dancer named Miguel, born of assimilated Raramuri parents in Mexico, to guide us in building, in a sacred manner, a sweat lodge out of overarching saplings and draped in many layers of blankets. Several times I was asked to be Firekeeper, which meant that in the afternoon I tended the fire and heated the Grandfathers, soccer ball-size, terminal moraine rocks carried and pushed southward by the mammoth glacier which had formed Cape Cod. Participants brought these rocks from various beaches to the sweat lodge.

On one such occasion we gathered after dark without clothes inside the pitch black lodge with drums or other instruments for prayer, seated ourselves in a twelve-foot-diameter circle around the perimeter of the space and Miguel cried out, "Firekeeper! Bring in the Grandfathers!"

Opening a blanket flap and with a spade shovel in hand, I ventured out to the pit and carefully carried five or six red hot rocks one at a time on the spade back inside the lodge to place them in another pit located in the center of the lodge. With each rock carried in Miguel exhorted us, "Welcome the Grandfather!" and we loudly responded, "Welcome, Grandfather!"

He then poured several ladle-full quantities of water on the orange glowing orbs radiating the power of fire and ancestral spirit from within. The water violently hissed and spat, quickly transforming into unseen clouds of hot steam. The temperature in the lodge quickly rose and Miguel cried out in his indigenous tongue and encouraged us to cry out while beating on our drums. He then threw small handfuls of copal, sage, and lavender onto the glowing rocks and sweet, earthy fragrances filled the darkness and mingled with the smell of our sweat, while our shouts, improvised songs, chanting, and the din of our drumming all coursed through our bodies and the blackness.

Again water sizzled on the rocks and the heat intensified. Some of the participants had to lie down on the cooler ground to avoid a near scalding at the higher levels within the lodge. Those who could stayed seated and combined their heated pain with corresponding devotional enthusiasm for Great Spirit, the healing of Mother Earth, self and others, or for some psychic expiation and forgiveness of personal or collective sins and wrongdoing.

In the months following the eagles' visit my relationship with the natural world became more animated both during my waking hours and in my dreams. Miguel had taught me to never remove anything—a rock, a feather, a bough of cedar—from Mother Earth or from her creatures without prayerfully asking permission of the object, for all such objects were sacred objects imbued with their own spirit. If I intuited an affirmative answer, I was to leave a few strands of my hair or some corn meal, as a reciprocating offering of respect. I soon found myself in communication with trees, birds, insects, squirrels, and all living things. Miguel told me that he saw in a vision a white owl around my head, and eventually during periods of evening prayer in my hut, the white owl rested on my left shoulder; a skunk, whose medicine was respect and right balance of sexual energy, rested on my right shoulder; a wild turkey, whose medicine was generous giving, stood below; a buffalo within my heart taught me right prayer and action leading to an abundance of Spirit; and a dolphin, sometimes a pod of dolphins, swam round and around me, while overhead an eagle circled. A distinction between the "real" and the imagined or imaginal realm was disappearing.

One evening after my prayers I stood outside my hut among the pine trees. I heard two great horned owls calling to one another, their hoots echoing in the dark woods. One voice seemed to come from down behind the old house in the hollow near the marsh. The other voice was coming from somewhere atop the hill where my father's studio dwelling had stood before the fire had consumed it. I stepped into the sandy driveway and began slowly walking down toward the old house while calling to the owls with my own soft hoots. In a moment, out of the darkness a breath of air whooshed over my head, passing down the driveway ahead of me in the form of a broad-winged silhouette darker than the night around me. My heart quickened and I continued to walk and to call. I came to a rest on the rough lawn in front of the old house. Standing in front of the house alongside the driveway is a sixty-foot-tall cedar tree whose lower boughs drape the ground within the circumference of the twenty-foot-wide circle delineating the tree's lower expanse. Two small boughs protrude into the air at the top of this great tree, resembling the horns of an owl. First one then the other great horned owl alighted between the boughs. With my arms spread wide before me in supplication, I gazed up to them and softly hooted my gratitude for their appearance and for their presence upon the land. After a few moments of mutual acknowledgement I walked slowly back up to the new house on the hill.

That night I had a vivid dream: *I'm slowly walking down the driveway, calling for the owls. Suddenly, out from under the tall cedar tree, a skunk darts across the driveway.* I pondered the meaning of this dream for some time afterward until finally coming across it in one of my books, *Animal Speak*, which stated, "Skunk is the favorite food of great horned owls and their balancing medicine." Not long after this encounter I was able to purchase two skunk pelts from an obscure shop in Provincetown whose proprietor was a mortician and a practitioner of Santaria. The shop contained many unusual objects, including a small crate of 500-year-old buffalo teeth acquired from a standing jump in Alberta. I purchased some of these, as well.

••

I'm not sure how or when I met Frank James, but I believe it was when someone suggested to me that I contact him regarding giving my 5th grade daughter Grace an alternative interpretation of the Thanksgiving story to the standard one of peaceful Indians and Pilgrims sharing a meal at the table of brotherhood. Frank, now retired and in his early seventies, had been the music director at Nauset High School for thirty years and my daughter was learning to play the trumpet. With Grace's instrument in her hand we set out one fall day to Chatham to meet Mr. James. When we arrived at his house a fire engine red Corvette was parked in the driveway. Beneath the rear license plate a bumper sticker proclaimed CUSTER DIED FOR YOUR SINS.

Sitting in Mr. James's kitchen, Grace played a rendition of the Mickey Mouse Club theme song, while Frank, politely listening, sipped a glass of whiskey and smoked a cigarette. 'Not bad" he said, offering a few pointers, "You're getting there."

Short of breath and small in stature, he stood up with some difficulty and reached across the clutter on his kitchen table and grabbed hold of a tape recorder and a cassette.

"This is how you could play someday," he said, inserting the tape into the player. "This is my son playing," he beamed with pride as we listened to the opening first movement of a Mozart trumpet concerto.

"Mr. James, do you think you could tell us about the real Thanksgiving, not the one Grace here is learning about in school?" I asked after the music ended.

"First of all you may call me Frank. Second of all Thanksgiving is a holiday created by the white man to alleviate his guilt about the atrocities committed against native peoples and the theft of their land. It's an institutionalized myth created by Lincoln in 1863. The attitude, the behavior of the white man from the get-go is right there in *Mourt's Relation* where those Pilgrims stole our corn, robbed our graves, and fired upon our people with their guns in Eastham. The plaque there says it all: 'Hostile Indians had their First Encounter' with Bradford and company. Now you tell me who's hostile? Strangers coming onto your land, stealing your food, digging up your graves, then shooting guns at you? Pour me another whiskey, if you'd be so kind." Frank then proceeded to give us a history lesson, personal as well as a broader Native American history and his role in setting the record straight.

Frank, also known as Wamsutta, was an Aquinnah Wampanoag elder and very much an activist. The son of a fisherman, he rose up from poverty, encountering the hurtful obstacles of racism. He recalled how kids had called him "nigger" when growing up. Graduating from the New England Conservatory as a brilliant trumpet player, he was told he would be unable to secure a job with any major orchestra because of his dark skin and segregation. A founder of the United American Indians of New England (UAINE) and the annual National Day of Mourning held in Plymouth, Massachusetts, Frank spent much of his life studying and researching the history of the Wampanoag Nation and the English invasion of New England. Over the years he participated in Native American protests across the United States, including the Trail of Broken Treaties in Washington, DC in which activists took over the Bureau of Indian Affairs building and the Longest Walk from California to Washington, DC.

In addition to his music and activist interests, Frank was also an accomplished artist and craftsman, specializing in scrimshaw, intricate model sailing ships, and painting. Now quite infirm and somewhat housebound, Frank spent most of his days reading, chatting with occasional visitors, and once and a while writing fiery letters to the editor. He smoked too many cigarettes, despite the onset of emphysema. He drank too much and knew it, declaring at the end of our visit, "I'm a bitter man, Leon." He had been considering the pervasiveness of racism and inequality in the world. "And there are no longer any pure-blooded Wampanoag," he added with some despondency. "We're all mixed now." He paused, staring into the distance. "But you keep at it, Grace, and someday you'll get a lot of enjoyment out of that horn of yours. You might even play with the Boston Symphony."

"Thank you very much, Frank. I'd like to come visit you again sometime, if I may."

"You certainly may, Leon. I'd like that."

I came to know Frank as a cantankerous fellow, full of piss and vinegar, not unlike my father. I felt drawn to him. I longed for some mutually respectful friendship of a paternal sort without my interest in earth-based, animistic spirituality coming across to him as Indian wannabeism for which he had nothing but disdain. Therefore, as a "paraminister" for my UU church, a role hidden from Frank entailing a selfless giving back to my community under the guidance of Reverend Jim Robinson, I began a four-year period of bringing a lunch to Frank once a month. We would eat together and talk. Sometimes we made music. He played the guitar and I would play his recorder. I never discussed Native American subjects unless Frank brought them up, which he often did. Frank's unpredictable rants could be angry and passionate with a dangerous aura to them and a potential to be directed at me, qualities not unlike my father's diatribes. But I had become practiced at dodging my father's more hurtful onslaughts and did not, therefore, feel intimidated by Frank. Over time we developed a friendship, and I was able to derive some replenishment for the empty well of yearning I experienced with my father.

I did fear onetime that that replenishment might be jeopardized when I brought Miguel to visit Frank. On an annual visit to the herb farm to lead sweat lodges and do individual sessions meant to heal spiritual wounds and bring one closer to Great Spirit, Miguel had asked to visit any member of the Wampanoag nation. I was reluctant to make an introduction. Miguel, who had kinky, slightly graying hair and did not look particularly Native American (an appearance sure to arouse Frank's suspicions), had committed some transgressions with a few women in individual sessions, namely having sex with them while disguised in the shapeshifted form of an American bison. I knew this "form", as he had wrapped me in his arms in one of my private sessions while breathing heavily, pawing the ground with his foot, and emitting whispered whistles, grunts, and words of an indigenous tongue, all such cues conducive to a surrendering to Great Spirit and possibly to Great Buffalo should he wish to mate. In a later session with Miguel I gave him a skunk pelt to get his libido under control. Along with the fact that Miguel was now in his second of four years of Sundance Ceremony on the Rosebud Reservation and had the scars on his pecks and back to show for it, I allowed that he was in process of redeeming himself for having violated the trust of women. He now even carried the Chanupa or sacred pipe given to him in South Dakota, and he wished to smoke with a representative of the People of the First Light. That person was Frank Wamsutta James.

Frank went after Miguel. "You don't look Indian. What do you want from me? You a wannabe?" he asked, taking a belt from a glass of whiskey. "You sellin' ceremony to white people?"

"No, sir. I come in peace and wish to smoke and pray together." He shared how he had been drawn to South Dakota to participate in the Sun Dance Ceremony.

Frank softened some and the three of us smoked, and I felt privileged and filled with a sense of Spirit, the breath of all existence, as I followed Frank and Miguel's example, drawing on the pipe, dipping it to each of the Four Directions and then slowly twirling it above my head before passing it around our circle. In my unconscious mind and in my heart an unbounded space was opening, inviting me to enter into an accepting and natural world where no being was an outcast, where all things of the earth and the universe—the animals, birds, fish, ancestors, trees, and stars—were imbued with energy and relatedness and could be called into benevolent conversation and infinite communion.

During this time of intensifying mystical involvement and abating parameters of conventional white man's reality, my mother, who was living alone in Bethesda, Maryland and with whom I shared few if any conflicting emotions, suffered a stroke in her eighty-fifth year. In the preceding decade she had remarried a longtime friend and labor journalist from her earliest days of working with the labor, peace, and feminist movements and for the ideals expressed by Socialist Party leader and presidential candidate Norman Thomas. She had been happier than I ever remembered. When her husband passed away, she remained defiantly independent. Now stricken, she had lain on her bathroom floor incapacitated through the night and well into the next morning unable to call for help as her ability to speak and move waned away. She was discovered by a concerned neighbor and transported by ambulance to Washington Hospital.

More medical complications followed and prospects for her recovery were fading. Kate and I decided to have her placed on a Medivac flight to Cape Cod to be near us in what would be her final days.

As she gazed up at me without affect from her Cape Cod Hospital bed, I asked, "Do you know where you are, Mom?"

"Near ... the circle," she murmured through motionless lips in a soft monotone with her patrician Boston accent.

"Oh my god," I thought, "Could she be referring to the cosmological Medicine Wheel? 'Do you mean like the, the Sacred Hoop, the ... u-hum ... the Circle of Life?'" I tentatively queried, feeling a wave of subversive, apostatic foolishness roll through my belly.

She looked at me with leaden, penetrating eyes, which seemed to ask, "Have you lost your mind?"

"The Bourne Circle," she whispered dryly, referring to the traffic rotary at the Bourne Bridge foot of Cape Cod.

Within the next two days her gastro-intestinal system shut down. The doctors considered surgery but felt she would not survive. They recommended "making her comfortable." With Kate and me by her side through the night and an IV morphine drip in her arm, my beloved mother, whose sometimes excessive mothering had countered my father's privations, left this world. It was December 22, 1995.

Soon after that stressful time, Kate, Grace, and I traveled to New Hampshire for a few days of rest with friends in my old stomping ground in the Bristol area.

One afternoon by myself I sought out an old, single-story house with rolled asphalt roofing and waterlogged wooden shingle siding on Route 3A in Bridgewater occupied by two very old sisters. There, in the winters of '88 and '89, working as a Dead River truck driver, I had regularly delivered and pumped kerosene into two outside fifty-five gallon drums which gravity-fed a cook stove. The sisters would invite me in to warm myself and have a cup of tea and a cookie or two. One of the elderly sisters would sit propped up with pillows in a slightly reclined wooden wheelchair with a cane seat and back. Now I hoped to have a brief reunion with a bit of motherly condolence.

As I drove up to the house, a large sign with a blue background and gold letters surrounded by a spray of gold stars and a comet came into view over the snow-covered lawn. It read MORNING STAR ROCKS AND GEMS. Clearly this was not the work of the sisters. I went inside where display cases of rocks and minerals lined the room. Above each case words were written on index cards describing the energetic properties of the rocks or minerals. I felt an affinity for rocks ever since high school when I had taken a geology course. I had also been intrigued by Teilhard de Chardin, the Catholic theologian and geologist, and his conceptions of spiritual evolution within the context of vast distances of geologic time, a context making the human experience infinitesimally small. Rocks held so much more history, a history back to the beginnings of time, the universe, and before, perhaps. I asked a girl behind the register counter about the two sisters and learned they had both died. I then began perusing the display cases and the written descriptions of their contents: "Rose Quartz—Soft vibrations of rose quartz help experience love. The energy of pink carries the universal energy of love"; and "Obsidian—Powerful. Changes negative energy into positive. DO NOT MISUSE."

I picked up a piece of the quartz and held it for a few moments. Then I picked up a larger, baseball-sized piece of obsidian.

"Hmm, might come in handy," I thought. I purchased the obsidian from the girl and left the premises.

Back on the Cape my solitary nightly rituals in my hut had become more vigorous and thorough. Trudging from the house through the snow to my little building in the woods, I first turned up the electric heat. Then I would light and place a softly burning votive candle on the rose window sill, illuminating a white buffalo Zuni fetish on either side of which were other fetishes—a snake, a lizard, a horse, a standing bear and a carrying bear, a turtle, a small wooden statue of St. Francis, a cast lead figurine of an Arthurian knight on horseback, a scrying crystal wrapped in purple velvet and encased within a tiny silver box. High within the wild rose window casing two more fetishes, a golden eagle on the right and a raven on the left were perched on glued-on, nickel-size wooden platforms; another votive candle was lit and placed within a hollowed-out chunk of rose quartz on the desk, and a soft pink glow filled the hut; a candle in the shape of a dolphin shone next to a miniature crèche on the window sill opposite the rose window; and still another candle was placed on the bookcase before new volumes on vibrational medicine and Reiki, beneath postcards of Martin Luther King, Nelson Mandela, Geronimo, tiger-riding Durga, and Krishna.

With soothing strains of Nawang Khechog and Carlos Nakai's playing Tibetan and Native American flute music I would then smudge myself with smoking sage, copal, tobacco, sweetgrass, and lavender lit in an abalone shell. I would then pass the fragrant smoking shell before, over, and under the skunk pelt atop a basket holding a feathered owl wing; I gently blew smoke from the shell onto a heavy silver and gold Navajo ceremonial necklace bearing the ten claws of a once-living bear attached to Mexican fire agate stones with ten mother-of-pearl bear fetishes on top of each stone. High in another corner of the hut I brought the smoke to the pelt once encasing a bobcat's head; and continuing to circle around the feather-adorned hut's interior all things were smudged and the Circle was opened to the spirit of my ancestors and all whose courage and love has made this world a better and more just place. Setting down the abalone shell and picking up the hand drum and mallet stick, I then began to pound a steady beat whose vibration reverberated through the walls of physicality and reached far out into the universe, and I began to call in the Four Directions, facing each in turn as they came.

"Welcome Spirit Keepers of the East, the color Yellow, Rising Sun, the element of Fire, the season of Spring, Golden Eagle! May your light illuminate the dark places in human souls and warm the hearts and bodies of the lonely and cold! Bring us together! Welcome to our Circle! Aho!

"Welcome Spirit Keepers of the South, the color Red, the element of Water, the Summer season, and the source and quality of emotion, welcome Mouse and your medicine of scrutiny and Raven, great shapeshifter! Overturn destructive patterns of thought, help us face our demons and reveal a deeper world of Spirit! Welcome to our Circle! Aho!

"Spirit Keepers of the West, the color Black, the element of Earth, season of Fall, coming darkness, and great Bear! Protect and guide us through our dreams, carry us, if it be your will, along the Red Road, restoring our focus on Great Spirit and standing tall against the dark ones who would cut us down! Welcome to our Circle! Aho!

"Spirit Keepers of the North, the color White, the element of Air, the Winter season, and White Buffalo Calf Woman! Help us and all our Relatives in right prayer and right action! Our hearts cry out! Lift our spirits and join us as One! Welcome to our Circle!

"White Owl on my left! Skunk on my right! Turkey below! Eagle above! Buffalo within! And Dolphin all around! Welcome to our Circle!

"Black Elk! Warriors! Angels, Rabbi Joachim (the dwarf who came to me in a dream)! And John the Cobbler, Maker of Green Shoes (who also came to me in a dream)! Welcome to our Circle!

"We pray for our Mother Earth that she may not be exploited and damaged! We pray for those who are sick and suffering from war, hunger, loneliness, and disease! We pray for our Ancestors and thank them for bringing us forward to this gift of Life, and always we remember (raising aloft the glass box holding the seven white eagle feathers):

We are One people on One Earth.
All life is sacred. The Earth is sacred.
We cherish and protect
Our Mother Earth, Father Sky, and Sacred Waters.
The Generations of Humankind from the Four Directions
Must live in harmony and balance
With each other and all living things.
We are all related.

We respect and honor the Sacredness of all Life and all
Creation
So Seven Generations from each Generation,
Unborn future Generations, will live.
Seven Eagle Feathers represent future Generations and
Sacred Ceremonies.
They carry our Prayer to Creator.
We pray that Mother Earth and all of her Children will
live.
It is One Prayer:
Peace"

And then with only the soft sound of Nakai's flute I would sit
in silent prayer and meditation.

I would place my mother's photograph before me, offering her prayers of peace, gratitude, and well-being. I did this
many times over the ensuing three months and felt obliged
to place my father's photograph before me. But I would feel a
deep discomfort and inability to offer him my prayers. I then
put his photograph away behind some books on the shelf.

Twelve

SEVEN EAGLE FEATHERS (PART II)
CLEANSING

After concluding my ritual one snowy night in mid-March and sitting in prayer and meditation with my mother, I once again set my father's small photograph before me. It was an innocuous picture, sweet really. He was neither posed nor irritated at being caught off guard by the camera. In blue searsucker pants with broad red and white stripes, a rumpled red and white striped shirt (A.I.M. Thrift Store purchases, no doubt), and a western-style kerchief tied around his neck, he looked out with an unusual vulnerability and slumped shoulders, as if asking, "How did this all happen to me, legless with a colostomy bag, old and dying? What a peculiar wonder," he may have been thinking with boy-like, lifelong curiosity. I took a deep breath, sighed, and focused on the image.

Within moments my heart rate quickened and agitating thoughts, like devilish voles, skittered through my mind in contradiction to my peaceful intentions: "You're still here; we're not settled; you've always shat on me, you coercive, twisting son of a bitch; you always set yourself first; it's all about you. FUCK!"

Try as I did, I could not fend off these recurrent mental intrusions. They mocked me, snickered at my spiritual yearnings, as he did, and called me weak.

"If this does not end," I thought in near final exasperation, "I'm done with Cape Cod. Fuck this inheritance shit! To hell with fond childhood memories! Fuck him! There is no going home again. I'm outta here! Where's that fuckin' obsidian?"

I rummaged through a box beneath the hut's built-in bunk and pulled out the rock I had bought in New Hampshire. I set it forcefully in front of his picture and declared, "Get him the fuck out of here! Get him OUT!"

At the end of my school bus run the following morning, I backed the bus seventy-five yards up into my driveway and shut it down. As I stepped off into the snow-covered walkway, I looked up and saw smoke pouring out of the soffit vent in a line straight across the front of my new house. "What the fuck? The house is on FIRE!"

I ran to the front door and threw it open. There was no fire or smoke in the living room. "You fuck, you fuck," I muttered as I went upstairs.

Smoke was drifting out of the tiny bedroom, which also served as an office and Kate's place of meditation. I ran back downstairs, grabbed a fire extinguisher and double-stepped back up to the room. Small flames, oxygenated by the open front door, were beginning to lick the walls as I pulled the trigger lever and swept the baseboard with dry chemical. The extinguisher quickly emptied its contents with little effect on the spreading fire. I ran back downstairs and called the fire department.

"This is Perlman! Leon Perlman! We have another fire right now at our place!" I exclaimed with some embarrassment, this being the third time within the past decade the fire department had been called to our property, for a brush fire, a fatality, and now this. I quickly began to take my paintings off the living room walls and carried them outside along with a couple of photo albums. I put them inside the nearby tool shed, repeatedly thinking, "You fuck, you fuck, I know you did this."

Within minutes I heard the sirens along Route 6 and then their engines heading down my road. I ran out to the school bus and backed it to a spot beyond the far side of the frozen-over lap pool which remained intact after my father's studio fire. A pumper truck pulled up into the driveway, followed by another. Donny Snow jumped out of the first truck's cab, clad in helmet, cumbersome rubber boots, and a heavy black firefighter's coat with reflective yellow and silver stripes. He began barking orders to the other emerging firefighters and within a minute they were carrying a three-inch hose with nozzle, axes, and fire extinguishers forward into the house. All the firefighters were familiar to me. I followed them into the house to grab one more picture and was immediately ordered back out. In a moment I heard breaking glass, looked up, and saw a red axe breaking out the mullions of a smoke-belching window.

"You fucker! I know you are doing this!" I said out loud to my father. I began to laugh. "You're unbelievable, you SHIT!"

On the other side of the house a smoking file cabinet was tossed out a window and burst open onto the snowy ground. Papers began to fly about from opened folders.

"You can burn down my house, but why fuck up the landscape with paper?" I knelt down and picked up a sheet. It was a photocopy of a newspaper clipping, "Vincent Perlman, Noted Author Dies in Wellfleet Fire." I picked up another piece of strewn paper, "3 Towns Respond to House Fire," and another, "First House Fire Fatality in 25 Years, Early Morning Fire Fully Engulfs Author's Home." A tumble of papers were blowing every which way across the snow, all from a file folder Kate had assembled in remembrance of that day more than five years before.

"FUCK YOU!" I cried with maniacal laughter, rushing to the tool shed. Grabbing a heavy splitting maul, I ran with it to the eight-foot tall cement male figure which stood in the open space between the house and my hut. Its flat body had been poured by my father into a piece of corrugated metal roofing, giving it its rippled form, painted in faded pink and draped in nylon fishnet like a toga; the head was a bearded self-portrait of my father; and a rebar-supported, extended arm projected off the body and pointed to the great long view to Cape Cod Bay, proclaiming its ownership as his and his alone for eternity.

"Burn down my house, will you, you cocksucker! GET OFF MY LAND!" I howled, swinging the mall into the belly of the statue, reinforced with heavy wire mesh. I swung again and again, sending chips and chunks of cement flying. "This is MY land now!"

Finally the great hulk teetered and fell over with a thud, a mangled demon-Satyr-god broken in the snow.

The fire was soon extinguished. The trucks and firemen left. Water damage was extensive. The living room floor buckled. The walls were streaked with rivulets of smoke-blackened water. The upstairs, Grace's bedroom, the office, the bath, closets, clothes were destroyed or severely smoke damaged. The house was uninhabitable. Power was shut off from the pole on the road.

That evening Kate, Grace, and I spent the night at my cousin Rachael's house down the road. We had thought of opening up the old house in the hollow, but the pipes were drained and we had no coal.

Although in shock I nevertheless felt determined to do battle with this turn of events. After speaking with our insurance agent in town the following morning, she referred me to the owner of an empty summer rental house a mile away from our place. We were able to move into it within a day for the remainder of the winter and spring. We would then move back into the old house for the summer. I called Disaster Specialists of Cape Cod and made arrangements for cleanup and reconstruction of our house, which all too clearly was no longer new. I then called a lady from our church, Dede Bucklin, reputed to be a gifted psychic and healer. I made an appointment to see her.

Feeling a need to call upon all my resources in a confrontation with the ghost or spirit of my father, I also phoned Patti Devereaux, the owner of the herb farm in Harwich. Because Miguel was back out West, she advised me to get in touch with Malcolm Crowley, a Wampanoag also known as White Feather who lived in Falmouth. She told me he was a modest man who made an income as a plasterer, but his work was in quiet service to Great Spirit, Mother Earth, his community, and those seeking help along the Red Road.

At this point I was well beyond seeking reasonable solutions to my paternal psychic logjam. Reason and all its therapies had been suspended for quite some time in order to fill a spiritual void left vacant by my more rational efforts to feel success, accomplishment, or satisfaction in this white man's life in accordance with the expectations of my confused breeding. Furthermore, I rather enjoyed escaping into and believing in an alternative reality with magic and wonder omnipresent in the natural world. The eagle had confirmed my belief, as had owl, skunk, and all my allies who journey with me.

"You need to clear your land and help your father's spirit to move on," White Feather spoke over the phone.

"How do I do this? Will you help me?"

"Yes."

"How much will it cost?"

"Money doesn't enter into these matters. This is the work of Spirit."

"Will you come to my land?"

"It's not necessary. You live in Wellfleet. I live in Falmouth. I will meet you halfway in Hyannis in the parking lot of the main post office at noon a week from this Sunday. I'll show you what to do."

Two days after my conversation with White Feather the investigator from the fire department called. He surmised that the fire had been caused by a piece of burning stick incense which had broken off and gone unnoticed during Kate's morning meditation and lodged itself between the carpeting and the baseboard. It had smoldered for at least three hours before I had returned in my bus. Given my father's misogynistic inclinations, I thought it quite plausible he would attack by way of Kate and her place of meditation, revealing himself as the perpetrator by the scattered newspaper clippings released from the tossed file cabinet.

Later that afternoon I met in Brewster with Dede Bucklin, an attractive, well-dressed, intelligent woman in her mid to late forties. Her enormous Great Dane Winston lay at our feet and was a soothing presence. That her house was well-kept, comfortable, and in a nice neighborhood assured me, as if I were on a visit to a respected doctor's office. She presented a very professional and kind demeanor.

I told her there had been a fire at my house and I suspected my deceased father might have had a hand in it. I briefly described my difficulty in letting go of long-held feelings of resentment toward him. I did not go into detail.

"Please give me something that holds your energy, something you carry with you."

I gave her my wallet. Clasping it in both her hands, she held it beneath her chin and closed her eyes. A minute of silent anticipation followed.

She gasped.

"He's here. I've got him," she whispered. She grimaced. Her eyes and mouth clenched shut. "This isn't me speaking," she said quickly. "He says he's going to burn down the whole fucking place!" She opened her eyes, looked at me, then closed them again.

"What's his problem?" I asked contemptuously.

"He says you keep pulling him in and pushing him out. He wants you to come out and fight him like a man!"

"Fine! Where? When?" My immediate response to his challenge allowed for no show of weakness or hesitation;

there was truth to the message she was conveying. My struggling antics with his photograph were evidence.

"You have an open space, a field on your property?"

"Yes," I answered, thinking of the area a short distance from my hut between the new house and the old house down in the hollow.

"He'll meet you there this Friday night at eleven o'clock.

Two evenings later at around ten-thirty I left our Cannon Hill rental and went over to Lieutenant's Island Road. The car's creeping tires crunched in the snow as I drove very slowly up the driveway. I passed the burned house to my left. A murmur tinkled from the old wind chimes left dangling years ago from a high branch above the lap pool to my right. I stopped and walked down into the grove of trees to my hut and went in.

Neither praying nor meditating, I sat for a while with one candle burning. I was calmly preparing for the appointed hour. Soon I took off my down jacket. I thought of removing all my clothes, but the winter cold dissuaded me. I removed a dolphin amulet from around my neck. I would not need allies or prayers to fight my nemesis like a man. I went out into the night.

Walking a path through the pitch pine, locust trees, and choke cherry bushes, I came to the edge of the open space and stopped. I stood motionless and listened. I looked across to the surrounding black trunks of locust trees silhouetted within the dimly lit tangle of thickets behind them. Scanning from my left to my right and back again, I slowly lowered down into a warrior stance. I thrust my right leg before me, left planted behind, and extended my right arm and hand straight out before me with palm down, and my left arm curled up behind me with hand and fingers straight up. In this warrior pose I stepped into the small field.

"Alright, come out!" I bellowed. "I am here!"

Maintaining the warrior stance, I moved into the center of the clearing and began to slowly rotate, keenly looking into the darkness. "Come out, I said! When challenged, are you afraid? You gave this land to me and my family! I did not expect you to be hanging around! Now come out, goddamnit! Or are you a coward?"

I heard a branch snap and swung toward it in my stance.

"He is hidden behind that tree!" I slowly stepped toward him, each foot staying in contact with the ground as fear welled within me.

"Kill me if you must, but I am here!" I bellowed once more. "Now show yourself!"

I reached the tree and he was not behind it. He was not in the woods. I turned around and he was not behind me. I rose out of my stance and walked to the center of the clearing. With my fists clenched and my arms spread wide from my expanded chest, I stood erect and roared skyward, "Listen, Pop! I want you outta here! You may think you have some secret codicil to your will giving you the right to float around here in perpefuckintuity, but you don't! Now get your fucking ghost-haunted ass the hell on outta here!"

Taking a deep breath, I puffed out my cheeks and let out a long sigh. The foolhardy sciamachy was over. "I'm insane," I thought.

I walked back to the hut, hung the dolphin amulet on its thin leather thong back around my neck, put on my jacket, and drove home to my rental.

On Sunday of the following weekend at noon I pulled my Corolla wagon into the empty parking lot of the Hyannis Post Office and parked. In my hand I held one of my 500-year-old buffalo teeth from the Alberta standing jump. Waiting, I rolled it round and round in my fingers. In a few minutes, a small, putty green Datsun pickup parked a few feet from me. White Feather, looking to be in his early fifties, and a small woman I took to be his wife, emerged. A large man dressed modestly in work clothes, he walked toward my car with his wife by his side. I got out to meet them.

"We'll sit in your car, Leon. My wife can sit in the back seat."

We shook hands and got back into my car. I unlocked the back door for his wife where she sat quietly and listened. I handed White Feather the buffalo tooth and thanked him for coming. As he handed me a six-inch long bundle of sage tightly wound on each end with yellow, red, black, and white thread, he said, "You will need this."

"So tell me again what happened on your land," he began. He had a pencil and piece of paper in his hand.

"My father died in a house fire in 1990. I've been feeling his presence on the land ever since. Sometimes I walk by the spot where he used to sit on his deck and my hair stands on end. I didn't always have an easy relationship with him. I don't think anybody did, unless they were drinking buddies, and even then, you'd never know how that might turn out. Anyway, I've been praying for months trying to make peace with him. I put his picture in front of me and try praying and after a minute or two, I get too uncomfortable and put the picture away. Finally, I got sick of trying a couple of weeks ago and I put this piece of obsidian I had in front of his picture and—"

Just then White Feather's wife in the back seat gasped and loudly whispered in alarm, "You put obsidian in front of your father's picture? Whoa-shhhhit!"

"Yeah, well, that's when the second fire happened."

White Feather, who had been writing something on his piece of paper, said, "Alright then, this is what you need to do and I'll write it down for you. Your father's spirit is definitely still there on your land and he needs help moving on. First thing," he began to write again, "You need to fast for four days. No food. No water."

"No water?"

"Well ... You can have eight ounces of water a day. Then you need to gather up four saplings from your land and plant them, like poles, in each of the Four Directions along with the colors on top of each sapling. These will surround a stone circle." He drew a circle on the paper. "In the middle of the circle put a white rock. Then take small stones and mark a path from the East into the circle. That's where you'll walk in. And when you enter, you'll walk clockwise and pray to the Thunder Beings in the West for their help. Do this everyday. At the end of the fourth day, or better yet, first thing in the morning of the fifth day, before you eat, take that bundle of sage I gave you and set it on fire right on the spot where your father died. Let it burn down into ash and then rub the ash into the ground there. After you do this, get some spring water and mix in some sea salt. Take a feather, dip it in the water, and go about clearing the land, sprinkling the water with the feather wherever you feel you need to, sending your father's spirit on his way. Then you'll be done. But most important," he said with emphasis, "you need to do this with love in your heart for your father."

White Feather handed me the piece of paper. While opening the door and beginning to step out, he said, "Aho, Mitakuye Oyasin! That'll do it. We are all related!" He exited, as did his wife, and I called after him, "Thank you! We are all related!" Together they walked to their truck.

After my Monday morning school bus run I cut down four cherry saplings, planted them on the hilltop where my father's studio had stood, and hung the colored cloth strips from their tips. I then drove out to Lieutenant's Island two hours after high tide and gathered a bucket of small stones and a larger one, which was white. It was a windy, crisp day with a cloudless blue sky.

I sat by the small boat shed at the "baptismal" beach, remembering the ritual of welcoming Grace into the world as my father had done for me forty-seven years before. Recalling his inveighed interruption when I tried reading from the ocean-inspired 107th Psalm, "What good has religion ever done for the world? It's only a crutch anesthetizing the soul!" I shook my head in spent exasperation and chuckled at his incessant chutzpah.

"I got your fuckin' crutch, Pop, right here, up your ass."

In the distance white caps frosted the surface of Wellfleet Bay while gulls dipped, soared, and circled above and black ducks, geese, and bufflehead bobbed in the waves. Only a few weeks before the bay had been frozen over with jagged blocks of ice, some of which flowed out in the ebb tide channel like a slow-moving armada of a thousand or more ships. I wondered if this latest phantasmagorical struggle might be the one which would finally set me free. I had watched then as the tide went out until the flats were again a broad debris field of immobile blocks and thick plates of ice stranded on the mud.

On Tuesday I began the fast, so that I would be done on Saturday morning and not have to drive the bus. I did not experience hunger; I was determined enough to be able to ignore any pangs to the point of not noticing. Safely driving the children to and from school was not a problem. Each day

I entered the circle within the flags of the Four Directions and prayed to the Thunder Beings, not that I was at all clear as to who they were. Throughout the fast the thought of love for my father did not occur to me.

On the morning of the fifth day, however, I woke from a dream clear in my mind: *I am on a broad expanse of water near what might be Jersey City looking through the fog in the direction of a not-visible Ellis Island, Statue of Liberty, and Lower Manhattan. Out of the monochromatic dark gray mist a figure moves across the water toward me. He is dressed in an ill-fitting black immigrant's suit, wearing a black fedora, and walking gingerly with a cane. He is an old man. He is my father. He stops next to me and looks into my eyes, and his eyes are soft, gentle, and loving. He speaks, "I have to make peace with your oldest brother." He smiles sweetly and self-effacingly at me, as if apologizing for all the years of family turmoil, pain, and loss. With finality he points his cane out across the dimly lit water and says in farewell, "And then I'm crossing over."*

Grace went over to a friend's house and Kate and I gathered at the stone circle on top of the hill. It was a sunny day with a spring thaw in the air and the ground was beginning to exhale an earthen fragrance through the grass. The bright yellow banner of the East and the red of the South, along with their black and white counterparts atop the sapling poles, fluttered festively in the breeze against the cloudless blue sky. I remained mindful of the tender feeling I felt for my departing father in that morning's dream.

On the ground next to the circle sat a pail of spring water, a box of sea salt, a seagull feather, the sage bundle, and a
dry cedar shingle with some newspaper. Kate held the hand
drum and I asked her to softly pound a heartbeat rhythm.
Carrying the abalone shell filled with smoking sage, I entered
the circle, followed by Kate. I called in the Four Directions
and we then exited out of the stone enclosure, slowly walking
in expanding spirals, which widened to encompass the entire
hilltop area where my father's studio had stood.

We came to a halt at the spot where his burned metal
bedspring had lain on the ground under the open sky. To
the thump—thump-thump of the drum I retrieved the
sage bundle, shingle, and paper. Separating the shingle into
shards and breaking them in half, I arranged them on top
of crumpled paper placed where my father's body had slept
and perished. I ignited the pile and then set the sage bundle
within the flames, and the flames soon grew higher. Kate
stopped drumming. We watched in silence until the pile became ash.

After pressing the ash into the ground with the rotating
sole of my shoe, I walked slowly with Kate back to the center
of the hilltop. I raised my arms high and wide and faced the
long western view, his last view, across the marsh and Loagy
Bay to Lieutenant's Island, Great Island, and Cape Cod Bay
beyond.

"Great Spirit! Ancestors! All benevolent spirits of this
beautiful earth and loved ones! We are here today to present

to you the magnificent soul and spirit of Vincent Perlman, who has loved this land so much he hasn't wanted to leave. But today, Great Spirit, we offer him to you with great love and appreciation for the good, kind, and generous man he hoped to be and in many ways he was. He is a man's man, a brave warrior! Take your son, O Great Spirit, and give him peace! Celebrate him! He deserves this! He has made well of the life you have given him! Aho!"

Kate resumed drumming and I mixed the sea salt into the pail of spring water and we began a long walk, first around the hilltop, casting droplets of water with the feather, then through the woods, around my hut, the old house in the hollow, the new house under reconstruction, and along their roof peaks, down their chimneys, and at their foundations, water droplets cast everywhere.

And it was done.

Thirteen

SEVEN EAGLE FEATHERS (PART III) THE CIRCULAR TIDE

I was not expecting to be freed of my father's presence on the land or in my psyche, but over the next few months and even into the following years, I dwelled on him less and less, choosing to ignore thoughts which would pull me back into an entangling web of blame. My rituals in the hut subsided, and I did not endeavor to seek out or sustain a magical or shamanic relationship with the Earth Mother, the animal world, or with spirit guides, although I knew such a relationship is readily available if sought and one's heart and mind are open to it. I rebuilt our house, and eventually, a new addition. I began to accept the land as my own.

Over the next four years I did continue to bring a lunch to Frank James once a month as part of my paraministry work with First Parish Brewster. I never shared my father struggle with Frank, yet I did derive from him some soul sustenance that had been lacking with my father.

Near the end of Frank's life the Sun Dancers, Sonny and Elayne, who had visited our church over five years before, returned to Cape Cod. They wanted to reconnect with the parishioners and see what progress we had made in healing our relationship with the Mashpee Wampanoag Tribe. As they had said, the Earth Changes were now upon us, and as the genocide had moved from east to west, now was the time for healing to move westward.

Our church had become an ally and friend of the tribe. We actively supported their housing assistance program. We advocated for the abandonment of Nauset High School's use of the name Warriors and Indian mascot logo for its sports teams. We worked to have the wording changed on the First Encounter Beach plaque referring to "hostile Indians." Wampanoag culture and history were taught by native teachers in educational programs sponsored by our church.

Sonny asked if he could meet with Wamsutta Frank James. I agreed to take him and together we drove down to Chatham. At this point Frank had quit drinking and smoking, and he was getting supplemental oxygen through a cannula tube. He was growing gaunt. He was far more vulnerable and receptive than the time I had brought Miguel to visit, when Frank had nearly thrown him out on his ear.

The three of us ate sandwiches. Sonny and Frank playfully bantered and we all laughed a good deal. Then Sonny asked if the three of us could smoke his pipe. We were quiet as Sonny removed the red cloth in which it was wrapped. He filled it with kinnikinnick. I shut off the oxygen tank and we smoked in silence several times around our circle.

"Leon," Frank said, "go in the other room and get my Wampanoag pipe." I fetched it and Frank took it and held it aloft for a moment and smiled with satisfaction. "Now this here's a real pipe. A real Wampanoag pipe. It was stolen from us by the white man and was stuck up in the Peabody Museum for people to gawk at. But I got it back!" He pointed at the small bowl at the end of the pipe. "This here bowl is affixed to the top of a genuine Pilgrim axe head over three hundred years old. Now the old wooden stem rotted out and I had to make a new one. Sonny? Fill her up, if you'd be so kind."

We smoked once around our circle and then Frank held the pipe aloft one more time. Sweeping his hand beneath the stem, he declared, "Now all I need to finish off this pipe are seven feathers to hang underneath the stem." He smiled. "Seven feathers to represent Seven Generations."

I had never once mentioned the eagle and its offspring who had visited the marsh behind my house five years before.

The following week, after Sonny and Elayne had left the Cape, I returned to Frank's house. This time I brought with me the leaded glass box containing the seven feathers resting on a bed of lavender, sage, cedar, and tobacco with kernels of corn and small rocks and crystals around them.

Sitting at his kitchen table, I held the box in my hands.

"The feathers in this box were left by an eagle in the marsh out behind my house. It's a funny thing, Frank. Five years ago Sonny and Elayne taught me a prayer. I said it everyday, and after a month or two, this eagle and its immature offspring came and left seven feathers out there in the snow, but I think maybe they weren't left for me."

He looked at me sharply through squinted eyes. His breathing had become more constricted with advancing emphysema and now his exhaled breaths quietly whistled through his pursed lips. I knew he would not be in this world much longer.

"Now I know you and I have never regarded one another by the colors of our skin," I said. "Let's just say we've disregarded the colors and seen one another as human beings, and I've appreciated that that bullshit hasn't come between us. But now, and I feel pretty awkward saying this, I want to say this as a white person." I placed the opened box on the table before him. "Because I believe these feathers were meant for you and have come by way of me so I can give you a message." I cleared my throat and continued. "So I'll just say it and that will be that." I paused and sat up straight. "On behalf of my white European ancestors and those still living with that white heritage, I apologize for all the disease, hardship and loss of life, theft of your land, racism, slavery, and disrespect suffered by your people as a result of our presence here. I'm sorry, Frank. I give these feathers to you in peace and I'm sorry."

"I'll tell ya what, Leon, that's one helluva lot of stuff for you to be sorry for. And quite ceremoniously, I might add. I don't hold you responsible. It's the goddamn history and all the ignorant sons-a-bitches who robbed ... No, sir, Leon. You've been a good friend and I appreciate your friendship. You're a regular human being, a kind fellow. But, like I told you once, I'm a bitter man, an angry man, and I don't think I can just let it go to posterity what was done to Indians and is still being done to Indians all across this land and around the world. No, sir! The white man is a rapacious beast and he's damn near destroyed this planet and won't likely stop 'till he's succeeded in killing off everyone and everything. So personally, from you, Leon, I accept your apology, but from the white man in general? No!" He was breathing harder and his exhaled breath whistled more audibly. We sat in silence for a few minutes. He glared off into a distance, as if he were surveying four centuries of his past.

For a moment my thoughts went with Frank into that past and I saw the man originally known as Wamsutta, who was the eldest son of Massasoit, the 17th Century leader of the Wampanoag, as if Frank were his reincarnated form. After Massasoit's death in 1661, Wamsutta became grand sachem and worked to consolidate Wampanoag power against the widening encroachment by the white man. In violation of Plymouth Colony laws making it illegal for colonists to do commerce with the Wampanoag, Wamsutta had sold a parcel of land to Roger Williams who lived outside of Plymouth Colony's jurisdiction. In addition, Wamsutta was suspected of secretly forming a hostile alliance with the Narragansetts. He was arrested by the Plymouth Colony governor Josiah Winslow. While in custody he died suddenly and it was suspected he died of poisoning. I thought of Wamsutta's younger brother Metacom, who became known as King Philip and fought for his people's survival in one of the most ferocious and deadliest wars in American history. Metacom's head was placed high atop a pike for more than twenty years in Plymouth to instill fear in the Wampanoag. I considered the necessity and humiliation of surrendering to the white man's racist ways in order to survive, the violations and compromises of personal dignity which had to be endured, as one's history and culture were drained away into oblivion or at best confined to reservations, museums, or secrecy. I also remembered that Frank had been invited to speak before the Massachusetts legislature in 1970 on Thanksgiving Day, an honor quickly turned insult when his prepared speech was censored by his hosts, and that he consequently refused with pride and anger to share his deeply felt and understood version of the so-called Thanksgiving feast. I understood why Frank would not accept an apology on behalf of my white ancestors. Still, I wished he might find a smidgen of forgiveness in his soul for the injustice residing in his genes, some means of relinquishing his pain that he might find some peace.

"Please, Frank. Accept these feathers. They're not even from me. I don't know how or why they got here. They just came on a prayer. May I share that prayer with you now, Frank?"

"Go right on ahead, Leon." He listened politely as I recited the One Earth One People Peace Prayer, but I'm not sure how much of it entered into his heart. I didn't want him to leave this world angry or bitter. I wanted him to know he had fought one helluva good fight for justice and truth and done good work helping young people develop their musical talents. I wanted him to know he was loved and that he shouldn't feel bad about himself. Even if the fight hadn't been won, it sure wasn't lost. I wanted him to know I loved him.

"That's a very fine prayer, Leon. Thank you for sharing it," he said. I could see he was tired and that the prayer hadn't set off any fireworks. It was just a prayer.

"Well, I best get goin', Frank. I've got to do my afternoon school bus run."

"Keep the little ones in line, Leon. Keep 'em in line."

"You bet. I'll stop by next week. See ya later."

"Thank you, Leon. Be safe."

I did stop by the following week, but Frank was sleeping in his darkened bedroom with a big oxygen tank nearby. I tiptoed in and sat in a chair next to his bed for a while. After about fifteen minutes I left and that was the last time I saw Frank. He passed away the next week.

Fourteen

THE OPEN SEA

It's been 14 years since Frank died and 25 years since my father left this world. If I've learned anything from my struggles of late, it's this: acceptance is one thing, forgiveness is another more difficult, and peace is no still pond, at least for me. And learning that they're all choices is one difficult nut to crack. But I keep working at it.

I'm grateful for the beautiful land my father gave me. I still live on it with my patient and loving wife of forty-two years. I'm grateful for the good times we've shared. I'm grateful for my lovely daughter who has grown into a strong and successful woman. I have friends and relatives who love and care for me. I'm clean and sober and I have good health. I am blessed with a good life and I've had time to write about it. I am learning to give more weight to what I am grateful for and less to my resentments and self-deprecations. I am breathing more easily.

My father provided me with much—a good education, despite myself in my younger years; an appreciation for the arts; a sense of humor; a taste for the wild; a desire to look beneath the surface of things. Yes, he was impossible, outrageous, boundary-crashing, and still, very insightful. He was my hero and I'll love him forever, even as he does at times piss me off to no end. I accept him for who he was and I forgive him his shortcomings—most of the time. I am letting go of my long saga of living in relation, reaction, and comparison to him. Resentment and blame have only kept me trapped in the past for far too long. I am moving on.

I am grateful for the privilege of having had a friendship with Frank. Like my father, he was a great man and a warrior to the end. Were I his son, I'm sure it would not have been easy to grow up under his shadow.

I apologize to my Native friends for my wannabeism. I have never tried to sell or publicly promote your culture and spiritual beliefs. I have greatly admired them and felt their value in my bones. Our Mother Earth and all her people need your prayers more than ever.

I thank Sonny and Elayne for what they shared with me, and especially Elayne, also known as Bluebird, for her prayer.

Thank you, friends, for reading my story. For any of you who may have been hurt by me in any way, I apologize for my indiscretions. May we all remember

We are One people on One Earth.
All life is sacred. The Earth is sacred.
We cherish and protect
Our Mother Earth, Father Sky, and Sacred Waters.
The Generations of Humankind from the Four
Directions
Must live in harmony and balance
With each other and all living things.
We are all related.
We respect and honor the Sacredness of all Life and all
Creation
So Seven Generations from each Generation,
Unborn future Generations, will live.
Seven Eagle Feathers represent future Generations and
Sacred Ceremonies.
They carry our Prayer to Creator.
We pray that you, Great Whales and Dolphins,
Stranded on these Outer Cape beaches and beaches
everywhere,
Suffocating under your own weight,
May be lifted on the floodtide
And set free to swim again in open seas.
O Great Spirit,

We pray that Mother Earth and
all of her Children will live!
It is One Prayer:
Peace!

The Author, Age 6 or 7

The Author's Father
In New York City Brownstone

Author's Father on Studio Deck
South Wellfleet, Cape Cod

Author and His Father
on Studio Deck

Author with Family, 1984

Don Quixote   Thrift Store Attire

Surveying the Wild Horses of the Sea
How They Foam and Fret

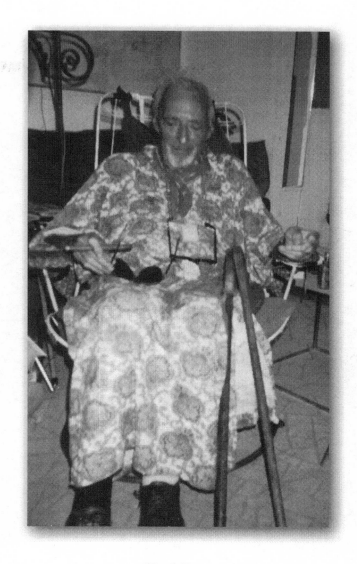

Final Days

Family on Winter Beach, 1990

Thou wast not born for death, immortal Bird!
No hungry generations tread thee down;
The voice I hear this passing night was heard
In ancient days by emperor and clown

John Keats
Ode to a Nightingale

19544656R00208

Made in the USA
Middletown, DE ·
25 April 2015